SHOW DOWN IN LAS VEGAS

"What are you doing in Las Vegas, Leech?" The man spit the words, adding extra venom to the term "Leech."

"Same as everyone else. Minding my own business." Jack paused a second, rolling the lump of tobacco across his tongue.

Last I checked, it was still a free country."

"Not for you." The man changed as he walked toward him. Jack's bad feeling grew far worse. Gray-and-black fur grew across the man's skin as his body expanded. The ragged clothes didn't tear, but suddenly seemed to fit, as the leader stopped a few feet away. "We don't like vampires in this part of town."

Dawson stared the werewolf square in the chest and decided he should have run. "Well, since you put it that way, I s'pect I ought to just run on home."

The monster looked down from a full three feet above the top of Dawson's hat and smiled. Thin black lips peeled away from a set of fangs Dawson just knew could take his head off with one chomp.

"Too late, Leech. You were rude. Now you're gonna die."

THE WORLD OF DARKNESS

WEREWOLF
Wyrm Wolf
Conspicuous Consumption
Hell-Storm

VAMPIRE
Dark Prince
Netherworld
Blood Relations

MAGE
Such Pain

WRAITH
Sins of the Fathers

Strange City (an anthology)

Published by HarperPrism

ATTENTION: ORGANIZATIONS AND CORPORATIONS

Most HarperPaperbacks are available at special quantity discounts for bulk purchases for sales promotions, premiums, or fund-raising. For information, please call or write:
Special Markets Department, HarperCollins*Publishers*,
10 East 53rd Street, New York, N.Y. 10022.
Telephone: (212) 207-7528. Fax: (212) 207-7222.

THE WORLD OF DARKNESS
Werewolf

Hell-Storm

James A. Moore

HarperPrism
An Imprint of **HarperPaperbacks**

If you purchased this book without a cover, you should be aware that this book is stolen property. It was reported as "unsold and destroyed" to the publisher and neither the author nor the publisher has received any payment for this "stripped book."

This is a work of fiction. The characters, incidents, and dialogues are products of the author's imagination and are not to be construed as real. Any resemblance to actual events or persons, living or dead, is entirely coincidental.

HarperPaperbacks *A Division of* HarperCollins*Publishers*
10 East 53rd Street, New York, N.Y. 10022

Copyright © 1996 by White Wolf Publishing
All rights reserved. No part of this book may be used or reproduced in any manner whatsoever without written permission of the publisher, except in the case of brief quotations embodied in critical articles and reviews. For information address HarperCollins*Publishers*, 10 East 53rd Street, New York, N.Y. 10022.

Cover illustration by Mike Chaney

First printing: June 1996

Printed in the United States of America

HarperPrism is an imprint of HarperPaperbacks. HarperPaperbacks, HarperPrism, and colophon are trademarks of HarperCollins*Publishers*.

❖ 10 9 8 7 6 5 4 3 2 1

ACKNOWLEDGMENTS

Special thanks to Robert Hatch for his insight and kind words. Also, to my wife, Bonnie, for her patience with my eccentricities and her endless support.

This story is dedicated to Joe R. Lansdale and Stephen King for reminding me that the "Old West" was always a lot of fun to visit; to Lisa Cantrell for all of her help when I was just starting; and to the officers of the Horror Writers' Association both past and present for all of their efforts. In differing ways, you have all made my task much easier. Thank you.

Prologue

Twenty miles beyond the Las Vegas city limits, Norman Louder was digging his own grave. Three figures stood behind him, guns in hands, and watched impassively. Norman's body dripped a thick, greasy sweat, and he gulped air raggedly as he continued to move the arid soil from the deepening hole in the ground. He'd been digging for over five hours, and his fingers were blistered from the rough work. Forget his arms; they'd stopped feeling anything but pain a long time ago. His back was a knot of burning muscles, and even his legs were starting to give out. Sweat ran down his forehead and splashed into his right eye. He simply continued on, knowing that if he stopped without permission, the goons would beat him black-and-blue. His ribs were still tender from the last time.

Norman Louder had learned too late that some people didn't take well to blackmail. Michael Giovanni, his latest attempted victim, took the attempted extortion personally. Victor Humes was Giovanni's personal enforcer. Humes was the largest of the men standing above him now, and certainly the meanest of the lot. When he'd first met Victor, he'd thought for certain he'd made a friend. The man's big, easygoing smile and booming laughter had set Norm at ease in a matter of seconds. But as soon as word came down from Giovanni, the smile vanished. In the place of the friendly man he'd met a week earlier, there was now a silent, brooding giant with murderous eyes and a feral sneer. Looking up at the man, Norm knew the meaning of fear.

Michael Giovanni was a powerful person in Las Vegas. Norm's mistake was failure to realize just how powerful.

Norm sighed heavily, forcing his arms to lift the shovel up and drive it deep into the hard soil at his feet. He heaved with both of his arms, and just managed to lob the dirt out of the pit. Something hot flashed through the corded muscles in his right shoulder and made him cry out in pain.

"Okay, Norman. That's deep enough. Hand me the shovel."

Vic's words were like the songs of angels after the last five hours, and from the last reserves of strength, he managed to hand the digging tool out of the pit. His hands came short of actually reaching the hole's edge by a good four inches. Part of his mind wondered how he'd ever manage to climb out of the excavation, but a louder, more desperate voice screamed that he would never have to worry about actually leaving. He tried to ignore the panicky screams that echoed through his very soul.

Victor Humes looked down at him, his face buried in shadows and surrounded by the star-filled night sky. From this perspective, the man looked impossibly tall. "Nothin' personal, Norm. You were a nice enough guy." Vic turned and called to his two friends. "Hey, boys! Finish it."

Victor disappeared from view, replaced by the other two men. They, too, were little more than silhouettes against the sky. Norman Louder was still staring upward when the first clod of dirt struck him in the face. The dirt sent knives of pain into his eyes, and spilled into his parched mouth. Right around the same time, the shrill mind-voice he'd been trying his best to ignore finally won the battle. It went from just loud to a maddening scream, and Norm started thrashing in response. He begged for mercy, but the two men continued to toss more dirt on top of him. He tried climbing out of the pit, but his one successful attempt at the edge of the hole ended with the impact of a heavy foot smashing his fingertips into a bloodied pulp.

Inside of ten minutes, the hole was filled completely. Inside of fifteen, there was little to prove that anyone had ever been in the area. What little moisture the dirt held was greedily sucked away by the desert winds, and the topsoil looked as dry and unchanging as the rest of the area by the time the sun rose.

From above, the Mojave Desert was a vast, motionless ocean of gray. The only break from the endless darkness came as an island of light: Las Vegas. In the city, people moved on with their lives or tried again and again to beat the odds in a never-ending game of chance.

Though few among the living could have heard them, Norman Louder's screams continued on long after his physical form was dead. His was only one of over a hundred enraged screeches that split the air in that little section of the desert. One of the many who had attempted to cross Don Michael Giovanni's path in the last forty years. They all screamed. And twenty miles away no one heard their cries.

No one felt the turbulence in the desert's frozen ocean of bone white sand, but that too would change.

1

I

SAN FRANCISCO

Gabriel White shoved the last of his bags into the rented truck, scowling the entire way. Life had taken a severe turn for the worse over the last few months, and he no longer felt as carefree as he once had. In the last six months he'd had damn near every aspect of his life turned around and then smashed into so much dust.

Bad enough he was a werewolf—*No, Garou,* he corrected himself—Christ knew that was something he'd never expected: That was the least of his problems. The man he'd always thought of as his father was dead, murdered by the man who really was his father. The man who really was his father, aside from being a twisted bastard, was also dead, murdered by a man who was once his mother's lover.

Gabriel was fairly certain that his life had fallen into a nightmarish version of *General Hospital*, complete with a cast of twisted monsters where the actors should be. He knew his mother felt about the same way. For a while, Diane White seemed to take the more demented aspects of her new life with a grain of salt, but that had changed. Where she once went around trying to keep a stiff upper lip, she now sat in the house and stared blankly at the TV. The most she'd said in the last two weeks was one sentence: "Gabriel, make sure your room is clean, you know how your father gets when you leave a mess." He'd dutifully cleaned his room, because not doing so would have meant another confrontation, another screaming match over nothing at all.

Gabriel could learn to hate his mother at this rate.

On the brighter side, the letter she'd received earlier in the week had helped cheer her considerably. It wasn't the letter she was hoping for—not from Samuel Haight, her onetime lover—but it cheered her anyway. An invitation to the grand opening of the Platinum Palace in Las Vegas.

What the hell, the change of pace will do us both some good. Not that Gabriel could think of much a sixteen-year-old could do in Vegas. *Gambling is out of the question. Or is it? With a little practice, I can easily make myself pass for thirty or so.*

Gabriel looked around, making certain the street was clear of onlookers, and willed the change to occur. He did not permit the change to complete itself. He made himself stay mostly human, instead. His body shifted, warping and growing. His jaw stretched slightly, and his lean form filled out substantially. Not quite Mr. Universe proportions, but closer than he'd ever hoped to achieve. Then he looked in the window of the truck and stared with satisfaction at the changes in his form. Taller, heavier, and looking to be in his mid-thirties. Yep. This would work just fine. He allowed himself to smile, but closed his lips upon seeing the fangs growing from his mouth.

"Have you lost your damned mind, boy?" The voice was angry, and Gabriel immediately willed himself back to his completely human form. Shaun Ingram stared at him, his face set like stone. Once again the man had succeeded in sneaking up on him in broad daylight. How Shaun managed the feat was still a mystery. "When did you throw away the brains God above put in your thick head?" Shaun's Irish accent was sneaking into his voice, and that was a bad thing. His accent only showed itself when he was angry.

"I'm sorry, Shaun. I just wanted to—"

"You just wanted to let the good people of this neighborhood know that you're a bloody freak, is that it?" Despite being a good four inches shorter than Gabriel's six feet, Shaun carried himself with an air of authority that lent importance to his every word. When he spoke, Gabriel listened. It didn't hurt that Shaun was also the only teacher he had for the dos and don'ts of being a werewolf.

"No, I just wanted to see if I could do it. If I could take on the Glabro form and keep it from fluctuating." That sounded like the sort of crap Shaun would accept.

"That's fine, Gabriel. But not in public. It's asking for grief that neither of us needs." Shaun sounded calmer, and Gabriel was already hating himself for the lie. But it had been necessary. The truth would have gone over poorly at best. "Use your common sense, lad. We don't want anyone to know what we are. It's a surefire way to get hunted and killed."

"But you said the Delirium would stop them from seeing us for what we are; I thought it would be safe."

"I said the Delirium helps to keep us safe, but it doesn't always work. There are plenty of humans running around who can take one look at us and see past whatever lies their minds want to make up." Gabriel started to object, but Shaun quieted him with a gesture. "Sure, most will convince themselves they saw a bear or a man in a gorilla suit, but there're always a few who can accept what they see and decide that we need a couple of hundred bullets put through us. Take it from someone who's been hit a few times: the bullets might not always kill us, but they always hurt like three kinds of hell."

Gabriel turned away, trying to stop the anger building inside of him. The man was right, of course, but that didn't make it any easier for him to swallow his pride. Before he could go far, Shaun's hand rested on his shoulder. He resisted the urge to slap that hand away and tear into the throat of his teacher.

"Look, Gabriel. I do understand what you're going through. I know this is hard. It's certainly not what you wanted for your life. I never wanted it either. But we've got to make the best of it. There are a lot of bright sides to being Garou."

"Like what? So far all I've been dealt by you is 'don't do that' and 'when are you going to grow up.' When the hell does it get a little brighter, Shaun? What's the purpose of being something special if you're not allowed to be what you want to be?" Gabriel felt the stinging in his eyes, and fought back the tears trying to escape from him. Damn, but he hated wanting to cry.

Shaun looked at him with eyes that had seen too much of the world and sighed. "It's the moon. Almost full again, and that means you'll be wanting to change." Gabriel could have laughed. Wanting had little to do with it. When the moon was in his Auspice, he *had* to change. Denying the transformation and the need to become more than human was like trying to stop menstrual cramps. It just didn't work. The only good news was that his mind was still his own. He didn't go off on a rampage and kill innocent people like all the movies portrayed. Shaun spoke again, and Gabriel listened. "We'll be in the desert in a few days; when the moon grows full we'll run for a few hours, learn a bit more about the world. Does that sound like a deal?"

Gabriel smiled, already excited by the prospect of running through the night with no one to see and no fear of attracting unwanted attention. "Yeah. That sounds wonderful."

Shaun smiled in return, his wide face crinkling with joy. Diane White always compared him to a leprechaun when he smiled, and Gabriel had to agree. With his bright red hair and scattering of freckles, the man looked the part. "Wonderful. Now let's get this tank loaded with bags and be on our way." Shaun looked over at him again, casting a knowing wink. "Who knows? Perhaps we can pass you off as an adult and get you into the casinos. Assuming the Glabro is just the thing, I suspect."

Gabriel felt himself blushing. He was still lousy at telling lies.

II

Dawson watched from the shadows, waiting for the proper moment to make his next move. In the last two nights he'd placed a total of seventeen calls to

Hell-Storm 9

Jason Worthington's home, and he always left the same message, whether the man answered the phone or his answering machine or another member of his family answered. He simply said, "Rachel Simpson sends her regards." Finally, the man could take the calls no longer. He fled from the safety of his home, moving into the late-night streets in the hope of escaping Dawson's voice.

Dawson intended to make sure that never happened.

Worthington slipped from the house in silence, trying his best to sneak over to his battered Ford Pinto without being noticed, if the almost-exaggerated steps he made were any indication. He slid into the front seat and gently closed the door. The driveway was on a hill, and the man carefully backed away from his home with only gravity to power his descent. At the bottom of the drive, he turned the wheel sharply, and Dawson watched patiently as the man used his car's momentum to back the car up the slight incline of the street. By the efficient way he handled the Pinto, Dawson guessed he'd done this many times before.

Dawson lowered his Stetson slightly, sauntering in the direction his target was traveling. He was in no hurry, knowing full well the car wouldn't start. Damn hard to turn the engine over when the car's Diehard battery was sitting in the back of Dawson's truck. No hurries, no worries, just a little walk down to see how Jason liked being stalked. He whistled as he walked, the heels of his cowboy boots making a nice counterbeat to the tune he let slip past his lips.

"You sure that's the one, Rachel?"

Though no one stood near him, he cocked his head and listened. A whispered voice replied, "Yes, Jack. That's him." Even if someone had been right next to him, they'd have never heard the faint answer.

"Okay then. Let's get this done. Whattayasay?"

"Yes, Jack. And thank you." Her voice was soft, sweet.

His own deep voice responded, filled with the good humor he felt. "Hell, sweetie. Ain't no problem as I see it. Just another asshole in need of educating." He smiled tightly, his eyes narrowing. "I'm a damn fine teacher, if I do say so myself."

He walked on in silence, listening to the sounds of Jason Worthington's vain attempts to start the car. From ten feet away he could hear the man's mumbled curses. He stopped right next to the driver's side door, grinning widely enough to damn near split his own lips.

"Howdy, sport. Looks like you're having a mite bit of car trouble. Why don't you pop the hood and we'll see what we can see?"

The man nearly leaped out of his seat, a squeaky little gasp escaping from him as he realized that Dawson was there. "Jesus Christ! You scared the hell out of me, mister!" Up close the effects of two nights without sleep were more obvious. The man's face was pale, except for the dark circles under his brown eyes. His black hair was wild, not at all like it had looked when Dawson started his hunt. On a good day, the punk would likely be pleasant to look at, but right now he looked like death warmed over. He was almost as skinny as the Grim Reaper, too.

Dawson chuckled good-naturedly. "Sorry about that, Bubba. I tend to walk real quiet for the most part."

"Oh, hey. No problem. Thanks for stopping." The man was silent for a moment, looking past Dawson with a slightly blank stare. After a few seconds, he asked the question that most people would ask in his situation. "Do you know anything about cars?"

"Oh, I know a bit. Why don't you pop the hood for me, and we'll give 'er a look-see."

"Thanks. I barely know how to drive, and I'm useless with anything harder than putting gas in the tank." He almost sounded apologetic, but the desperation in his voice leaked in just the same.

The man obliged him, and Dawson lifted the hood, exposing the engine. He made the appropriate noises, reached inside, and fiddled with a few wires. It took a little effort not to laugh, but only a little. Right now the anger was building inside, the anger that demanded payment for what had occurred before.

"I think I see your problem, buddy."

Jason Worthington stepped out of the car, walking around to take a peek himself. "Yeah? What's the matter?"

"You ain't got a battery. Someone must have stolen it right out from under your nose."

The man's eyebrows knitted together, his face growing darker with righteous anger. "Fuck. Only in this city." Dawson looked at the dark hole where the battery should have been and shook his head, *tsking* his condolences.

"Yeah, I know what you mean. But don't feel too bad. I'd be willing to bet a smooth operator like you can find a replacement without too much trouble."

"Not without an extra hundred bucks or so."

"Money problems?"

"You bet. Everyone's got money problems these days."

"Hey. It could be a lot worse, y'know."

"Yeah? Well this sucks enough for me, thanks."

"I mean, you could be dead. Am I right, or what?"

"Yeah. There is that."

"Oh, hey, before I forget..." Dawson made his voice sound casual, but he was waiting for this, the look that would come over the man's face when he heard the next comment.

"Yeah?" Jason Worthington looked at him quizzically.

"Rachel Simpson sends her regards."

The man's reaction was instantaneous. He went from a relaxed, casual posture to a rigid fighting stance in the blink of an eye. "You're the one's been calling my house?" His voice was heavy with threat.

Dawson smiled, nodding his head. "Right the first time, buddy."

"Well, you've got the wrong house, asshole. I don't know any Rachel Simpson."

"That ain't the way she tells it."

"Yeah? Why don't you call the bitch on the phone, and we can talk it out?" His voice had grown slightly shrill, and his pulse had increased noticeably.

Dawson shook his head, a mock frown covering his face. "Shoot, Bubba. I'd love to, only she ain't got a phone."

"Yeah? Well, then, maybe you can pass a message on for me. If I hear from you or her again, I'll call the cops on you. How's that sound?"

"Well now, you never let me tell you why she ain't got a phone, pardner." Dawson stood up a little straighter, aware that his voice had dropped into a threatening tone.

"Fine. Why doesn't she have a phone?"

"Well, I'll tell you why. She hasn't really had much use for a phone since the day you killed her."

Jason Worthington stepped back hastily, his voice cracking as he spoke. "What the hell are you talking about? I never killed anyone." His voice quavered, and Dawson knew he was lying.

"You trying to tell me it wasn't you that cut her little body into pieces and fed her to the sharks?" Dawson laughed out loud, his voice still filled with humor. "Shit, son. I'd hate to think she's been lying to me. I mean, she said you did some awful things."

"I-I don't know what you're talking about." The man's voice was faint; his skin had gone even whiter, until it fairly glowed in the light of the moon.

"Hell. She said you broke into her house and killed her daddy. She said you did some awful nasty things to her momma, too, before you cut the poor woman's throat." Dawson placed an arm companionably over the man's shoulder, locking him in place when he tried to squirm away. "But you know the part that bothers her the most? Why, it's the same thing that bothers me." He added pressure to his grip, and the man cried out as his muscles bruised under the onslaught. The smile dropped from Dawson's face, and his voice grew menacing. "She's real pissed about what you did to her innocence. What you did to her shouldn't even be done to a three-dollar whore." He grabbed the man by both shoulders, bringing his face within inches of his opponent's. "You remember Rachel now?"

"I—"

"Do you remember her now, you little shit?"

The bastard started crying. Dawson pushed him backward, and he staggered back into his powerless Pinto, his scrawny backside slamming into the metal hard enough to leave a dent and make the whole vehicle rock.

"Did it bother you at all? Did you feel bad when she screamed? Or when she bled? Or when she died?" With every question, he shook Worthington's tall, angular body. "I can hear the Dead when they are in pain. I've been listening to her voice for five long months while I tracked you down, boy."

"I didn't do anything! I never touched her!" The man's voice cracked, and his breathing hitched as he started hyperventilating. Dawson looked at him and wondered if he'd somehow made a mistake. There was a wedding ring on Worthington's finger, and he sounded so sincere . . .

Then the man sealed his own fate with desperate, stupid words. "She wanted it! She liked it! I know she did!"

Dawson reached out and grabbed Jason Worthington's face in his hand, muffling the offensive, lying mouth. He bared his teeth, wanting to rip out the man's throat. But the thought of blood that foul being used for food was repulsive. "She sure ain't been tellin' it that way, Jason ole buddy. Way Rachel tells it, she begged you to stop until you gagged her." Dawson concentrated, forcing the black ichor that passed for his blood to run to his fingertips and spurting the thick, cold liquid across the mouth of the child molester. "Do you know the Dead feel pain, Jason? Do you know they can feel it for years on end without relief? She was six years old when you killed her. That was ten years ago. That means she's been suffering for what you did longer than she even lived."

Jason Worthington started thrashing, his voice lifting upward from his mouth and scaling the octaves as it came. Dark patches grew across his skin, bubbling and sinking into black ulcerations of decay. As if in a film played in fast forward, Dawson watched the skin and muscles putrefy. A bitter smile crept across his mouth.

"I know what they feel. I feel it every day." Jason's voice gave out as he fell to the ground, and

Dawson watched on impassively as the rot devoured all the healthy flesh on his body. "Rachel and me, we figured it was only fair that you feel it, too." He turned away from the decomposing man, looking back only once, to add a parting sentence. "If you stay really still, you might live through this. Just don't break the skin. 'Course you might not want to live; you don't heal as well as my kind does."

He whistled as he walked away, pleased by the wet, gurgling sounds behind him. "You're on your own now, Rachel. I got to get on the road soon, and I need to say good-bye to an old friend, too."

"Thank you, Jack." Her voice was fading. She was being drawn away from the world, released from the pain.

"My pleasure, sweetheart."

There was no response from Rachel, and Dawson expanded with his senses, struggling to feel her presence and—thankfully—found nothing. "You rest in peace now, okay?"

The following night, Dawson awoke to seven messages on his beeper. The miracles of modern science allowed him to keep one phone number, no matter where in the country he went—a convenience he'd come to love. Three were from Jeremy Wix, a friend with more troubles than anyone deserved, asking if Dawson could meet with him at the base of the Golden Gate Bridge. He noted the time for the meeting and decided he could. Three were from different collection agencies searching for the last tenant of the rented house. He ignored their politely angry inquiries, chuckling at their veiled threats. The last was from Michael Giovanni, the head honcho of Las Vegas. The message was short and to the point. "Jack. This is Mike G. in Vegas. I have need of your services. Be here as soon as you can."

Jeremy could wait. Business always came before pleasure, and Mike Giovanni did not like to be kept waiting. Of course, Jeremy was still wanted by the prince of San Francisco for allegedly passing around information regarding the existence of vampires, but Pretty Boy Wix was very good at hiding, if nothing else. Dawson had to assume that he'd be all right on his own.

Jack loaded up his traveling bags with everything he'd need and threw them in the passenger seat of his Ford Bronco. He paused in the kitchen, loading his Igloo cooler with four bags of blood and a six-pack of Budweiser, grabbing a fifth blood pack for his meal. He drank it cold, just the way he liked it, smiling to think how most vampires would react if they knew he only drank the blood of corpses.

Feeding was supposed to be a sensual experience, the closest most Kindred ever came to experiencing physical pleasures. The very idea of drinking the blood of a corpse was the equivalent of necrophilia for them. Dawson wasn't most vampires. He liked his food dead and cold.

Of course, most vampires didn't drink beer or chew tobacco either, and he did both with equal delight. Their loss for short-sightedness. He carefully closed and folded the plastic Baggie when he finished, slipping it into his pocket for recycling later. He erased the messages on his machine, grabbed his battered cowboy hat and his duster from near the door. Getting to Vegas would take most of the night, and he wanted to get there as fast as he could.

No one ever kept Don Michael Giovanni waiting, not if they could avoid it. Besides, work from the Don meant money, and lots of it. Killing humans was something Dawson did for free, a way of helping out the Restless Dead unable to avenge themselves. Killing Kindred, on the other hand, was how he made a living. After almost a hundred years of hunting down the vampires who managed to piss off their older or wealthier counterparts, he'd developed a reputation as a professional. Vacation was over, and the time was right for making enough money to live comfortably for a while.

The house he left behind was devoid of anything that could have told people more than the inhabitant's name. The few personal items he had acquired over the years were snugly set away in his bags. Jack drove at exactly ten miles over the speed limit as he hit the interstate.

III

TIJUANA, MEXICO

The border between the US and Mexico was well guarded, but not superbly so. Joe Hill didn't much care either way. If everything worked out, he'd never have to cross it anyway. He looked the area over, trying to find signs that his prey was in the area. So far, he'd had no luck. Beside him, del Gado stared at their surroundings with a look of raw disgust. Nothing unusual there, del Gado stared at everything that way. In this case, Hill could not blame him. Tijuana was, to be kind, a trash heap. The women he saw walking the street were young in years, some only just entering their teens, but moved like crones. All too often, they were forced to sell their bodies in the hope of making a little money. Just enough to eat, or take care of their next fix. In the twenty or so minutes since he'd settled in to stalk his enemy, six different girls had attempted to offer themselves to him. One look in his eyes was all that it took to drive them away, as often as not crossing themselves and muttering prayers under their breath. At a guess, the oldest was around twenty-five. She looked closer to fifty.

"Ain't this just a pisser," Joe sneered. He spoke aloud, but talked only to himself. "I know it came into Tijuana, but finding it's gonna be a bitch."

"Hey, man. I don't see why we got to follow this thing anyway. Leave it to the Sabbat in Tijuana." Joe looked over at his companion and managed not to hit the man. Del Gado was as nervous as he was stupid. How he'd managed to live more than a year beyond his Embrace was anyone's guess.

"Just do us both a favor, *hombre*, and shut the hell up before I shove them boots of yourn up yer caboose. I know I'm gettin' soft in my old age. Iffn I wasn't, I'd a' kilt you a long while back." He paused a moment, rolling a cigarette with deft fingers and tamping one end against his bony wrist to pack the loose tobacco.

"You don't have to be so nasty, Boot. I can say whatever I damned well please."

"Not around me, you can't. I don't much like dealing with yella-bellies. Only reason yer even here's 'cause you know what that blasted thing looks like." He was just striking a match against his thumb tip when the screams started. He looked in the direction of the agonized shrieks and nodded. "Let's get this done. I want ta get back to Mexico City." After the tip of his cigarette was burning properly, he started moving in the direction of the sounds.

Hill double-checked the pistols on his hips, reassured by their familiar weight. After a hundred-plus years, they were as much a part of him as his own hands. Since his Embrace—the night he'd been beaten down and forced to drink vampiric blood—he'd become very proficient with the weapons. Oh, the old pistols he'd once carried were gone, long since replaced by more modern weapons, but the feel of them was still familiar. The feel of murder at his fingertips was a sweet thing indeed.

He headed toward his quarry at a leisurely saunter. His steps were assured, confident. The screams came from only a block away, at a cheap little hotel that specialized in hourly rates for the rooms and the women alike. The scent of blood in the air told him he'd found his prey at last.

The vermin who passed for police in Tijuana surrounded the building, ready for whatever might come out. None of them were quite bold enough to go inside. They weren't paid well enough to die, not by any stretch of the imagination. Joe was having second thoughts about entering the building himself. The thing behind that door was certain to sense him as easily as he sensed it, and it was far more vicious than he. Also, despite their reassuring weight, his pistols wouldn't do him a damned bit of good against the monster.

The decision was taken out of his hands when the wall exploded outward in a blossom of debris. Several of the *policia* screamed, jumping in shock as fragments of brick and wood spewed away from the hotel. A spear of wood shot past Joe, impaling del Gado through his chest. What remained of the front desk stuck halfway through the stuccoed wall, spilling its contents across the ground. Joe looked down at the other vampire, where he lay twitching and stuck to the ground. "Well, that's one problem solved. Ya always wuz too eager ta run away. Let's see ya do it now." Joe backpedaled as he spoke.

Everyone backed away, Joe included, though not del Gado. Joe had lived a hundred years and won virtually all of his battles, not because he was immensely powerful, but because he believed in being cautious.

The humans seemed as skittish as newborn foals, and Joe took an odd comfort from their fear. At least he wasn't alone. On the other hand, he knew what was waiting inside the ruined hotel. From the second story of the building, a woman pushed past the shutters of her window, scrambling madly to escape whatever was in the room.

Even as she crawled through the narrow window, something wet and slimy wrapped around her throat, pulling her back. Joe stared, enthralled, as the tentacle stripped the flesh from her throat and face. He'd seen and done worse to many people. The mortals around him broke ranks, running in mindless panic from the shadowy hulk inside the building. A few, the truly brave, muttered prayers and crossed themselves, but stood their ground.

Joe respected their dedication, but knew it would only get them killed. The screams from the woman in the room upstairs trailed off and then ended abruptly. Joe's conscience screamed for him to save her. He forced himself to remember that she was only human, not really worth the trouble of rescuing. He did not like hearing her die, but he could live with it.

The silence that fell over the area was even more terrible than the screams had been. Every sense he had was heightened by the tension, and Joe felt a faint blood-sweat break out on his brow. He licked his upper lip, feeling the perpetual stubble there, and tasting the rusty flavor of his own perspiration. One of the nearby police officers wet himself. Joe sympathized with the reasons behind his sudden loss of bladder control.

His hands touched the grips of his pistols.

A demon from hell erupted from the window above.

The thing slapped down on the broken asphalt and Jorge del Gado with a sound like four hundred pounds of whale blubber crashing to the earth from a hundred feet up. It was a wet noise, and it filled Joe Hill with revulsion. The thing itself was a wild, chaotic mass of bubbling flesh, streaked with blood and dotted with what could only be called mouths. Great gaping maws filled with an odd assortment of teeth, cilia, and hooks moved in unison, filling the air with wheezing shrieks that surely had to reflect the monster's own madness. Small, circular sockets of black spread randomly across its mass, gleaming with an eerie intelligence. Somewhere under that thing, Jorge del Gado died. He would not be missed.

Even as Joe took in all of the changes in the freakish thing since last he'd seen it, the mass moved forward with terrifying speed, wrapping itself around one of the uniformed men and burying his struggling form.

Joe Hill took his hands away from the comfort of his weapons, preparing to face the creature. His battle cry was an equal blend of bloodlust and fear.

IV

LAS VEGAS

Don Michael Giovanni understood the meaning of power. He was the most influential being in all of

Las Vegas. To call him a man was no longer truly appropriate. He'd been a living breathing human being once, but for the last four centuries he had existed among the Kindred, the vampires. His life was very different from what most humans could ever comprehend. For four hundred years he had fought against undead rivals in an endless battle for power. These days he left the fighting to others. A word or a gesture from Don Michael, and the unfortunate who had displeased him was as good as dead.

He missed the good old nights. It all came too easily. There was no challenge left. Oh, to be sure, many vied for his position, but none had been able to take it from him. His security was far too tight and his power over the human rulers of Las Vegas was absolute. Everyone had a price. Loyalty came easy when you met and exceeded that sum. Some wanted money, others wanted satisfaction. Any who refused to play by Michael Giovanni's rules found themselves buried in the desert, lost for all time.

Like all of his clanmates, the vampire prince of Las Vegas was ruthless to a fault. He had to be. The Giovanni did not belong to any of the political factions in Kindred society. They paid homage neither to the Camarilla, nor the Sabbat—though they dealt with both groups on a fairly regular basis. The two warring factions fought for cities and territory all over the world, and Las Vegas had the dubious honor of being close to the border between the two sects' domains.

The Camarilla held sway in most of the United States and controlled virtually all of Europe and Africa. The Sabbat held a few strongholds in the Northeastern US and claimed all of South America as its domain. While the two factions fought over territories in dispute, the Giovanni established their power bases where no one really bothered to look.

Las Vegas, for example, didn't even exist until he had decided to end the grief he suffered in Santa Monica. Back in the forties he'd run most of his financial empire from a handful of gambling ships off the coast of California. When the Ventrue clan of vampires decided they would seize control or use their pawns in the human political arena to destroy the Giovanni power base, he'd let them. Before the bastards even knew what hit them, he had finalized plans for building the city where he now ruled. Getting the capital up for such a venture was simplicity itself. He just talked to his superiors within the clan and, *voilà*, instant city. Just add water and let human greed do the rest.

There had been some work involved, but not much. In a matter of only a few years he'd established a stronghold for Giovanni interests, one that even the Ventrue could not destroy. Simple economics kept them from taking over or shutting the city down. Nevada needed the money it received from the casinos, and the Giovanni owned them all—lock, stock, and barrel. Every one of the casinos belonged to someone else on paper, to be sure, but those people needed Don Michael and his money. He owned them, body and soul. Without ever lifting a finger, he generated money for his clan and expanded his own personal influence within the Family. Indeed, he was one of the clan's golden children. He could do no wrong in the clan leaders' eyes.

That was the main problem. He no longer needed to do anything at all. He was bored. Without a challenge in his life, the night-to-night mechanics of holding his city together meant nothing at all.

Perhaps he should have taken up a hobby. Surely

if he had, his thoughts would not have drawn so much unwanted attention. While Don Michael Giovanni contemplated the meaning of his existence, other forces listened in. Surely his thoughts were an invitation if ever there was one. Once invited, they moved into Las Vegas to stay. The prince of Las Vegas's life was about to get a lot more interesting.

V

Las Vegas

Tourists found the city lovely. Glittering casinos arched luminous spires into the heavens to compete with the night sky. Within a few blocks of the Strip, however, the real world rudely interrupted and the dreams became a cesspool. Statistically speaking, there were more gang members roaming the streets than in any other part of the country. Drugs were rampant, and violence was a way of life. Alcoholism soared; drug abuse was the rule, not the exception. There were places where the police simply did not go, because they did not dare.

The crimes committed in Vegas were the sort you hear about every day. Murder, rape, rampant gang activity, violence in levels never dreamed of by people only twenty years ago. They never made it to the newspapers, however, or to the television either. Bad press could slow down the influx of new money into Las Vegas, and that would never do. Instead the crimes were hidden, buried in the darkest corners of the city and left to fester and bloat.

Hell-Storm

The city was ripe with corruption and ready to spill its foul seed across the ground for all to see.

Jude thrived on the bad parts of the city. He loved to walk down the darkened streets in his jeans and muscle shirts and wait for someone, anyone, to try their luck. Unfortunately for Jude, word about what happened to those foolish enough to attack him had already reached the street. He seldom had a chance to mangle anyone.

Which was just as well; lately the idea of hurting someone just for kicks wasn't as satisfying as it used to be. Indeed, Jude had a bad feeling about the city of late. There was something intangible in the air, something making him a little edgier than he usually was.

When he'd reached Vegas a year earlier, he'd decided that the city held everything he needed for his comfort. He still felt that way, but something else was here as well. Something vile and dangerous. Jude loved the danger aspect. It was the secretive nature of the threat that bothered him.

Down Anderson Avenue, where the seedier aspects of Las Vegas nightlife liked to stalk each other and anything that got in their way, Jude walked with a predatory gait. Not far away, a cluster of punks, dressed in gang colors—blue bandannas and black shirts and pants, one of the new gangs coming in from LA—was hanging at the end of the street. They saw him and shifted their eyes elsewhere. Last time they'd tried their luck with Jude he'd left two dead and three hospitalized. Everything that should have gone well went wrong. Guns exploded in steady hands and healthy members of the gang ended up dead. None of them dared retaliate. The consensus among the gang was simply that Jude was not human, at least not like any human they'd seen before. Their opinion was very accurate.

Seeing the reaction his appearance caused made Jude smile. He liked having that effect on people. "Hello, ladies. Nice night for a walk."

One of the group advanced, fists balled, and was pulled back by the others. Jude laughed and continued on his way. A low-slung Cadillac oozed down the street, blaring a Latino beat. Several shadowy figures sat very low in the deep seats, wearing sunglasses despite the late hour. Jude watched them go by, nodding to the man in the passenger's seat. The man nodded back, pointing his index finger like the barrel of a gun and mimicking a firing hammer with his thumb.

Jude stood watching the car as it faded away, an odd smile on his handsome face. His ice blue eyes stared at his reflection in a window across the street. As always, the face staring back seemed very wrong. Anyone looking at him just then would have thought he was a little slow. His black hair was pulled back in a ponytail, and the wind clutched the thick cord of hair, flipping it wildly into the air. He turned just in time to see the boy coming at him, knife held ready to thrust down into his neck.

Jude stepped smoothly to the side, raising his left arm to block the blow. The impact was jarring, but nothing he wasn't used to from countless other attacks. His right elbow slammed into the boy's face, loosening three teeth and smearing his lips all over the place. Using the momentum he already had going, he backhanded his target's nose halfway into the next week. The boy dropped bonelessly, and Jude kneed him once more as he fell.

"Well, that was fun. Want to try it again?" Already unconscious, Jude's attacker opted not to reply. Jude waited politely for a few seconds and then shrugged. "Maybe tomorrow." He looked over to the rest of the gang, face set in an expression of challenge. No one moved. The world went soft for Jude, his mind grew cloudy. He looked from his victim to the group watching him cautiously. "Hey. Tony fell down. You think you guys can get him home okay?"

"Yeah, man. It's skippy. No problems." The leader's voice was shaky, nervous. Despite the cool night air and gentle breeze, he was sweating.

"Cool. See ya around." Jude walked on, oblivious to the strange looks the gang exchanged. That was Jude's biggest problem. He didn't understand how different he really was from the world around him. He seldom pondered why he couldn't remember his life before coming to Vegas. He simply accepted that he was here now and saw no reason to move on. On a few occasions the lack of memories bothered him, drove him into a frightening rage. When that happened, his normally cheerful demeanor vanished, replaced by silent brooding and a need to hurt people. The gang behind him had made the mistake of bothering him when he was in that mood the last time.

Jude continued his stroll through the most dangerous part of the city, enjoying the sounds of the night and nodding his greetings to complete strangers. Some people actually held their breath until he'd passed, afraid that even the slightest noise might set him off. Every last person, some of them guilty of murder and worse, was glad to see him go.

Jude always had that effect on people.

2

I

Gabriel White sat in the back of the Ford Bronco and listened to the sounds of his mother and Shaun going round and round over who was paying for what. Diane wanted to pay for everything; Shaun wanted to pay for everything. *Like either of them could afford to pay for it all*, he thought. Neither was willing to take "no" for an answer.

He was hot. The desert sun seemed so very much warmer than the same celestial body felt when he was at home. Even this close to nightfall, the area was a furnace. The Bay area just didn't get this warm. Despite the open windows and the sixty-five-mile-per-hour breeze flinging his hair across his face, the heat from outside stuck to him like a wet blanket. He looked down at the picture of Teri he held in his hands, missing her already. They'd only left a few hours ago, but that didn't matter. Teri was his girl, and being away from her was like trying to break a bad drug habit. He wanted her with him all of the time.

Looking away from the photo, he turned to view the rugged terrain outside the moving vehicle—a vast spread of rock and sand, with the occasional cactus to remind a person that there was life out there. Out of the corner of his eye he caught a coyote dashing away and felt the old familiar thrill of seeing something new. Then the blur of motion disappeared and the wastelands spread out again in silence. Except, of course, for Shaun and his mom's constant arguing.

Up ahead, a signpost held the simple legend:

LAS VEGAS 75 MILES

He felt the excitement twist his insides again. Finally, a place where he could have a little fun.

They could actually see the city limits just after sunset. The lights of Las Vegas burned brightly, igniting the sky with a thousand colors. Even this far away, the powerful beam from the top of the Luxor's pyramid-shaped main building was noticeable. Just before they reached the city proper, Shaun pulled the truck to the side of I–95. He climbed out of the driver's side door and stretched his stocky, athletic form. Diane looked over at Gabriel for a second, shrugging at his unvoiced question: *Why have we stopped*?

Shaun looked around for a moment, nodding to himself, and then peered through the open door. "Diane? Would you be a love and drive the car over to the Palace?"

"Well, sure, but what are you . . . ?"

"Not just me. Gabriel and I are going to get a little exercise."

She looked puzzled for a second, then her eyes

widened, and she nodded. "Okay. Are you sure you two will be all right?"

Shaun put on his winning smile and nodded, the crow's-feet at his eyes crinkling with humor. "Of course, dear lady. We'll be just fine." When Diane nodded again, Shaun looked into the backseat and stared at Gabriel. "Come on then, lad. Time to do a bit of running."

Gabe slipped from the backseat and winced as his muscles protested the lack of activity. Despite the heat and the sweat, he couldn't help but feel a thrill race through his muscles. "Sounds great!" After a second's hesitation, he leaned back in his own door, staring at his mother. "You sure you'll be okay, Mom?"

Diane nodded, her pretty face showing more worry than he suspected she'd have liked him to see. "I'll be fine, Gabe. Just you be careful, okay?"

"That's a deal." He reached into the car as his mother slid over to the driver's seat. When she was comfortable, he wrapped his arms around her and gave her a brief hug. "See ya in a while."

Diane's return smile was sad, haunted. "See you soon." Gabriel and Shaun stood by the side of the road until the car disappeared from sight. They stood that way for several more minutes before walking into the darkness leading in the opposite direction from the city.

After almost a full hour of walking, pausing from time to time while Shaun pointed to a particular plant or stone and commented on its purpose in Gaia's world, they stopped and took off their clothes.

"Why do we take off our clothes if we don't have to?" Gabriel asked.

"Because I don't want you getting too comfortable with the clothing on your back. Each item of clothing you wear must be prepared before you can wear it and change without causing it damage. You've got three pairs of jeans and four T-shirts that've been properly dedicated. Everything else will tear apart when you change." Shaun looked over at Gabriel with a friendly smile. "What you've got on hasn't been dedicated as yet. Imagine what your mother would say if we came back wearing nothing but our birthday suits."

"I keep forgetting about that."

"Aye. That's why I'm your teacher. To help you remember."

He and Shaun both meticulously wrapped their clothes into bundles, using their shoestrings and belts to make certain the packages were tightly bound. Then they made a loop of the belt ends and set them carefully on the ground. Gabriel felt his adrenaline increasing, felt the blood in his body grow warmer.

"Let's do this," said Shaun. "The Crinos first, and then the Lupus."

The first time Gabriel experienced the change, he thought he'd lost his mind. Several hours of heavy sweating and agonizing convulsions culminated in the release of a monster from his worst nightmares. He could remember the night if he concentrated on it, but often as not decided to forget.

That was in the past. A few weeks of training sufficed to allow him the freedom to become a werewolf whenever he desired. Changing forms was a rush like none other, and he looked forward to the times when he was allowed to roam the wilds. It only took a few seconds, and though the pain was like a hot knife while his bones stretched and his muscles reshaped themselves to match the change in his skeleton, all five of his senses grew sharper and the fine hairs on his body grew longer and thicker. The sheer power of his changed shape was intoxicating. The increase in his senses made him feel heady.

Beside him, Shaun Ingram's body changed also. The man's broad torso grew longer and even broader as well; his forearms stretched even as his calves did the same. The thick muscles of his neck bulged, while the bones in his spine curved at a new angle, forcing his head into a lower position. The red hair on his body grew wildly, all but erupting from his body in a wave, darkening as it did so to a rich auburn color. His nose and chin stretched outward and his brow grew more pronounced. Fine, even teeth lengthened and sharpened as the bones and muscles in his jawline swelled. The only part of his body that remained unchanged was his eyes. They were as sky blue and intelligent as ever.

In human form, Gabriel White stood six feet tall. In the Crinos, he loomed to a height of nine feet, seven inches. Beside him, Shaun Ingram grew to just under eight feet in height. Shaun was smaller, weaker than he. Gabriel also knew the man could tear him apart.

The voice coming from Shaun's muzzle was distorted, warped by his mouth's shape and the odd changes in his vocal cords, but his words were still comprehensible. "Let's move. I want to make it to the mesa before we change shapes again."

Reborn as nature's most ideal killing machines, the two of them started running. They lowered their arms and ran on all fours, charging across the desert floor. The animals they encountered froze in their tracks, petrified by the sight of Gaia's protectors.

When Gabriel could no longer hold back his savage joy, he howled to the full moon above him, praising Luna in a thunderous voice. Shaun joined him. For a while, they were free.

II

SAN FRANCISCO

Just after eight-thirty, Teri Johannsen used the key Diane White had given her and entered the White residence, armed with her trusty watering pail. Diane needed someone to water the plants while they were away, and Teri was more than glad to do it.

Gabriel was gone less than a day, and already she missed him. He was nice to be with and a gentleman to boot. He never tried pushing her farther than she was willing to go in the physical aspects of their relationship. She liked him a lot, but going all the way was still a few years off in her eyes. Sixteen was too young, no matter what Melissa Jackson had to say about the subject.

She moved around the living room, watering the small plants along the windowsills and the plum tree standing in the bay window. After that, she moved toward the back of the first floor, pausing at every windowsill and then continuing on to water the plants in John White's study.

The room had not been altered in any way. Everything was exactly where it should be. The only element missing was John White—dead for the last year and a half.

She'd always liked John. He was the sort of man she would have chosen as a father if she'd been given any choice in the matter. Her own father tended more toward the sort one heard about on talk shows—she loved her dad, but she also hated him on the nights when a twelve-pack and a half of Budweiser disappeared from the refrigerator and he got violent. How he managed to keep a job was something of a mystery to Teri—in the movies the alcoholic parent always got fired—but one she tended not to think about. He was drinking tonight, had been since the minute he came in the door and dropped his shoes next to the hallway closet. Dear old dad was in a "whuppin' mood," and so she used the excuse of watering the plants to get the hell out before he started slipping the belt from his pants. Lately, he tended to prefer beating Teri to slapping her mother around. With the way he looked at her sometimes, she almost suspected that wasn't the only thing he'd prefer to do with her. She rubbed the tender area where he'd taken out his drinking frustrations the last time—*"What the hell are you lookin' at, little missy? Where's your mind?"*—and finished with the plants in John's den.

Teri left the study with a feeling of loss unlike any she'd experienced before. John White was long dead, but only now did that fact really strike home. Part of her felt guilty about taking so long to really understand that the man was gone forever. Most of her just felt sad.

She moved through the kitchen, pausing to water the ferns hanging over the table where the Whites ate their meals, and moved up the stairs to where the bedrooms were. There were no plants in Gabriel's room, but she stopped there anyway, feeling his presence in the room and catching the familiar musky smell of his body in the air. On the street outside, a car idled for a few moments and finally stopped. The doors slammed, and then the silence returned as she drifted on thoughts of her boyfriend.

Gabriel was special. His shy smile, his clumsy way of walking. Everything about him made her happy to be alive. She hated that he was out of town, almost as much as she hated the idea of going home to the anger of her father. After ten minutes of sitting on the edge of Gabriel's bed, Teri moved on to Diane's room and watered the plants there.

Every step down toward the first floor of the town house filled Teri with dread. She didn't dare stay here for too long, or her father would accuse her of sleeping with one of the neighborhood boys. That was his favorite excuse for "giving her a whuppin'" of late. Right around the same time she started developing breasts, he started looking for any excuse to call her a whore or a slut. *"Come here, sweetie, let Daddy look at his little angel . . . "* He started beating her. She'd toyed with telling the police, but her father was a good man, and she didn't want to see him in jail for being a little angry when he drank.

Not often, he didn't drink very often at all, but when he did, Lord help the person foolish enough to get his attention. Lawrence Johannsen was a mean drunk, and, lately, he almost always seemed to notice Teri when she passed him in the hallway or the living room. A chill rippled up her spine and gooseflesh crawled across her arms and back. She had trouble remembering how to breathe and had to force herself to inhale and exhale as she walked toward the front door.

She knew from experience that the next two blocks from Gabriel's place to her own home would seem like a thousand miles. She wished Gabriel were here to hold her. He always made her feel better.

She opened the front door just as a very tall man was reaching out to grab the exterior doorknob. Teri let out a little gasp of surprise, dreading for just an instant that the man was her father. But he was much taller, and leaner as well. Athletic, but lean. A shaggy mane of gray hair fell down from his head in wild waves that drifted across his shoulders and half obscured his eyes.

"Oh, Gawd! You scared me half to death." Her voice was shaky and strident, a tone she hated because it sounded too much like her mother's normal tone. She smiled to take away the sting of her words.

The raspy quality of the man's voice sent warning notes across her mind. That he also sounded amused did nothing to help her feel calmer. "I'm so very sorry about that, Teri. It is Teri, isn't it?"

"Yes, it is. I'm sorry, have we met?"

"We've never been formally introduced, but I know you well enough. You've been dating Gabriel."

"Oh, are you a friend of Gabriel's?" She felt calmer knowing that the man knew Gabe. If he was a friend of Gabriel's, he couldn't be all bad.

"Not quite. We've hardly even met. I'm his father, Edward McTyre."

"His father?" She was confused. John White was Gabe's father. She'd known the family long enough to remember the man fondly.

"Yes. His biological father. Gabriel was adopted."

"I-I didn't know that."

The man chuckled, his voice growing deeper. "I'm not surprised. Diane and John White never bothered to tell him."

The silence stretched for several moments, and then Edward McTyre spoke again. "I've been waiting to meet him for a long time. Longer than most people could ever understand." He stepped forward, his aggressive manner forcing Teri back into the hallway of the White residence. "The time has come for Gabriel to meet his daddy."

"He . . . he's not home. The family left town." She felt the panic returning, felt her heartbeat increase and a thick fear-sweat break across her entire body.

"Yes. I know." Revealed in the full light of the

house, Edward McTyre was a monster. His hair was patchy, sparse in some areas and full in others. His flesh looked too smooth, as if he'd been hideously burned some time in his past, and the doctors attending him had never even bothered to try to limit the scarring. Large areas of his flesh were an angry red, while the rest of his skin was too pale. His watery eyes were charcoal gray and glittered feverishly in the artificial light. His head seemed too large for the rest of his body, and his thin-lipped mouth in turn seemed too large for his head.

Teri backed away from him again, stopping only when a wall barred her way.

Edward McTyre slammed an arm against the wall on either side of her chest and leaned in close. His wide grin was as mesmerizing as the eyes of a cobra. "Yes, indeed, I know he's not home. But I bet you can tell me where he is."

Suddenly, Teri very much wanted the comfort of her father's arms.

III

TIJUANA

Joe Hill could not remember just when the fight began. For some length of time, between an hour and a century, he'd been wrapped inside a moving wall of blubbery death. He clawed, he bit, he even tried firing his weapons, all to no avail. Certainly not too long, for parts of Jorge del Gado still floated in the crushing miasma that surrounded him. *Serves ya right, ya damned polecat,* he thought. *Worst mistake I ever made was hookin' up with a loser like you.* Another violent squeeze from the monster brought his attention back to the battle.

Hot, needlelike pains erupted across his face where the monster he'd pursued from Mexico City once again sank its flesh into his. He screamed, then pulled away from the pain as much as he could.

The weight of a hundred corpses seemed to press him into the ground as the vile thing convulsed and squeezed down on his body. "Boy, you really are starting to get on mah nerves," he panted, as another pseudopod reached across and started battering its way into his throat. Enough was enough. Come hell or high water, he was ready to end the battle.

Joe Hill reached out with his hands, struggling to grab hold of the main mass of his enemy. After a few moments, he managed to gain his prize. It only took a second to extend his claws. Once they were elongated, he shoved forward with all of his strength, ripping into the gelid mass and sinking his sharpened nails into the heavy musculature flowing beneath the creature's hide.

The scream which erupted from his enemy was both verbal and mental. The world of Joseph Hill collapsed, exploding into fragments as the monster retaliated. His last thoughts were simply that he had failed to stop the horror before it could grow again.

IV

Jack Dawson walked into the Palisades Casino as if he owned the place. He ignored the beefy security men all around the place and headed straight into the pit, where hopeless mobs desperately blew money in a desperate attempt to gain back much more than they had lost. The ringing bells and whooping sirens going off in the room told a tale of fabulous riches won, but the empty, bitter expressions on so many of the gamblers' faces told a different tale.

Dawson wore what he always wore in Vegas: blue jeans, cowboy boots, a light flannel shirt, a heavy leather duster, gloves, and his trusty battered Stetson hat. In most towns his attire would have attracted attention; in Las Vegas he was practically tame. The hat and gloves served their usual purpose. They kept his unusual physical deformities hidden from the dozens of security cameras mounted and concealed throughout the casino.

Most of the people either ignored him completely or got the hell out of his way. He moved with the cocky strut of a street turk ready for a fight. Now and then someone failed to move quickly enough and got knocked half off their feet as a result. One or two complained, but the noises were minor in comparison to the endless sounds of slot machines in action. A very adept pickpocket tried for his wallet as he moved across the floor, but thought better of it when Dawson stared into her face. There was something decidedly scary in the way he looked at a person.

On the other end of the main casino, a well-camouflaged door was guarded by two very large men in the uniforms of the Palisades security force. He stopped before the two and looked at the largest before speaking. "Hi there, fellas. Y'all be good and tell Michael G. that Jack Dawson is here to see him, if you please." His voice was filled with cheer, just as it always was.

"If you could wait one minute, Mr. Dawson, we'll check with the Man."

Dawson waited, looking around at the masses moving from machine to machine, thrusting coins into the slots and pulling old-fashioned handles or pushing buttons to make the digital fruit and symbols spin. A very bitter-looking woman well into her golden years shoved rudely past him, a Camel unfiltered stuck firmly in her mouth. He smiled, nodding and saying "excuse me, Ma'am" as if the entire collision had been his fault.

A few seconds later, the mirrored door in a mirrored wall opened, and the two guards stepped out of the way.

"Enjoy your stay in Las Vegas, Mr. Dawson." The guards were very polite; they were paid to be polite.

"That I will, good buddy. That I will."

He walked past the guards and down a corridor carpeted with a lush white shag and papered with gray satin wallpaper. There was only one door, and that was at the end of the hallway. The door was open, and Dawson appreciated the heavy steel vault he entered, remembering a time when the only barrier had been a simple fire door. After the collapse at the MGM Grand, Michael Giovanni had stopped taking chances.

Past the vault door and inside the massive room, a huge oak desk and several plush chairs were surrounded by paintings by some of the hottest new artists in the country. Michael Giovanni collected fine art the way some people collected comic books. His fascination with the art world was one of the few vices the man allowed himself, and the only real weakness Dawson ever heard him admit to.

Michael Giovanni rose from his seat behind the desk and opened his arms in greeting as Dawson walked toward him. "Jack Dawson! It's damn good to see you again!" He was a big man, with dark Mediterranean skin and darker hair, dressed in a suit as black as the devil's soul. His handsome Roman features were the sort that made women look twice, even if he did seem old enough to be the father of most of the women dancing in Las Vegas. Don Giovanni looked roughly forty, and moved with the ease and grace of a man born into money and bred for power. Other than being much older than he appeared, his looks were not deceiving.

The two men met and embraced, exchanging dry pecks on each cheek. "How the hell are ya, Mike? It's been too long."

"That it has, old friend, that it has."

"Lucy sends her love, by the way." Dawson grinned ear to ear, pleased to see the old vampire before him.

Michael laughed, his handsome face beaming with merriment. "Does she know you call her Lucy?"

"Sure. Same as you know I call you Mike."

"You've got balls, Jack. Maybe three people I know have ever called Lucretia Giovanni 'Lucy' and lived to tell about it." The man slapped Jack's shoulder and indicated the chairs set out around the room. "Make yourself at home, you old bastard. What's mine is yours."

Jack flopped down in one of the oversize leather thrones, setting his boots on the marble table resting in front of Giovanni's desk. Rather than taking his habitual seat behind the desk, Michael Giovanni settled down in another of the armchairs.

"Looks like the world's still treating you right, Mike. I like the new decor."

"Yeah? Well, now and then you just need a few new pieces to change the atmosphere. You stay with the old stuff, you start feeling like an antique, y'know what I mean?"

"Hell yes. Just bought myself a new truck last

week. The old one did me well, but she was getting tired, and I wanted a change of pace."

"I know what you mean about a change of pace. This place is starting to seem too small."

The two chatted on about everything and nothing for almost an hour before Dawson changed the subject. "Listen, Mike. I do love talking with you, but my guess is you didn't call me over here to shoot the breeze."

"Yeah. I called you 'cause I have work for you."

"What sort of work?" Both men lost the pleasant edges in their voices. The time for reminiscing was past, and both had to make a living.

"There's a new casino, the Platinum Palace, scheduled to open later this week." Michael Giovanni's normally pleasant demeanor changed as he spoke. His face grew darker, menacing. "Clan Giovanni owns this city, but the people opening the Palace don't seem to understand that. I want the place gone. If you can't remove the building, then I want you to remove the people behind its construction."

"That big place? The one right next to the Mirage?" Dawson looked hard at Giovanni. The Platinum Palace looked like it was already open, and the building occupied nearly an entire city block. Giovanni nodded his affirmative response. "That's a damned tall order, Mike. You'd just about be better off renting a Ryder truck and buying a half ton of fertilizer."

Michael Giovanni laughed, practically roaring with good humor. His eyes glittered with joy. "Don't think I haven't thought about it. But the problem with explosives is that they get noticed. When they get noticed, they get traced. I've been at this game too long to risk everything to make my point."

"So do you know who's behind the Palace? Is it the Mafia again?"

"No. Not the mob. We have a long-standing agreement about splitting the rights here in Vegas. I know most of my family has a problem with the human gangs, but I have an understanding with them. They get their share, and they do what they have to to cover up the mistakes. Besides, these days they work for me."

Giovanni stood up, pacing the large office like a jungle cat in a very small cage. He walked over to his desk after a few moments, opening the top drawer and removing a thick envelope. "No, this is a new player. Took a lot of looking, almost two months' worth, to find out who's behind the Palace. A business conglomerate called Pentex. Seems owning the fast-food joints and the movie chains ain't enough for these assholes anymore."

"Pentex?" Dawson revealed more than he wanted to when he spoke. Don Michael looked back at him with a brooding, curious expression.

"You've heard of 'em?"

"Yeah. They've had me pull a few jobs for them in the past. Nothing big."

"You have a problem dealing with these bastards?"

"No." Dawson shook his head, slipping his boots from the table and standing up. "I'll take the job. Me and a few of the boys at Pentex have unfinished business to settle anyway."

Mike beamed, his broad, handsome face once again looking as friendly as Dawson liked to remember. "This is a fine night, then, Jack. This is a very fine night. With you working the case, I have nothing to worry about."

Jack Dawson smiled back, his easygoing manner and his laid-back grin hiding the fact that he was worried very deeply by the implications. One rule he'd learned a long time ago popped into his mind even as he shook the prince of Las Vegas's strong hand: Wherever Pentex goes, werewolves tend to follow.

He didn't like the idea of fighting the Lupines, not one little bit.

V

Denise Merrick had a body built for pleasure. She was curvaceous, but with enough muscle to avoid having to worry about getting flabby. At the ripe old age of twenty-three she was well versed in the art of pleasing men. She wore the latest fashions and walked with the grace of a ballerina. Her second year as an escort, and already she'd made more money than most executives three times her age.

Denise was well paid to be the perfect date. She knew the right wines to order with any meal, the proper order in which to employ her forks, and the best places to eat in the city. She was also a veritable fountain of knowledge on the stock market and was licensed to work as a financial agent. Her clients were the very finest in the city.

Tonight she was going to meet a new man. He worked for a multinational conglomerate and had connections with the mob. Not that she cared in the least what he did for a living as long as he could meet her normal rates. The only time she discussed business with a man was when he wanted her to discuss business. She wasn't paid for her opinions, at least not often.

The escort service Denise worked for was owned by her and four other girls who were equally well qualified. The staff called her "Ma'am" and did as they were told without question. She did not abuse the privilege. Contrary to what most people thought of someone in her particular profession, Denise did not carry a beeper, nor did she have to check in with anyone before the night was over. The only person Denise had to answer to was herself. Oh, to be sure, she paid a share of her income for the privilege of working within the city limits, but she never worried about getting arrested or hurt. Every client who came to Denise was carefully screened before they met. Part of the substantial sum her clients paid went toward a background check.

Proposals of marriage came to Denise almost as often as junk mail comes in the average mailbox. She politely declined all offers.

Denise left her home at 9:30 P.M., prepared to meet with her latest client at exactly 10:00 P.M. at a designated location. She never made the rendezvous. The Wyrm caught up with her first.

When her body was found early the next morning, the flesh and bones had been warped far from their original shapes. The twelve-year-old boy who found her thought the strange-looking thing was some kind of snake, or possibly a nest of snakes. He poked it with a long stick and ran away when it screamed at him. After only a few hours, the snake-thing finally figured out how to rearrange itself into Denise's original form. The creature that had been Denise Merrick found her car and her home with little difficulty. All of Denise's memories were there for the taking. Its first objective after cleaning and showering was to call Denise's client from the night before and apologize for missing their date. It offered to make up for the inconvenience in any way the man wanted. After only a minimum of placating, he agreed. She was, after all, a very beautiful woman.

They met that night, and the Wyrm claimed its second victim in Las Vegas.

The Wyrm came home to the city, wondering how it had managed to miss the place for so many years.

VI

Four hours after her arrival, Diane White still couldn't quite grasp the luxury of her suite. The king-size bed was perfect. The view was stunning. Even the bathroom was like a slice of heaven on earth. At present, she floated in the warm waters of the private Jacuzzi, where the pressurized streams moving beneath the bubbles were making mincemeat of the steel bars that had long since replaced her back muscles. The stereo system belted out an endless stream of torch songs. The chilled champagne was just tart enough to cleanse her pallet without making her mouth feel dry. Given the chance, she'd stay in the suite forever.

The last eighteen months had not been kind. When Diane was growing up she'd expected her life to maintain a nice, stable course. But from her college years on, everything in her life just crumbled when she least expected it.

Samuel Haight was her first love. They'd seen each other in high school and even then their mutual attraction was obvious to anyone who knew them. Sam always kept his distance, remained quiet and by himself in high school. When they both attended the University of Wyoming, the spark between them became a flame. By the last year of school they'd made plans for getting married and living happily after.

Then Sam's knee got ruined in a football game. She visited him in the hospital faithfully, until the day she entered his room and found the bed empty. Just like that, their dreams were gone.

Life went on, and then she met John White. John was a lot like Sam, handsome in a rugged way but still kind and almost frighteningly gentle. Unlike Sam, John stayed around for the long haul. They were married and should have lived happily ever after, but Fate threw a few more unexpected surprises Diane's way. Life went well, but finances were always appallingly low. Despite a solid education and a gusto for his work, John never seemed to make enough money to cover all the bills. Diane went to work for all of a week before John exploded in a fury the likes of which she'd never seen. She quit her job and his temper faded away again. Simply put, John White could not stand the thought of not being a good provider. Adding to the tensions in their marriage, they soon discovered that Diane was infertile. Both of them wanted a family, but it was not meant to be.

They applied for adoption several times, always being turned down because they did not make enough to "support a child properly." Just when Diane was certain their marriage was doomed to failure, John got a new job, one that paid him handsomely for his expertise. The next time they applied for adoption, his new employer pulled a few strings and, *voilà*, instant family. Gabriel Thomas White was adopted into their family with full honors. The only sad note for a long while was the news that her parents had passed away.

After their death, she inherited a substantial amount of money—along with over forty letters written to her by Samuel Haight and postmarked from exotic locations all over the world. Her parents had never let her know of his attempts to communicate.

Much as she loved her mother and father, she cursed their names when she read through the letters. Sam's sorrow and regret were there on every page, along with a deep-seated anger for the life he'd been dealt. Despite everything, including her life with John and Gabriel, she longed to see him again.

Still, she was happy despite the few bad things she'd experienced.

Until Halloween night just two years ago. That was the night her sweet son vanished, kidnapped by unknown assailants. Then the monsters came. Edward McTyre—Gabriel's biological father—so like his son and so very different. Where Gabriel was kind, McTyre was a sadistic bastard. Worse still, he was a sadistic bastard who was also a werewolf. She remembered little after the man changed into a nine-foot-tall demon, but she recalled too well the sight of her husband dying as McTyre tore out his throat.

Then the noises came from outside the house, and the monster went to check. In its place Sam Haight entered the house a few minutes later and almost three decades late for their wedding. He was still handsome, but he was also so very different from the man she remembered. He was harder, meaner. Her world tilted madly from that point on. When next she remembered much of anything, Gabriel was back home and her husband's corpse was being lowered into the ground. Sam was nowhere around.

He called, even came to visit three times over the next twelve months. He always brought gifts and spent time talking with Gabriel. He also did something to her mind to let her accept that her son was a werewolf and that her next-door neighbor, Shaun Ingram, was a Garou as well. The mere sight of Shaun or Gabe changing didn't make her mind shut down anymore.

The last she'd heard from Sam, he was planning a brief trip to Mexico City, but he had promised to meet with her for Thanksgiving. He never made it. Almost a year to the day after he'd stepped back into her life, he vanished again.

Since then, Diane had learned the same lesson so many widows learn: When everything you own is in your dead husband's name, you effectively own nothing. The last six months had been a constant struggle to pay the bills and keep Gabriel from losing his mind. He was still a sweet kid most of the time, but now and then he reminded Diane of his father. His biological father. The similarities scared the hell out of her.

Now, just when she was certain she could fight off the bills no longer, she'd received an invitation to the grand opening of the Platinum Palace, Las Vegas's newest, brightest casino, designed by none other than John White.

She'd have come to the opening if only to honor her husband's memory. She loved him still, and could do no less. But as an added bonus, Andrew Montgomery, John's direct supervisor, had offered to extend a loan to the family. She needed the money. Oh, Lord, she needed the money so desperately.

Diane soaked in the water, relaxing as the warm jets caressed her body. She could stay here forever given a chance. For the first time in eighteen months, life was looking up again. She didn't even mind being alone.

VII

There were places in the world where animals refused to walk. People tended to grow nervous in those areas, and even the plants and trees leaned away from them. The unholy graveyard of Michael Giovanni's victims had become one of those places. The lizards, coyotes, birds, and even insects avoided the area. Far from the beaten path, people failed to notice the spot. Still, the animals knew, and so did the plants. A few small cacti grew in the area, but they did not prosper there. Wilted and beaten, the plants simply suffered and tried to survive.

The Dead were angry. In a small section of the desert only twenty miles from Las Vegas, the Dead were in pain and restless.

Jude could not say what led him through the desert to find the area, but the attraction was very strong. In this place, he could almost remember who he used to be. Not that he really wanted to, but he could just the same.

He could hear the voices screaming their rage into the wind, and even in the hundred-plus-degree temperatures of the noonday sun, he felt a chill run through his bones and caress every nerve in his body with a razor's edge.

"You are angry," he said.

The wind replied with a howl of despair, sending sand particles into his eyes and blinding him.

"Why?"

The Dead responded with images of pain and torment that dropped Jude to his knees. Lights danced before his closed eyes. Blood spilled across his tongue when he bit into the soft flesh of his inner mouth. Sweat crawled across his skin

Hell-Storm

and added an extra sting to his already-watering eyes.

Jude stood up after a time, his skin bleached white by shock. He nodded, looking around and carefully moving back toward the city. "I see. I'm very sorry."

He paused only once before leaving the area where no birds dared sing. Jude turned back to the desert floor where the Dead lay tormented and shook his head. "I make no promises, but I'll see if I can't fix the problem."

Jude started walking back toward the city he called home. He ignored the burning sunlight, neither tanning nor burning as he walked. With each step, something strange took place within Jude. Something strange and wonderful. For the first time since he lost his memory, he had a purpose. His mind opened up to the ways in which he could make Michael Giovanni suffer for what he'd done. Images of savagery far beyond what he'd been shown by the Dead ran through his mind in kaleidoscopic flashes.

His pace increased to a near run, but he felt no exhaustion and hardly broke a sweat. He grinned to himself as he moved, never noticing that the animals and insects of the desert were now avoiding him, too.

3

I

Shaun and Gabriel agreed; the Platinum Palace was amazing. The building defied logic, pushing the mind into overdrive as it tried to comprehend the sheer size of the place. Although the Palace was not officially open to the general public as yet, a full staff of servants catered to their needs and the needs of the other people wandering around the interior of the building. Just about everyone spent their time numbly staring at the massive chrome pillars and almost–organic-looking steel sculptures that adorned every free foot of wall space. Thick, plush carpets covered the floors on every level save the lobby. The lobby itself held a massive fountain, easily three stories high, which spilled iridescent streams of water from the mouths of a dozen metallic seraphim.

In short, the Platinum Palace made most of Vegas look tame in comparison.

Hell-Storm 53

Just the same, the two men and Diane White had a wonderful time running through the full-size amusement park in the center of the Palace, as well as sampling the fares from the dozen restaurants within the massive building. Despite the overwhelming heat of the midday sun, the interior of the Palace was a mild seventy degrees. Gift shops offering everything from clothes to candy to a thousand tacky knickknacks populated the building, and everything was available for the next forty-eight hours. Seven different camera crews were also running through the place, asking questions of everyone who would stop for them and taking moving shots of the panoramic interior.

Diane White smiled more that day than any in the last year and a half. She seemed almost like her old self to Gabriel. A stunning woman wearing more makeup than seemed possible spent thirty minutes talking with his mother about her late husband. Diane answered all of the woman's questions, pausing only once when the memories of his death grew too strong.

As the day progressed, Diane grew tired. Not surprising when Gabriel considered the distances they'd covered as they traveled the length of the massive building several times. When dinnertime came around, they were invited to eat with the manager of the entire Palace, Andrew Montgomery.

Andrew Montgomery was a decidedly handsome man, but Gabriel found him unsettling. Shaun apparently felt it too, as his normally friendly manner became more forced during the meal. He tried to hide it, but Gabriel knew him well enough to sense when he was not happy.

Diane seemed not to notice, but she was tired.

Despite Montgomery's odd presence, the night was as enjoyable as the day. The food was excellent, and the service staff included some of the most stunning women he'd ever seen. Of course, they only made him realize how much he missed Teri. By nine o'clock, Diane was ready to retire for the evening. She looked exhausted and seemed ready to collapse on her feet.

Gabriel and Shaun escorted her to her room. After the good-nights were exchanged, Shaun pulled him aside. "This place is a blight waiting to happen."

"Huh?" Gabe looked into his mentor's eyes, taken aback by the comment. "What are you talking about? It's a casino."

"Aye. That it is. It's also about as foul with the Wyrm's taint as any place I've ever seen."

Gabriel felt his hair rise along the back of his neck. But he also felt a blooming heat run deep into his chest as he thought about what was happening to his vacation. Part of him responded to his training, but the larger part wanted nothing to do with the enigmatic creature Shaun called the Wyrm.

"Can't someone else handle this crap, Shaun? Can't we just have a few days to relax?"

Shaun's face grew dark, his eyes all but blazed, and Gabriel heard the accent creeping back into his friend's voice. "Ye still don't understand, do you? Over a year now, I've been warning you about the dangers and ye still don't get it." He reached out gently and placed a hand on Gabriel's shoulder. "Come on, then. Let's go for a walk. I'll explain it to you again."

"I don't want you to explain anything to me, Shaun. I just want to relax." Even to his own ears, Gabriel sounded whiny.

"I know. But that will change soon enough."

The two of them left the Palace, stepping into the furnace left behind when the sun set. Even now the air was cooling, but several hours would have to pass before the air truly chilled again.

The night was filled with flashing lights and the distant sounds of music, merriment, and laughter. Gabriel White stepped into the darkness, wondering what secrets lay beyond the sounds of happiness. He suspected he'd find out all too soon.

He was right, of course. More right than he knew.

II

Jack Dawson walked the streets of Las Vegas as if he owned them. He did not feel nearly so confident as he acted.

Dawson felt a fondness for Las Vegas. He had passed through the city on countless occasions over the last century, spending spare time and a lot of money in pursuit of a little safe excitement. Still, the city had changed since last he'd been here. Despite the pretty colors and pretty faces, the air seemed filled with a deep tension. Violence waited nearby, ready to explode.

Once away from the main strip, the caliber of people changed as surely as the quality of lighting. Where the big casinos faded and the lights dimmed, the night people made themselves known. Drug users and pushers. Desperate, desolate souls looking for anything to fill the void where their lives had once been. Some of them still looked sane enough to escape if they tried. Some were too far gone down the road to damnation. Even the animals in these darkened streets seemed far removed from their counterparts in the world of the financially secure.

The battered street sign proclaimed the road's name as Vegas Valley Drive. The proper name should have been Road to Nowhere. Nowhere was exactly where the people living here were going. Dawson reached into his duster's pocket and drew forth a can of Red Man Chewing Tobacco. He slipped a wad of the stuff into his mouth and let the black juices seep between his teeth.

Gangs infested the area. Some rode around in cars as old as they were, others loitered on the corner near this bar or that convenience store. Predatory animals looking for easy prey. Dawson felt the familiar weight of his trusty old pistols and was reassured. The laws of the Camarilla frowned on using vampiric powers in public. They said nothing about defending yourself with guns. Jack Dawson had been born and raised with firearms nearby and, like many of his generation, nothing would ever replace the feel of his personal arsenal by his side.

Still, he preferred to avoid conflict whenever possible. Just because you can kill a man doesn't mean you like killing. In Dawson's case, that was especially true. Every death sent another soul into the realms of the Dead. Most faded away, heading on to their final reward. Some stayed behind, growing angry and feeding on the impotent emotions of the people around them. Wraiths. Some called them ghosts or spirits, but they called themselves wraiths. The wraiths did not like the living, but they held a special place in their spectral hearts for the ones who killed them.

Jack made a point of helping the wraiths escape from their bonds to the world of the living. He hunted down their killers or those who did them wrong while they were alive. He tracked down loved ones and passed on one last message. He avenged the Dead. Jack Dawson did as all of his bloodline did; he aided the Dead whenever possible. The Samedi felt far more pity for the Dead than they ever would for the living.

Most vampires spent their time devising new ways to outmaneuver their counterparts. The great Jyhad revolved around the machinations of clans who sought to rule over all of the Kindred. The Samedi simply moved along cleaning up the mess the others left behind.

Don Michael Giovanni was a friend, but he, too, had left a mess behind. A mess that fell to Jack for cleaning up.

Giovanni was different now than he used to be. The man's face showed signs of exhaustion. His eyes burned with an odd, feverish light. Jack took no comfort in the thought. Mike Giovanni was a longtime friend, one of a handful of Kindred whom Dawson would assist in any way he could. But there was something wrong with Mike. Something was missing from him. Perhaps his will to live, perhaps his all-consuming passion for unlife, power, and intrigue. Mike played the Jyhad like a professional, because he was a seasoned veteran of the vampiric holy war. But his gusto for the game seemed lacking.

The early hours of the night were spent staking out the Platinum Palace. The MGM Grand seemed almost petite next to the newest casino in town. Finding basic information about the Palace was easy enough. Every store in town, every paper of any note, had ads or flyers for all of the casinos. Finding a map for the place was as easy as spending a few minutes walking. Dawson loved to walk.

Whoever was behind the Palace had money to burn. The complex dwarfed everything around it, a testimony to what human beings will do in the pursuit of money. Three thousand rooms in the hotel. A full-size amusement park, five stages for floor shows, a dozen restaurants, enough stores to fill a mall, and seven full-size casinos specializing in everything from penny-ante to megabuck bets. The cost of building the place was probably near a billion dollars.

Scarier still, the investors would likely start seeing returns on their capital within a year. His mind boggled when he considered the sheer volume of money flowing through the city. Not long ago he'd heard a fire-and-brimstone street preacher screaming to an audience composed almost entirely of pigeons about the foul nature of Las Vegas. The dirt-encrusted old bastard declared that Vegas was "the Sodom and Gomorrah of the modern world." The street preacher didn't know the half of it.

And Michael Giovanni wanted the place brought down like a house of cards. Jack Dawson walked on, lost in thought. He did not notice the group of street people following him.

III

The area away from the lights and sounds of the main strip made Gabriel feel mildly nervous. He and Shaun walked on just the same. Several times, women dressed in clothes designed to emphasize their natural—and often artificial—assets called out to the two of them, promising a good time. Gabriel blushed whenever that happened; Shaun just kept walking. They'd been on the move for almost a full hour.

"Are we actually going anywhere? Or are we just

Hell-Storm 59

walking?" The impatience in his voice was as subdued as he could manage.

"We're going somewhere." Shaun's voice was gruff, a sure sign of his own discomfort. The people in the area were less than friendly. Walking here all but invited a fight. Part of him wanted to slink away, but a dark voice in the recesses of his mind reveled in the very idea.

"Would you like to let me in on the big secret?"

Shaun actually looked over his way, his brooding eyebrows warning Gabriel to show a little respect. "We're here."

He looked around. More of the same thing they'd been seeing for the last twenty minutes: bums, winos, junkies, and whores. They were the same people he could see in the bad parts of any city; the faces changed, but not much. After a very short while, you could pretend they weren't even there. "Looks like the same shit we've been passing for an hour or two."

Faster than he could blink, Shaun's hand reached out and swatted him harshly across the mouth. Gabriel reared back, shocked and outraged. "What is the matter with you?"

"I was going to ask you the same question, boy." Shaun was angry—not just upset, but downright pissed off. "This isn't 'shit.' This is real life. These are real people. You've had it easy your entire life, Gabriel. You've had a roof over your head and you've had a stable environment. Never take for granted what you have. Instead you should count your blessings."

"Why did you slap me?" His own anger was growing, despite his best efforts to remain calm. "Where do you get off hitting me?"

Shaun grabbed a double handful of his shirt and shook him vigorously. Gabriel's head snapped back and forth a few times, and then his whole body moved sideways. Without so much as breaking a sweat, the man hauled him into the shadows of a nearby alley, his face a study in controlled anger. "You need to understand something. You need to understand what respect means."

"What are you talking about?" He pushed against Shaun's hands, breaking the grip and squaring off into an awkward fighting stance. Despite his posturing, he could feel his knees beginning to shake.

"I'm talking about your foul-mouthed comments. You said this looks like 'the same old shit.' You weren't talking about the streets and buildings, boy. You were talking about the people. So help me God, Gabriel, if I ever hear you talking about people that way again, I'll beat you within inches of your life. Do you understand me?"

Gabriel started to speak, and Shaun shoved him against the wall again. "Do you understand me?" His voice was a roar, thunderous in the confined alley.

Gabriel wanted to roar back, to swing and rend and tear. After a few seconds of staring into his mentor's eyes, he nodded his head. "Yeah. I understand you."

They stood in complete silence for several seconds. Finally, Gabriel shrugged his shoulders and looked away. "I understand. I'm sorry."

Shaun Ingram nodded his acknowledgment of the apology. "It's done. It's settled and forgotten. Now then, look around this alley and tell me what you see."

Gabriel looked. "Garbage. Lots of garbage." The area was half-buried in discarded wrappers and boxes. Several trash cans spilled their innards across the ground, attracting insects and the occasional stray animal seeking food. At the far end of the alley, a cat's eyes glowed in the darkness, staring at them.

"Then you still haven't learned to look. I see so very much more."

"Like what?"

"I see life. I see the remains of a hundred lives, and I see the Wyrm." The man walked over to the closest trash can, shifting the garbage around with his foot. "These are the remains of people's lives. Discarded clothes, a broken bottle, a used syringe." He hunkered down next to the waste, never touching anything, but looking carefully. "The syringe is a U–100 insulin syringe, disposable. The needle's been broken off. I'd bet money the person who did this is actually diabetic. With the needle gone, no junkies can use it to shoot up. The bottle's label says MD 20/20. Cheap wine for a quick drunk. More sugar and alcohol than flavor. I can smell the sweat from the man who held it. He's dying. He stinks of death. The clothes are almost new, but someone threw them away. There's a label on the inside of the jacket; it says the jacket was designed to fit a child. Most people give the clothes their children grow out of to someone else. My bet would be that either the child is dead and the parents wanted to remove memories as quickly as possible, or the child is dead, and the person responsible dumped the clothes here and the body somewhere else. Probably the latter."

"Why do you think the child is dead?"

"There are bloodstains on the cuffs of the sleeves. I can smell the blood and fear. I can see the spots where the fabric stretched when the clothes were removed. Somebody's little boy is never coming home again."

Gabriel felt the hair on his neck rise and the flesh

on his body crawl into goose pimples. Shaun stood up and walked a little farther into the alley, looking intently at the debris. "Three Baggies, crack cocaine by the looks of them. They held cheap drugs." He sniffed at the air just above the Baggies. "No. Heroin, poorly cut. Some poor fool spent their money on this shit and it probably only satisfied their habit for a few hours." He stood back up and walked out of the alley, his face saddened and old-looking.

Gabriel followed, amazed by the man's perceptions. Before he could speak, Shaun started talking again. "I see pieces of lives. You just see shit. You've got the same senses I do, Gabriel. You just need to learn how to use them. You're still too dependent on your eyes. You haven't let yourself start using your other senses. My fault, really. I haven't taken the time to teach you."

"So teach me. How hard can it be?"

Shaun looked back at him, a mischievous grin on his face. "I think I will, then. I'll start your training tonight. But not here." Shaun looked around the area. "This place is too dangerous. Let's go out into the desert."

IV

The night was getting old, and Dawson had wasted most of his time lost in contemplation over his latest dilemma. It took quite a while for him to realize he was being followed. When the knowledge sank in, however, his actions were almost instantaneous.

When he saw a suitable side road, Jack slipped

into the shadows and practically froze in place. Long years of practice, mixed with his vampiric nature, allowed Jack to hide in plain sight. His abilities to hide were so well developed that he could even alter his external appearance. He normally chose to appear as he did before the Baron Samedi brought about his change from mortal to Kindred. Best not to let the humans see him for what he was; humans tended to react poorly to his current condition.

As he waited, motionless and patient, the figures stalking him came into sight. A more unusual group of bums he could not recall seeing in his many years. The obvious leader was a scrawny man dressed in clothes large enough to cover half the people following behind him with ease. His hair was mostly gone, not so much from age as from a simple receding hairline. At a casual glance, he hardly seemed worth noticing, save for his massive, scarred hands.

Behind him, a gathering of the unwashed and unwanted crept down the street, looking about and sniffing the air. A young woman wearing a floral print dress some twenty years out of fashion turned his way and sniffed suspiciously at the air. Dawson liked the group's unusual behavior less by the second. He liked even less that every last one of them was sporting a weapon. Seven of them in all. The odds were hardly even.

The grubby leader of the group sniffed the air and then dropped to the ground, sniffing the street where Jack had stood only a few seconds before.

Jack contemplated running. If they were what he suspected they were, his life was worth approximately the same amount as the worn-out sneakers on the youngest of the bunch. Instead of doing the sensible thing, he stepped out of the shadows.

"Ain't no reason to sniff the ground, old son. I'm

right here." He placed his hands on his hips, resting them near his six-shooters.

The man rose up in one liquid motion. Despite his apparent age, no arthritis seemed to hinder his movements. *The desert air works miracles*, Jack thought. The reason was bullshit and he knew it.

"What are you doing in Las Vegas, Leech?" The man spit the words, adding extra venom to the term "Leech."

"Same as everyone else. Minding my own business." Jack paused a second, rolling the lump of tobacco across his tongue. "I couldn't help but notice you fine folk following behind me. Is there a problem I should know about?"

"The casinos belong to your kind. You should go back there. Now."

Dawson shrugged his shoulders. "Don't much feel like it just yet. Got things to do and people to see."

"It wasn't a request."

"Didn't figure it was." The tension was palpable. Dawson did a head count and came up with seven opponents. "But last I checked, it was still a free country."

"Not for you." The man changed as he walked toward him. Jack's bad feeling grew far worse. Gray-and-black fur grew across the man's skin as his body expanded. The ragged clothes didn't tear, but suddenly seemed to fit, as the leader stopped a few feet away. "We don't like vampires in this part of town."

Dawson stared the werewolf square in the chest and decided he should have run. "Well, since you put it that way, I s'pect I ought to just run on home."

The monster looked down from a full three feet above the top of Dawson's hat and smiled. Thin black lips peeled away from a set of fangs Dawson just knew could take his head off with one chomp. Jack looked away long enough to confirm his own worst suspicions. The other six were changing too. "Too late, Leech. You were rude. Now you're gonna die." The words were distorted thunder, but Jack got the message just the same. He tried to step back, but the massive arms, covered with salt-and-pepper fur, reached out and lifted him from the ground before he could take even one full step.

Jack thrust back with his elbow as hard as he could, feeling a satisfactory crunch as the vulpine nose broke. The monster dropped him, howling in pain. Rather than wait around to see if the bearlike thing would recover, he bolted down the street at top speed. Snarls from the remaining werewolves broke out immediately. Even as he gathered speed, he heard the sounds of claws scrabbling for purchase on the asphalt behind him.

Three times in his long life, Jack Dawson had been obliged to run out of a sense of self-preservation. Twice he'd managed to get away cleanly, with little or no fuss. The litter in the street and his own footwear conspired to foil him this time. The greasy remains of a fast-food burger managed to end up under his heel at the worst possible moment. He saw the foul, flyblown package before his foot landed, but could not avoid the collision despite his best efforts. Despite the comfortable feel of his well-worn cowboy boots, Dawson cursed them for their lack of traction when he tried to round a corner—sliding along on a sheen of special sauce and waxed paper—and fell flat on his ass. As he was somewhat on the bony side, the impact hurt more than he expected.

Oh shit, he thought as the monsters rounded the same corner, some on all fours and some running like human beings. *I am not ready to die tonight. I. Refuse. To. Die.*

The pack of wolf-things apparently did not share his sentiment. The leader, looking fine save for a rapidly drying trickle of blood across the left side of his muzzle, most especially did not agree with his decision.

Sitting in the mucky remains of some asshole's late-night snack, Jack didn't know if he should be embarrassed or afraid. He opted for both. *I always hoped I'd go out with just a mite more dignity.* "I surrender."

Old Moldy Clothes apparently decided not to accept an honorable submission. His guttural reply was direct and to the point: "Fuck your surrender! Your ass is mine!" Once again, while the words were slurred by the awkward shape of the monster's mouth, the general meaning was pretty easy to catch.

Dawson started shaking and, feeling like a fool, rose to his knees in a begging position. The werewolf leered down from his full height, nodding his head with enthusiasm. He started to speak again, "I'll rip you limb fro—" but stopped abruptly when Jack reached out with his right arm and clutched a handful of his privates.

Jack squeezed, and the big bad wolf let out a shriek that set his teeth on edge before dropping to its knees. "You just might tear me apart, old son, but I'll make sure you pay for the pleasure. Do you understand me?" Jack's voice dropped about three octaves as he spoke, and a sadistic grin spread across his face. To make his point understood, he squeezed again and twisted his hand to the left. A hundred years as a creature who no longer needed genitalia had not removed from him the memory of what a good shot to the *cajones* felt like. "I expect I'm about to die. Yer too chickenshit to accept my surrender, and that's okay. But I demand a fast, painless death. Understand?"

The beast was still head and shoulders taller, but he nodded his lowered head and closed his eyes against what Jack knew had to be intense pain. Jack scanned the rest of the group, looking at their indecisive postures. None of them was quite willing to risk their leader's privates for the satisfaction of breaking him in half. Hoping to keep it that way, Jack yanked his hand hard to the right. The brute fell even lower, whimpering.

Jack started reaching for his pistol with his left hand, but never made it. A hot tearing pain started at his back and then exploded through his chest. He looked down just in time to see the flattened end of a crowbar rip through his shirt.

V

Gabriel White sniffed the air, paying close attention to everything he smelled. His eyes were closed, and to make sure he did not cheat, a bandanna was securely tied over them. Cheating was the farthest thing from his mind; the experiment was too interesting for him to want to sneak a peek at what Shaun Ingram held before him. By the biting, almost-painful aroma, he could tell that he was catching the scent of a pepper. The vinegar odor told him the small vegetable was pickled. "A jalapeño?"

"Very good. Now try this." Something else was held in front of his face, far blander than the pepper. He inhaled deeply, rearing back and sneezing as the fine powder tickled his nostrils. Shaun laughed.

The scent was very familiar, but it took him several seconds to identify the odor just the same. It was not a lack of scent that confused him; rather, it was the intensity of the aroma. Shaun was right. He really did depend far too much on his eyes. "Is it baking flour?"

Shaun's voice sounded exceedingly pleased. "Very good! Do you understand now what I've been trying to explain?"

"Yeah. I think I do." Gabriel pulled the blindfold away from his eyes, blinking at the intensity of the moonlight after an hour of complete darkness. They sat in comfortable silence for several minutes, neither of them feeling the need to speak. Then Gabriel asked the question haunting the back of his mind. "Shaun? What does the Wyrm smell like?"

Shaun looked at Gabriel for only a second before answering. "It has no smell. You cannot find the Wyrm by using your nose; you must learn to use senses you don't even know you have."

"I don't understand."

"I know, but I'm going to teach you. Or rather, I'll introduce you to someone who can."

"Who?"

"We've talked about the spirits of Gaia, the ones you still cannot see. I will have one of them teach you."

"Okay, so where do we have to go to find one?" Shaun spoke of the spirits constantly, almost as often as he spoke of the Wyrm. Gabriel opted not to make any derisive comments this time, as it would only lead to another fight.

"We don't have to go anywhere. They're all around you. You just have to know how to look."

Gabriel stared hard at the air around him, but saw nothing. He was about to speak when Shaun started chanting under his breath. Gabriel opened

Hell-Storm 69

his mouth, but Shaun held up a hand for silence. Despite the lack of any immediate manifestation, he remained silent as his mentor continued.

Almost an hour passed. Gabriel did not feel restless. He felt awe. Something beyond his comprehension was happening: He saw nothing and heard only Shaun's chanted comments, but he felt a change in the air around him. Finally Shaun stopped speaking and reached in front of him with his hands. He gestured, and the air in front of him shimmered as if a sudden wave of heat was rising. Gabriel still saw nothing, but something powerful appeared just the same.

A part of him quailed at the thought of the powerful entity he could not see or hear. That part wanted to run fast and far from the energies Shaun brought forth. He forced himself to remain still. Curiosity won over fear.

Shaun spoke to the ethereal force, talking softly with a reverence Gabriel had never before heard in the man's voice. Shaun turned to him, eyes moist with emotion. "We are honored tonight, Gabriel White. The spirits have decided to aid us. You will feel a presence soon, in your mind. You have but to listen, and you will learn to use one of your other senses."

Gabriel stood, afraid that by sitting he might offend the presence. "I do not know her name, but she is a spirit of Gaia. Do not be afraid, Gabriel. She won't hurt you."

The wave of feeling that came over Gabriel in that moment was like nothing he'd ever felt before. A warmth flowed through him, revitalizing and invigorating every atom of his being. For one brief instant, every part of his body and soul was at peace. No muscle hurt, no sound was unpleasant, and nothing around him could do less than please.

He felt himself smile with a joy few experience past their first year in the world. The pleasure was as pure and innocent as the nurturing pleasure a baby feels when surrounded by the protective arms of its mother. His mind opened to the comfort, and in that instant the understanding came to him: Once all the world felt this way all the time. Gaia ruled and all was well. Then the stain of the Wyrm came, and with it came pain and suffering. Finally he began to comprehend the meaning behind Shaun's words.

The feeling faded quickly, a gentle dream fading as consciousness returned.

Shaun spoke and blew the remnants of the dream away. "Now you understand Gaia. Now you can understand the Wyrm." Shaun walked over to him, looking saddened by the loss of the spirit's presence. "Look around you and know that Gaia is still alive, even if she is weakened by the Great Corrupter's presence. Then look with your spirit-eyes, and see what the Wyrm has done."

Gabriel stared into the desert night, reveling in the clarity of his senses. He turned to speak with Shaun, and immediately stepped back, offended by his mentor's very being.

"You? You are of the Wyrm, Shaun?"

"Yes and no." The man stepped closer, and Gabriel stepped back. "I've helped you learn to see the Wyrm's poisons, Gabriel. I did this because you *must* see—you must be aware of the dangers. Yes, I am poisoned by the Wyrm, as are all who have danced the Black Spiral that circles the Great Corrupter's heart. But I do not follow the Wyrm's beliefs, nor do I want anything to do with it or its creations. I choose to fight the Wyrm. My body and soul are tainted, but my heart and mind belong to Gaia alone."

Gabriel stared hard at his mentor, mixed emo-

Hell-Storm 71

tions of loyalty and revulsion wrenching his heart with merciless fists. Shaun stepped several paces away, his face unreadable in the distance.

"Open your senses again, and see yourself for what you are."

Gabriel did as the man commanded and cried out with terror. His mind was numbed by the implications of what he sensed, and he felt a sickening tide of dread wash through him. Somehow he wound up on the ground, staring up at the moon so far away. His eyes were wet from tears and his breath hitched in his chest every time he inhaled. Shaun sat nearby, head lowered and arms wrapped around his knees.

"It's true, Gabriel. You were born of the Black Spiral Dancers. You are something of a freak. Your genes and spirit belong mostly to the lost White Howler Garou from whence the Dancers came. You are not a Black Spiral Dancer. You are a Garou whose tribe died long ago."

The man came forward and offered his hand. After a moment, Gabriel accepted the assistance and climbed back to his feet. "It's good that Gaia saw fit to let you come into this world. You are a hope that should not be. Just the same, your father is a Dancer. He has danced the Spiral many times, seeking greater power and a deeper understanding of the Wyrm's madness. You bear his taint as surely as I do."

There were no words for several minutes. The two of them walked to the east, in the direction of the city they'd left behind. A mile passed, then two and then three. Shaun spoke again after Gabriel had considered his plight for some time. "But it doesn't have to be this way. I've heard rumors of ways to destroy the taint. I've heard of places in the Umbra where Gaia's spirits can take the Wyrm's influence from our bodies and cleanse away the sins of our heritage. We have but to find them. Then, we have but to survive the cure."

VI

There are few important organs in a vampire's body. The brain and the heart are the only ones that truly count. Remove the head, and the vampire dies. Pierce the heart, and the vampire is immobilized. Hollywood got that last part wrong nine times out of ten. The Kindred made sure of that. Once immobilized, any powers the vampire might be employing are shut off as sure as pulling the plug on a TV stops the idiot box from showing any more pictures.

The werewolves of Squire's Park saw Jack Dawson for what he was and decided that he must be destroyed. But they could leave no evidence of what they had done, for fear that the other vampires of the city would destroy them. So they climbed into the rusting van that was also the home of their leader, and took with them the withered form of Jack Dawson.

He could not move. He could not speak or fight back in any way. But he could hear. The leader of the group, called Father RipThroat by the others, recovered completely from the tortures Jack had performed upon his privates. He also swore to gain revenge and settle their little dilemma with equal ease. The desert is full of endless miles of nothing. What better place to end the Leech's miserable unlife? Jack knew the end would only come quickly if he did not hurt the man. He was lucky; they did exactly what he'd hoped they would. Miles from the city, the deceptively human-looking monsters carefully laid his motionless form on the ground, making sure the stake stayed in his chest. They parked the van to his west, and he heard their jokes and rude comments about what an ugly bastard he was—their actual words included such lovely phrases as "butt-ugly corpse, mummified snake, and two miles of bad roadkill"—intermingled with the sound of cans being opened. Even from a dozen feet away, he could smell the beer they poured down their throats. The woman in the baggy flowered dress popped a can and spilled half the contents into his mouth, wishing him better luck in his next life. Her voice overflowed with merriment, but her eyes said she actually hoped his next incarnation would be a better one.

As the sun rose, the burning rays igniting his flesh, Jack Dawson swore to make her death as painless as possible. The golden light of morning kissed his frozen body with unspeakable agonies. He burned for several minutes before consciousness faded, replaced by the soft embrace of death.

VII

Joseph Hill rose from the ground like a vengeful demon erupting from the pits of Hell. His face burned, but the pain was nothing next to the hunger he felt in every fiber of his being—a massive, gnawing wound that would not let him rest.

The last thing he could remember was the monster he'd been fighting. It was everywhere, surrounding his body and trying to rip him to shreds. He'd sensed its anger and desperation just as surely as it had sensed his.

Then the world went blank.

Finally—after who knew how long—he was conscious again. Conscious, and ravenous. He crawled from the place where he'd buried himself—*Hell, I must have buried myself*, he thought. *Who else would have done such a shitty job?*—and dusted off what remained of his clothing.

A quick look around told him he was still in Tijuana. The same glance told him he'd been spotted crawling from his temporary haven. A young girl, surely no older than twelve, looked at him with wild eyes as she started backing away. He moved before she could take three steps. His strong hands wrapped around the soft flesh of her shoulders, and his teeth raped the delicate skin of her throat. She managed one scream before he started feeding. Hot, salty blood filled his mouth, and with every anxious gulp he felt the strength returning to his body.

In a matter of less than a minute, she was dead. He threw her emptied body to the side and moved forward in search of more prey. His hunger demanded more sustenance, and he was in no shape to deny the primal urgings.

The next victim was an elderly man who opened his door in response to the girl's scream. A quick twist of his wrist and the man's neck snapped like a twig. When he had finished, he tossed the remains aside. "Sorry, *hombre*, nothin' personal."

Twice more he killed, draining his victims completely and then tossing aside their worthless remains. Unfortunately for him, the last one screamed the most. That much noise was almost certain to bring unwanted attention.

Moving again, he broke into a small house. The people inside stared at him, shocked, no doubt, by his unruly appearance. Without conscious thought, he drew his pistols and fired, wasting one bullet on each member of the family, seven in all. Their deaths were quick, almost merciful. He then chose the clothes best suited to replace his ruined shirt and pants.

As he was preparing to leave the corpses to their business, he spotted his reflection in the mirror mounted to their living room wall. He saw his face, and what the monster had done to it. Vicious, arching wounds made a mockery of his once-handsome features. The old scars were barely noticeable behind the angry red welts that were crosshatched over them. For all the world he looked as if he'd been beaten with a lead-tipped bullwhip.

"Now, you ugly bastard. Now it's personal."

Joe Hill walked away from the lives he'd ruined, following the strange pulling sensation coming from his new scars. The one attempt by the local police to stop him left five more dead. The tugging sensation was weak. The monster he'd battled was long away from the area. Still, it was only a matter of time before he found it again.

And when he did, there would be hell to pay.

4

I

By ten in the morning, the streets of Las Vegas were already hot enough to bake flesh. There was no breeze today to aid in evaporating sweat. Being outside was like standing in an oven. Jude barely noticed. He was far too busy looking at the cracks in the sidewalk. His mind refused to remember, no matter how hard he tried to recall, what his life before Vegas had been like. There were no painful memories best forgotten, no reflections of happier times in the past; no thoughts of his parents or siblings were available for him to contemplate. Today he found the situation very frustrating.

He could remember everything since he arrived in Las Vegas, however, with near-perfect clarity. The names of all the Dead he'd spoken with the night before were clear and sharp, as were the memories of how they'd died. He knew they should be avenged, but he could not grasp why it was so important to come to their aid. He understood on a very basic level that Michael Giovanni, the man responsible for their deaths, was a vampire from Clan Giovanni. But where the knowledge and confidence came from was a complete mystery.

Thinking about the situation hurt his head.

Rather than consider the problem any longer, he decided to do something about it. He walked over to the Palisades Casino and stepped inside the cool, air-conditioned world of glitz and greed. His clothes were not the best, but plenty of others walked around in even shabbier states of dishevelment. The security guards couldn't care less what he was wearing, so long as he was willing to spend money.

Jude dug into his pockets, pulling out three dimes, a well-folded twenty-dollar bill, and two quarters. The dime went into the first ten-cent slot he found. He pulled the handle down and concentrated. Five seconds later the machine was making loud whooping noises and dropping a load of dimes into the coin bowl below. Jude scooped the double handful of dimes into his palms and carried them over to one of the cages, where a bored-looking man with a plastic smile exchanged them for the equivalent value in silver dollars. Jude added the twenty in at the last second and carried his rolls of coins over to the dollar slot machines.

In another hour, he'd won close to four thousand dollars. Management was starting to look at him suspiciously, but seemed satisfied when he exchanged the coins for forty hundred-dollar coins.

Then he went to the biggest slot machine in the entire casino—the Megabucks Marathon Machine. Nothing smaller than a hundred-dollar token was accepted, but the winners took home a million dollars if they bet ten coins. Jude bet ten coins and won. An honest-to-God police siren complete with flashing lights announced his winnings for everyone in the establishment. Indeed, when the Megabucks went off, half of the people on the Strip heard the sirens.

Jude never even batted an eye. He just fed ten more coins into the machine and pulled the massive handle down a second time. And won a second time. The crowd surged around him in an enormous, cheering mass. Management went into a cold panic around the same time, rushing forward in a desperate attempt to prevent what had to be a malfunction in the Megabucks from giving away another million dollars. They were too late by about three seconds. Jude had won three million dollars before they could get there.

"We're sorry, this machine is broken. There must be a malfunction." The pit boss kept his calm, despite growing growls from the patrons. No one liked to see a winning streak shut down.

Jude smiled and nodded. "That's okay. Can I have my money now?" One look at the crowd made clear that denying the scruffy man would result in a riot as sure as actually throwing thousand-dollar bills across the floor. It took around ten minutes to get everything taken care of, but Jude got his check, less the amount demanded by the IRS. He did not have any identification, but he knew his social security number by heart.

Jude was happy. He opened a bank account half an hour later. He also moved into a suite in the Palisades Casino.

Content for the first time since he'd spoken with the murdered souls lying in the desert, he settled down for a nap. Tomorrow, he'd hit the Sands Casino and do the same thing all over again. By his calculations, Michael Giovanni would come to him within forty-eight hours.

He was wrong. It took less than thirty-six.

II

Nature makes demands of everything. One of those demands is simply this: Everything must die. Nothing can escape from death, for that, too, is a part of nature's way. Some creatures break the laws of nature, but only a very few. At 6:17 P.M., a rather large and very old bobcat managed to step onto the hot tarmac of Interstate 95 at exactly the wrong time. The tour bus full of people from Los Angeles en route to Las Vegas never even slowed down. The aging predator lay in the hot sun for almost two full hours before nature demanded payment for services rendered.

The sun finally set. The broken body jerked three times and then rose from its prone position. The mind was long gone. The heart did not beat and the lungs did not draw in or breathe out air. But, despite a ruined left forepaw and broken pelvic bone, the dead cat walked.

After almost three miles—a distance that would surely have killed the old cat even if it had lived through the accident—the feline fell to the ground again. After a few moments of inactivity, the beast tore its own belly wide open with its hind claws. It stood back up, uninterested in the entrails it leaked along with its bodily fluids.

The beast had lost a great deal of blood after the accident, but what it had left was enough.

The cold red liquid spilled across the desert floor, mingling with the sand and with the ashes that were all that remained of Jack Dawson when the werewolves finished their task. The effect was instantaneous. The ashes seethed from their resting spot—where the strong desert winds had failed to move them in the least—greedily absorbing the blood and ichor released from the feline's bloating corpse. The ashes then rose in a gray wave, gathering into a towering mass and re-forming into the solid body of Jack Dawson.

Dawson looked down at the tightly drawn, leathery flesh coating his form and smiled. His clothes lay where his body once rested as ash. He made short work of getting dressed. The werewolves had taken his boots, his Stetson, and his pistols with them. They were nice enough to leave his coat, shirt, and jeans. Even his wallet was untouched.

"Now that's just about enough to chap my ass." He started walking back toward the city, glad they'd left his chewing tobacco alone. He stuffed a wad of the shredded leaves into his mouth and started humming. Upon occasion, his hands reached of their own volition to where his holsters should have been. "Don't that just beat all," he mused. "Bad enough to take a man's weapons and hat, but the fuckers went an' took my boots, too." Almost absentmindedly, he sheathed his body in illusion, reestablishing his appearance as an average man with handsome features and café au lait skin. The black hair was real; the rest was a fake, but looked as he had before his body decided to mummify on him. He added proper attire to the illusion and headed toward the distant road, following the faint tracks left behind by the van the night before. "I can't believe they'd take my boots. Goddamn it, how's a man supposed to have a proper grave if every asshole in town is willing to steal his boots?"

Less than ten minutes after he'd hit the interstate, a nice, elderly couple coming in from Utah stopped and gave him a lift. They refused his offer of gas money, but thanked him for his advice as to which casinos were best for winning and which would rob them blind. They were so grateful, in fact, that they let him off right next to his truck. He wished them the best and waved a fond farewell as he located his truck keys.

From the concealed storage spot beneath the false floorboard of the truck, Jack Dawson removed a pair of small and highly illegal automatic weapons. He also pulled out a fresh pair of socks and four long clips, each of which held exactly thirty silver-filled glazer bullets. Lastly, he took out the spring-loaded shoulder holsters for what he liked to refer to as his "heavy artillery."

When he was properly attired for the upcoming confrontation, Dawson started walking along the same path he'd taken the night before. They'd see him. He knew they would. They'd see him and they'd be very, very pissed to discover he was just fine.

"Took my goddamned boots," he said, still shocked by the revelation. "Now I'm gonna have to kill 'em. Can't have a bunch of damned thieving varmints stealing from a corpse. Nothin' ruder in the whole damn world."

He continued mumbling to himself all the way down the Strip.

III

Michael Giovanni sat in complete darkness. His body was motionless; only his eyes blinked occasionally. Three million dollars was a lot to lose, but not enough to make him worry. He owned at least a portion of every casino in town, either legitimately or through blackmail. Clan Giovanni specialized in the art of necromancy; learning exactly where every skeleton in the entire town was buried was child's play when the skeletons themselves were forced to tell you where they were hidden. He seldom made demands on the moneys owed him for secrecy, but he could if he had to.

Three million dollars was actually little more than a drop in the bucket. It was not the monetary loss that concerned him. It was the blatant act of defiance. He understood the powers of the mages all too well. His family members had been mages long before they became vampires. But, oh, the act of "winning" so much money so quickly was either the act of a very stupid sorcerer, or a very brave one.

He'd wait. If the fool made so obvious a move again, he'd be joining a long list of stupid and cocky fools in a very exclusive gravesite.

The door at the far end of his office opened, and Giovanni recognized the towering shape of Victor Humes.

The man started to speak, but Mike beat him to it. "What is it, Vic?"

"I'm sorry to bother you, Mike. But you said you wanted to know if we located the guy who shook down the Megabucks."

"Yeah. Where is the little turd?"

"He's on the penthouse level. Suite 1703. He's staying here." Vic's voice sounded a little nervous, and Giovanni could not blame him. Lately he'd been less than a pleasure to deal with. The closest he'd been to calm in the last month was when Jack Dawson came to visit him. Michael Giovanni accepted his own temper as a curse he was stuck with forever. He just had to remember not to take it out on Vic anymore. The man was only human. He would not forgive the vicious and undeserved tongue-lashings Giovanni threw his way forever. Much as it pained him, he also knew that Vic was as proud as he was ruthless. The man was far too important to lose, and far too powerful to abuse.

"Thanks, Vic." He squinted a bit and then flicked the switch on his desk that controlled the lighting in the room. Lately, the light had become almost painful. He didn't like that. Pain showed a weakness that he did not want to accept. "Listen. About last night. I'm sorry. I shouldn't take out my frustrations on you. You've been a good man, and I apologize for hitting you. I'm not worthy of your friendship."

"Hey, Mike. It's not a problem." Vic grinned, the bruises on his face were almost completely gone, and apparently the bones had knitted properly. Being a blood-servant to the Kindred had advantages, not the least of which was a nearly miraculous healing rate. The giant shrugged his shoulders and then crossed his arms, while his grin grew even wider. "I knew the job would be tough when I took it."

Michael Giovanni laughed at the old joke, glad to hear the sincerity in the big man's voice. "Just the same, I am truly sorry. I trust you more than most of the Family working under me, and I should never have struck you. You name your price, and if it is within my power, I will pay it. I want you to know that you are appreciated."

"You give me plenty already. Just do me one favor. Don't let this shit drive you crazy. Okay?"

Michael nodded. "I'll do my best. Now getouttahere. I need a little time to think."

Vic looked at him for a moment longer, then quietly slipped out of the room and closed the door. Giovanni turned the lights off again, enjoying the darkness and pondering his situation.

The prince of Las Vegas stared at nothing, his mind running over the last few years again and again. Everything in his world was in order. The Family's hold on Las Vegas was still strong, and his influence in Atlantic City was just as firm as his influence here. *So why*, he wondered, *am I so afraid?*

IV

When the lights went out and he was certain Shaun was sleeping soundly, Gabriel White slipped from his comfortable bed and crept from the hotel room. His mother would be furious if she found out, and Shaun would go through the roof, but he needed to be alone. To think over all he'd learned since his first change. Eighteen months seemed so short a time when your entire world refused to remain coherent.

He'd expected to have fun in Las Vegas. So far the trip had proved disappointing.

Gabriel walked out of the Platinum Palace and into the night without anyone trying to stop him. He followed the same path he and Shaun had traveled yesterday, content to see the same sights so long as he could do so alone.

Over the last year and a half, Shaun had been by his side almost all of the time. At least now Gabriel knew why. The man was afraid Gabriel would go completely to the Wyrm. He remembered the gift the spirit taught him the night before and used it. The people walking around him in the nighttime city were as diversified as they were in San Francisco, but now, using the special senses he'd never known existed until yesterday, they were more heterogeneous than ever.

Sounds were clearer and more diversified. The city's scents were even stranger than the sounds. The change was not so much physical as intellectual. He recognized several faces from the night before, but few of them appeared the same. A woman in her thirties watched him go by, smiling tiredly and nodding. She was dressed in cheap jewelry and was likely willing to sell her body. That, or she'd never learned how not to dress like a slut. Despite her poor choices in the clothing department, she was a very pretty woman. But Gabriel looked beyond what his eyes allowed him to see, and backed away. She smelled of long illness and death. She was dying and did not know or did not care. She was not Wyrm-corrupt, but she gave off similar sensations. Death and the Wyrm had much in common, apparently, but they were not one and the same.

He reveled in the scents of a thousand people and countless animals. Just by concentrating, he could separate the spoor of each. Some smelled young, others reeked of cheap cologne and cigarettes. Up ahead, he could smell the odor of others like himself. Garou, here in the heart of the city. Since his change, he'd been warned away from the others. Shaun constantly cautioned him that they would not understand just what he was.

Gabriel decided to ignore the warning and moved in pursuit of the werewolves' scent.

As he moved, he mentally recited the list of Garou tribes to himself. Bone Gnawer, Black Fury, Children of Gaia, Fianna, Get of Fenris, Glass Walker, Red Talon, Shadow Lord, Silent Strider, Silver Fang, Uktena, and Wendigo. And, of course, Black Spiral Dancer. He belonged to none of them, but he needed to know about each if he hoped to survive. The pack obviously lived in the city; he could tell that simply by the fact that their scents permeated the entire area. Judging by the squalid living conditions, he narrowed them down to one of two tribes: Bone Gnawer or Black Spiral Dancer. Their odor was not mingled with that of the Wyrm. They had to be Bone Gnawers.

The Gnawers dwelled among the poor, envisioning themselves as modern day Robin Hoods, offering shelter and food to those in need. If the rumors were true, many of them mated with dogs in lieu of wolves. Most of the other tribes tended to scorn the Bone Gnawers as lower-class citizens.

He followed their trail through a substantial shopping district. Most of the establishments had closed for the night, save a few stores dealing in items of questionable morality. Pete's Poster Hut was open, but seemed more interested in dealing pornography than posters. Despite the temptation to step inside and study the merchandise, Gabriel walked on. Not much later, he came across a lush green field. The grass was well manicured, and numerous trash cans spaced throughout the area carried the legend: *Please help us keep Squire's Park clean and safe*. There was little debris on the ground, and he was glad to see that most of the people actually managed to hit their target receptacles.

Off in the distance, several people sat gathered around a fountain. They were dressed poorly, but he remembered Shaun's words from last night and decided not to judge too harshly. He sniffed the air as the wind shifted, blowing past the group. The scent of Garou was unmistakable. They were like him.

Despite the warning bells ringing in the back of

his head, Gabriel stepped toward the group. Finally, he'd have a chance to meet others who shared his gift. Once and for all, he'd be able to decide if Shaun was telling him the truth about what other werewolves would think of him.

V

Three hours of trekking through the same areas as the night before proved useless in locating the boot-stealing polecats. Dawson was a bit calmer, but much more determined to hunt the werewolves down. He stopped in a touristy little shop and purchased a pair of sneakers worth far less than what the store charged. His skin was leathery by nature, but glass and stones still hurt like hell when they bruised the soles of his feet. He also bought an overpriced straw cowboy hat to hide his true visage from any cameras—minds he could fool, but not the technologies created by those same minds. Blue jeans, a flannel shirt, a leather duster, bright white tennis shoes, and a red straw hat with LAS VEGAS in blue sequins. Just the thought of what he was wearing was enough to send him into a rage of vengeful dreams. He thanked the powers that be for his ability to hide his true appearance: He'd never live it down if anyone he knew actually saw him this way.

Looking at his reflection in a darkened shop window, he spoke aloud for the sake of hearing a voice. "Now, if I was a bunch of low-down, oversize junkyard dogs, where would I be hiding myself?" His reflection refused to answer, but he came up with an idea just the same. "Anyplace where there was trees ta piss on, I reckon."

Looking over his map of the city and checking the closest street sign, "S. Las Vegas Boulevard and Fremont Street," brought a smile to his face. Squire's Park was only a block away. "Hot damn. Hunting season's on, boys and girls."

He whistled as he walked, hoping to gain the attention of any passing varmint.

The park was just where the map promised, and he had no trouble at all spotting his prey from the edge of the fine green lawn. At present they were hassling an all-American boy. The kid was genuine Boy Scout material, right down to his creased blue jeans and Members Only windbreaker.

At present, the boy was standing in the center of the group and looking around with wide, confused eyes while the entire group gave him grief and called him "worm-poisoned." Every time he tried to protest, old Father RipThroat—wearing Dawson's boots and holsters, the hat was sitting on flower-girl's pretty head—screamed for him to "Shut your fucking face, punk. 'Cause you're in enough trouble already!"

Dawson moved to within fifteen yards of the group, whistling and waiting patiently. The whole gang, seemingly intent on giving Biff the Wonder-Kid grief, managed to ignore him despite the obnoxiously loud tunes he played for their benefit.

Junior All-American was the one who finally noticed him. His eyes lost their glazed look, and he stared hard for half a second before turning to the old man. "Um, sir?"

"Didn't I just tell you to shut up? What? Are you deaf *and* stupid?"

"No. I just thought you should know there's somebody watching us." The edge in the boy's voice made clear that he was rapidly growing tired of the verbal abuse. "I thought maybe you should think about that before you push me any farther. Because, right now, I'm thinking really hard about whether or not I'm gonna break you over my fucking knee!" Even as he spoke, the boy grew in size. He swelled to over seven feet in height and about wide enough to have trouble hiding behind a barn. Dawson looked on, adding the half change into his list of things to remember about boot-stealing werewolves. He'd never seen one do that before.

Father RipThroat turned his head a few times, looking from the boy to where Dawson stood and then back to the boy again. Then his face lit up with recognition, and he focused all of his attention on Jack. "Sonuvabitch..." His voice was incredulous. "You're alive."

"Evening. Father RipThroat, ain't it?"

"Yeah. That's the name, Leech." The old baldy started pulling the same trick as the blond kid and shifted halfway. That confirmed it wasn't just Jack's imagination. "How'd you come back from the dead?"

"I'm real hard to kill, asshole."

"Yeah, we'll have to see about that!" He continued the transformation, and the rest of his group did the same thing. Dawson stood his ground, and the boy-*cum*-giant stepped aside as the group moved toward Jack cautiously.

"Y'know something? I'll just bet 'Father RipThroat' ain't yer real name. Why don't you tell me yer real name, so's I can tell 'em what to put on yer gravestone."

"Cocky little shit. This time I guess we'll just have to do it right." The pack of monsters moved forward, and Jack Dawson grabbed the butts of his heavy artillery...

VI

Gabriel White was still reeling, shocked by the hostile attitudes of the local Bone Gnawers, when the gunfighter showed up. He had darkly tanned skin and an outfit that made him look like he'd just walked off the sound stage for a spaghetti Western. His voice was friendly and insulting at the same time, but his dark eyes were narrowed and the big guns in his hands looked downright deadly.

Off in the distance, a church bell struck the hour four times, and it was all Gabriel could do to avoid laughing. The only thing missing to make the scene perfect was a hot desert wind and the theme song to *The Good, the Bad and the Ugly*. That, and maybe a little boy calling out after Shane.

The cowboy shook his head and sighed dramatically. He paused a second and spit a wad of tobacco juice across the thirty feet separating him from the approaching group of werewolves. "See? Y'all have the same manners as a herd of rutting pigs. I double-checked on yer name and you ain't even got the decency to return the favor."

Father RipThroat snarled and continued to approach, but he slowed down. "Fine, Leech. What should I call you?"

The cowboy laughed. "I thought you'd never ask, old man. My friends call me Jack Dawson. But y'all can call me Uncle Whup-Ass."

Without another word, the cowboy proceeded to open fire on his enemies. The only sound his weapons made was a gentle chuffing noise, not at all like the thunder Gabriel expected. The speed with which the conflict ended was equally surprising. Jack Dawson's hands and arms quite literally blurred as he attacked. The first one he hit was the one farthest back. The one called Trash-Eater by the others. The obese Garou never had a chance. Three small holes appeared in his torso, followed a half second later by three massive caverns that erupted from his back. The gunslinger never even moved his head; he just lifted his arm and fired.

Father RipThroat lost most of his stomach and privates to a single shot. He lived through the experience, but fell to the ground just the same. Gabriel stared in mixed terror and surprise as the single man fired again and again, opening gaping wounds in all of the werewolves save him and the girl in the flowered dress.

The girl started moving forward, nine feet of blinding speed and razor-sharp claws. She came to a stop when the barrel of one of the cowboy's machine guns pointed between her eyes. "I'm still thinkin' about whether or not I'm gonna kill you, sweetie. So why don't you just make yerself human again and stay right where you are." The cold menace in his voice stopped the girl from moving any farther. "Thanks. Now gently set my hat down and step back."

Most of the Garou had reverted to human form, and the rest were in the process. Dawson looked over to Gabriel and nodded. "What's yer name, son?"

"Gabriel White, sir." Simple rule: When a man with big, dangerous guns asks you for your name, you give it.

"Hi there, Gabriel. I'd like you to do me a favor."

"O-Okay . . ."

"See that dumb-ass over there, the one with nothing between his legs?" He indicated Father RipThroat with his left machine gun. Gabriel nodded. "I want you to take the pistol holsters from around his waist and put them with the hat. When yer done with that, I'd like you to do the same thing with the boots on his feet." Gabriel did as requested, trying hard not to vomit as his hands moved through the blood and entrails painted across the holsters. The balding old man moaned, but did not awaken.

When he was finished, Dawson nodded to him. "Much obliged, son. You a werewolf?"

"Yessir."

"Don't call me sir. Call me Dawson."

"Okay, Dawson."

"Gabriel, I'm askin' ya straight and I want a straight answer. You plannin' ta do anything stupid, like try an' tackle me?"

"Hell no!"

Dawson laughed. "That's good, son. You're smarter than all of them. I've been practicin' my shootin' for over a hunnert years. I'm pretty damn good at it." The man looked away and nodded to the girl. "What's yer name, sweetie?"

"Paisley."

"Yer momma stuck you with a name like that?" The man sounded incredulous.

"No. It's my Garou name."

"Uh-huh. What's yer people name?"

"Angie."

"Well, Angie. It's like this: I've got about twenty more silver bullets I can pump into you and the rest of your group. But these here ain't just ordinary bullets, they're glazers. That means that each one's gonna leave a hole about the size of yer average watermelon on the inside of whoever gets hit with one. Understand?"

She nodded, her chest heaving with every breath she took and her eyes watering, though from fear or anger, Gabriel could not guess.

Hell-Storm

"Good. Now the thing is this: I don't like using these here bullets. They're damned expensive and I really don't much feel like killing anyone just now. Also, yer a pretty little thing when you ain't bein' a furry Cuisinart. I try my best not to kill anything pretty, 'cause the world's ugly enough as it is. So I'm gonna leave you be, provided you promise not to follow me."

"I—"

"But you can't just promise. You have to swear by Gaia and Luna that you and your folk ain't gonna bug me again."

She seemed shocked by his request, and Gabriel was equally surprised. After a few seconds, she nodded and swore no retaliation against him. She made the oath on the names of Gaia and Luna.

"All right then. I'm letting all of you live, against my better judgment. Like I said, I don't like to kill unless I have to. I'm tempted though, 'specially where baldy here's concerned. He stole my boots, and that ain't a decent thing to do." He grabbed his hat, boots, and holsters, managing to keep one arm free in the process. "I'm leaving now. I plan on bein' in Vegas for about another week, on personal business. I meant no harm to you when I came here, and I mean none now. But I'm keeping the silver bullets around this time. Just in case."

Gabriel watched the man walk away, still numb from the encounter. He turned to Angie and spoke to her. "Do you want some help? I mean with trying to get them to a hospital? Should I call 911?"

Her pretty face grew ugly and hateful. "Just get away from us, damn you. Go away before you taint us all."

He didn't argue; he simply left. His first attempt at befriending other Garou was an abominable failure. Half a block later, he met up with Jack Dawson as the man dumped a cheap red straw hat and almost-new Reeboks into a garbage can. He had no idea where they'd come from, and was far too afraid to ask.

"Where ya headed, Gabriel?" Dawson's voice held the friendly, good-natured tones of a man who liked conversation.

"Um . . . the Platinum Palace."

"Yeah? I ain't stayin' far from there myself. Want some company on the walk back?"

Gabriel opened his senses as the spirit had taught him. There was no sense of the Wyrm on the man next to him, but he smelled dead just the same. "Sure. But can I ask you a question?"

"Ask away, son. It's a free country."

"How did you know about Gaia and Luna?"

Dawson smiled and winked conspiratorially. "Ya want the truth?"

"Yeah."

"I heard some werewolves talkin' once, when they didn't know I was close enough to hear. One of 'em made the other swear by those two, and it sounded so good I used it myself. I've been saving that one up, just in case I ever met with a pissed-off Lupine."

Gabriel felt himself smile for a second, then forced it away as he built the nerve for his next question. He still wasn't sure he wanted the answer. "I know you're not human. So what the hell are you?"

"Hell. I thought you already knew that. I'm a vampire."

"You mean the vampires are real, too?" His exasperation must have carried over into his voice, because Dawson started laughing out loud again, all the while shaking his head in amazement. Gabriel decided in that moment that he liked the gunslinger. His first attempt at meeting a vampire was far more successful than his first attempt at meeting other werewolves.

5

I

Teri Johannsen stared at the approaching figure with eyes that refused to believe what they saw. Thick, matted fur spread across the hulking form, broken by long scars carved into macabre patterns that seemed to swim across the flesh. The face was a nightmare of exposed veins and pasty white flesh, surrounding piggish eyes and a mouth capable of engulfing her entire head. Worst of all, she could see by the way the thing stared at her that it wanted her. Not as a meal, but as a mate. The stench of the creature was almost overwhelmed by the ripe odors of the caves where they were resting. The others couldn't be far away. She could hear them; even worse, she could smell them.

She was beyond screaming. She'd screamed as much as she could over the last two days, despite the gag in her mouth. The thing claiming it was Gabriel's father was not present, but she knew he wasn't far away. The bat-faced monster. *No!* her mind screamed. *It can't be Edward McTyre. That's just not possible!* Despite logic and what she'd seen with her own eyes, she could not accept the possibility that a man could become the bat-demon which ruled over the other foul freaks. She forced the possibility away.

The monster tried to touch her. She couldn't even bring herself to flinch. She was so tired. Since the moment Edward McTyre had dragged her from Gabriel's home, the things around her kept her awake. Every time she started to drift, someone poked and prodded her until consciousness returned. She was numb. Nothing seemed capable of evoking emotions in her any longer. No tears and no screams.

The bad thing came closer still, and finally she realized the danger on a conscious level. She could not accept what she saw. Her mind refused to believe it had once been human—surely it was a bear, hideously scarred to be sure, but a bear just the same—not a demon or werewolf. Whatever the case, it wanted to touch her and far worse than simply touch. It wanted to invade her!

Teri screamed past the sodden gag in her mouth and kicked back violently, squirming to avoid the thing as it approached. The creature recoiled as if scalded, looking over its misshapen shoulder to see if anyone noticed her screams. If she hadn't known better, she'd have sworn it was afraid. Just to be safe, she screamed again.

With a paw large enough to wrap around her head, the creature lashed out, striking her across the face. Her skull bounced against the far wall, rocking forward with enough force to topple her from her almost-sitting position. She stopped screaming, far too busy trying to remain conscious. Besides, her throat felt as if it were on fire.

The bat-monster came into the small cave where Teri lay and grabbed a handful of the smaller creature's fur. Her mind reeled as she recognized Edward McTyre's voice coming from that vile, fang-filled maw. "Now, Bobby. I know we've discussed this before." The Thing-That-Wanted-To-Touch-Her-Privates shrieked as its leader ripped a hank of matted fur away from its scalp. It tried to retaliate, only to receive another cuffing.

Teri pulled back, struggling in vain to force her body through the rock wall. Despite her fears, the larger monster won easily, wrenching the would-be molester to the ground and sinking its razor-sharp incisors into the throat of its enemy. The bite was not fatal, merely a warning. The smaller nightmare scurried back, growling deep in its chest. "Bark all you want, Thraglk. The girl is for Gabriel. You may not have her. She must be pure." He looked her way, and she cringed at the obvious lust in its eyes. "We must have Gabriel. He can breed. She is his chosen mate."

The smaller one spoke, talking in a language unknown to her. The tone of the words was clear just the same. It wanted something to play with. To mate with. Her fear abated only a little as a result of the whining she heard in the freak's voice.

"Soon enough, Bobby." Bat-Face spoke placatingly. Then its voice grew cheerful. "I know. You can have Gabriel's mother. She's older than you. You know what they say about experienced lovers." The both of them laughed, and Teri started crying again.

She was wrong. She still had tears left to cry, and she still had screams left inside as well. She prayed for the numbness to return.

II

He walked whenever the sun went down, drawn across the desert by some unexplainable need to find the thing he'd seen before. Joseph "Boot" Hill was in a very foul mood.

He'd remained in Tijuana for several days before the wounds on his body healed enough for him to walk unimpaired. Even now he felt an odd burning in the scars left by his enemy. Scars! In all of his time as a member of vampiric society—over 115 years, thank you very damned much—he'd taken enough bullets and been cut by enough knives to kill a full battalion of soldiers. None of them had ever left scars before. He sighed, scanning the sky for anything unusual and then examining the landscape around him. Nothing out of the ordinary. He supposed he should be glad his eyes had grown back without any scars.

An unnaturally even length of darkness grew across the land in the distance. He walked toward the black line, hoping his eyes did not deceive him. "Well, ain't that a sight worth singin' 'bout." Even as he watched, a matched set of lights appeared on the horizon. Joe grinned, his handsome features pulling tight where the new scars overlapped the ones left behind when he was dragged behind a horse while still mortal.

The last two nights he'd been without any food, and healing big wounds always took a lot out of him. Not far away, the skeletal remains of some poor fool or another lay half-freed from the sand. He had the look of an illegal alien. Hardly the first to die while trying to escape Mexico's poverty. Joe nudged the skull with his boot until its empty sockets stared toward the distant road. "Betcha I can peg them tires from here, Pepe."

The corpse opted not to reply.

"Naw. Why waste a good ride for a little blood." He nodded to his silent companion. "Y'all be good, Pepe. Watch out for them coyotes." Once again, Pepe ignored his comments.

Joe Hill started running, determined to meet with the truck in the distance. The truck tore down the road, traveling well over the posted speed limit. Joe matched its speed and even managed to pull ahead. He laughed at the look on the flabby driver's face when he pulled the man's door open. The young girl in the passenger's seat screamed loudly enough to half deafen him, but he ignored her until he was done with the driver.

After a very brief scuffle, Joe slowed the truck down and pulled to the side of the road. He fed deeply on the blood of his latest victim. The woman-child he left alive but broken. He had no idea how far he needed to travel, and extra food was always a plus.

With a full belly and a song in his heart, Joe Hill rode the rest of the way into Las Vegas, arriving just before the sun rose. He abandoned the truck outside of a greasy spoon diner and rented a cheap room a few blocks down the road. He could feel the creature's presence. He swore again that he'd have his revenge against the thing if it was the last thing he ever did.

Now all he had to do was figure some way to hurt the damned thing.

III

Diane White was half-convinced that she was falling in love with Andrew Montgomery. He was charming, friendly, handsome, and so very considerate of her needs. Andrew was a gentleman, and one of the finest she'd had a chance to speak with in a very long time. She forced her mind away from such notions, instead trying to concentrate on the rhythm of the music as he led her in a slow dance across the dance floor.

By this time next week, the Platinum Record Dance Hall would be playing music more to the liking of a younger crowd—a part of the appeal of the place was the changing motif: a different era every week. For now the songs belonged to the past. Diane enjoyed the past so much. It really was a time of innocence, free of pain and loss. For the present she could relive the past, even if she was dancing with the wrong man. It should have been Sam, or John. They were the only two who'd ever made her feel this way: giddy as a schoolgirl on her first date. Just the same, Andrew managed to make her feel special anyway.

She stifled the thoughts, guiltily, forcing herself to remember John. Eighteen months in his grave and still she missed him. The wounds were fresh enough to make her feel queasy. A small, selfish part of her wanted to move on with her life, but she didn't feel right about letting that happen. Not just yet.

Besides, there was still a chance Sam would come back. Hope does spring eternal, after all.

As she spun around the dance floor—a new song was playing, something by Bill Haley and the Comets, with a much faster tempo—she smiled toward Shaun and Gabriel where they sat together eating burgers and fries.

Gabe seemed so intense these days, always staring harshly at everything he saw. He studied every item that caught his attention with a nearly fanatical determination. A phase, she supposed. One he would likely grow out of in only a few months. Andrew drew her attention again, smiling and moving with a fluid grace. Despite the formal suit he wore, she could almost imagine him dressed in pegged jeans and sporting a leather jacket. His face was handsome that way. He looked dangerous, seductively so.

She stared deeply into his light green eyes, fascinated by the way the light reflected in their depths. She felt herself being lost in those reflections, and would have turned away if he hadn't picked that moment to look away himself.

"Your son's growing up to be a handsome man." There was that smile again, the one that made her weak in the knees. "If you're not careful, some young lady's going to steal him away."

"Oh. No worries there. One already has. Teri's her name. I think if I tried to separate them for too long, they'd run away together." She thought back on long-lost dreams. The half-serious plans Sam had made to steal her away from the dormitory and run away to Las Vegas in order to get married. The fantasies still hurt. Even after twenty-five years, the broken hopes still made her want to cry. She forced her mind back to the present. "I guess it's a good thing we're going back to San Francisco next week."

Andrew drew her in close, holding her in his strong, wonderful arms. "You don't sound thrilled about that, Diane."

"Oh. It's not all that bad." She shook her head, smiling wistfully as she looked around. Shaun and Gabriel were leaving, doubtless heading out for more training. "It's my home after all. But without John there, the house doesn't feel the same."

"It feels empty, doesn't it?" She looked up again, surprised that he understood how she felt. His rich voice was sullen, lonely enough for both of them. His eyes seemed so dark, as if they'd changed to match her despair. "It's a hollow facade. Not at all the same since John passed away."

"That's exactly right. Empty." Diane felt the tears start stinging at her tear ducts. She almost had them under control when the song changed again. This time the speakers played "Smoke Gets in Your Eyes" and that was all it took to make her break down. As the tears started in earnest, Andrew held her close. She took strength from the embrace.

In that one moment, she loved Andrew dearly. He protected her and guided her away from the dance floor.

They spent the rest of the night talking. She told him all the woes that bothered her, and he listened. He sympathized. In the end, he took her back to her room and kissed her gently on the lips. As she drifted off to sleep, she fell more and more deeply in love with him. Not a mad, passionate love. A deep, comfortable affection which, in time, could well become addictive.

Diane White slept like a baby, with no idea just how dangerous her thoughts were.

IV

"It's all well and good that you've made a friend of a vampire, Gabriel. I personally have no complaints about that. But every Garou for a thousand miles will take the matter far more personally than that."

"Jesus Christ. Fuck the other Garou! I'm tired of being afraid of a bunch of leftovers from the Dark Ages." He stopped himself before he said another word. The look on Shaun's face let him know he'd already pushed as far as he dared.

"Aye. Leftovers we may be, but there's a reason for the bias against the Leeches." Shaun walked hurriedly, looking all around and sniffing the air from time to time. "Was a time when the bastards walked around blatantly, ruling over the humans and feeding as they pleased. They held control over whole cities and were normally responsible for the damned places being built in the first place." His accent was back and growing stronger. Gabe prepared himself for another preaching session. He was beginning to like the sermons less and less.

"The vampires have always been our enemies. They kill with no regard for anyone. They'd kill you on sight, given half a chance."

"Yeah? Well, Jack had plenty of chances last night. He had silver bullets in his machine guns, Shaun. He could have turned me into roadkill. But he didn't. He didn't even kill the assholes who were bothering me."

"Speaking of that sorry lot, this is where they've come to lick their wounds." He looked around the area, and Gabriel looked as well. The building appeared empty. What little glass remained in the window frames remained mostly covered over by plywood, and the litter-strewn street was devoid of any other people. Gabriel felt his hackles rising and took in the rest of the area. Scattered debris littered the street, and graffiti covered virtually every surface. Abandoned, burned-out ruins occupied the spots where cars would normally be parked, and even those were covered with obscene scrawls and neon orange slogans. The words were only readable to anyone who could make out the primitive letters painted inside almost tribal designs. There were no pushers on any of the corners, but he was willing to bet the only thing that kept them away was the pack of Bone Gnawers who normally roamed the area.

Shaun hefted the two bags he'd carried along the way, and then pushed open the front door of the tenement with his foot. He handed one bag to Gabriel and removed a .45 caliber pistol from his belt before moving forward. Despite his best efforts, Gabe could locate no trace of the Wyrm's presence inside the derelict building. None save that which came from himself and Shaun.

"My name is Shaun Ingram. I'm a Ronin of the Fianna and of the Black Spiral Dancers. My companion is Gabriel White. He is a pup of the White Howlers. Neither of us means you any harm. We're coming into your building. Should you attempt to hurt either of us, we will defend ourselves to the best of our ability." Shaun's words rang through the building, echoing off the dry-rotted walls. Gabriel heard shuffling sounds, but no voices.

After a few seconds, the two moved forward into the darkness. Before his change, Gabriel would have been terrified. These days, the darkness held no secrets. He saw the figures lying on the ground long before he reached them. He smelled them even earlier. Halfway down the hall, Shaun set down his bag, moving into a predatory crouch. Fur spouted across his back, and he swelled in size even as his clothes stretched to accommodate his new form. Though still mostly a man, Ingram's features grew bestial, and his body grew fully half again as wide and tall as it had been. Gabriel concentrated, forcing his own body to change. The pain was intense for only a few seconds, but enough to bring a growl from his throat. Sháun looked back at him, scowling.

The air stank with blood and feces and death. In the actual room where the Bone Gnawers had once lived, the bodies of five humans and one wolf now lay. All dead; they were all dead.

Gabriel stared at the remains of the girl he'd known as Paisley, sickened by what had become of her. There was barely enough left of her dress to recognize. Her pretty face was gone. Only strands of flesh—looking all too much like molten mozzarella cheese for his liking, and complete with pizza sauce no less—remained where her features should have been. Her graceful figure was gone, replaced by broken bones half-buried beneath bloody lumps of meat and flesh. Once again, the remaining skin looked like molten cheese.

She had been the prettiest of the lot in life, but in death they were equally hideous.

The carnage only grew worse from there. Looking at the positions of the bodies and recalling the shape most of the Gnawers were in only the night before, Gabe could tell most of them never had a chance. The bones in some were fused together, welded by some unholy heat or force. No burn marks existed to indicate the former. In others, the skeletons were shattered, as if they'd fallen from a mile in the air. Whatever had done this had apparently wanted to play with them before they died.

Gabriel all but ran from the room, his foot striking the bag of groceries Shaun had set aside and sending an explosion of raw steaks and milk across the ground before him. His stomach heaved, and the hamburger and fries he'd consumed an hour earlier joined with the ruined food on the floor. Despite the supernatural strength of his body, his traitorous stomach flopped over again and brought

Hell-Storm

forth another torrent to add to the remains of his supper.

"Gabriel..."

He could not answer; his body and mind were still reeling.

"Gabriel."

"Go 'way. Leave me alone."

A hand grabbed him by the back of his hair and lifted him from the ground. The pain brought the world back into focus, even as his body flew across the room. He twisted in the air, managing to land against the wall without serious injury, but only barely.

"Snap out of it, boy. We've got a wyrmling to catch." Shaun's voice was cold, shivering with repressed anger. "It's time you met the Wyrm on its own ground."

"What? The thing that did this? This was the Wyrm?"

The laugh that came from Shaun's throat was enough to freeze Gabriel's heart. "No. The Wyrm has a new agent, that's all. And I need you to track it."

"Why me?" Fear bloomed in his soul, and his brave words from the night before faded before the terror. "I don't want to do this, Shaun. I'm afraid."

The man walked forward, standing directly before him even as he pulled himself into a fetal position. "You can be afraid, Gabriel, but you've still got to help me do this thing. This is why we exist. We must stop the demon before it can hurt anyone else."

They sat for several minutes in the darkness, silent and solemn. When Shaun spoke again, his voice was calmer. "You said there were seven Garou in the pack?"

"Yes. Seven." The words were an effort. He felt completely numb.

"I was afraid of that." Shaun sounded bitter.

"Why? What's the matter?"

"There are only six bodies, Gabriel. Whatever did this either ate a full body, or used to be a werewolf."

They left a few minutes later, but only after setting the derelict building aflame. "Most everything burns, Gabriel. Always remember that. Fire kills damned near everything. Even werewolves."

V

Jude was ready when Giovanni's muscle boys came for him. He'd showered, combed his hair, and even shaved for the first time in almost a week. Just to make sure he gave the proper impression, he'd even purchased a new suit.

Appearance, after all, was ever so important.

There were four of them, all looking so much like the Hollywood stereotype of a gangster that he had trouble not laughing aloud when he saw them. Still, they were intimidating in a very large and brutal way.

He opened the door after the second knock and stared one of the goons directly in the chest. He slowly craned his head up to see a broad face which looked as if it'd been chiseled from stone. The man weighed 270 pounds if he weighed an ounce and either had a very good tailor or was without a gram of extra fat on his body. "May I help you?" While he waited for a response, he assessed the brute's obvious weak spots. There weren't many to choose from.

"Yes, sir. I'm very sorry to bother you, Mr. Jude,

but my employer, the owner of this establishment, would like to see you."

"And you would be . . . ?"

"Victor Humes. I'm the head of security for the casino."

"It's nice to meet you, Victor. Please tell Mr. Giovanni that I'll be glad to meet him for dinner. My treat. It's the least I can do after he's so graciously given me so much money. Two days in a row. I have to tell you, I like Las Vegas a lot. Hey, how can you not like a town where you can make ten million dollars in two days?"

Humes looked rather taken aback, and Jude decided to play his surprise for all it was worth. "Why don't you have him meet me in that nice restaurant downstairs—Rafaelo's?" Jude walked out into the hallway, forcing the man to back up. He grinned with enthusiasm, and the gorilla in front of him stepped back again, apparently surprised by his aggressive attitude. "I'm in the mood for Italian tonight." Jude tucked a hundred-dollar bill into Victor Humes's breast pocket and patted the man on the chest. "I'll be waiting."

The giant sputtered a few times, and Jude chuckled to think what must be going through his mind. He started whistling an old tune about money as he headed for the elevator.

Fifteen minutes later, Michael Giovanni showed up in the restaurant and was promptly escorted to a private room, where Jude sat waiting. He was a robust man, filled with the joy of life and vibrant. At least he looked that way on the outside. But Jude had spoken with the victims of this man's machinations. He knew better than to let appearances guide his judgment.

"Mr. Jude? I'm Michael Giovanni. Thank you for taking the time to see me."

"Thanks for making it so easy to win in your casinos. Ten million dollars is a nice sum of money. I could live on that for the rest of my life if I wanted to." The smile Giovanni shot his way was one part venom and two parts ice. "I took the liberty of ordering for the both of us—I hope you don't mind. Would you rather have the baked ziti or the linguini in clam sauce? I made the choice easier on the appetizer. The waiter suggested the pasta fagioli, so I ordered two." Without missing a beat, Jude poured them each a glass of red wine.

Giovanni accepted the wine graciously, inhaling the aroma. He then took a deep swallow of the liquid, obviously savoring the taste. "Thank you, my friend. Your choice is excellent. Oh, and if it's all right with you, I'll take the ziti. I haven't had a good baked ziti since I left Venice."

"My pleasure, Mr. Giovanni." Jude expanded his senses, seeking outward to check for duplicity. The man was a vampire, all right. But he was managing to hold the wine in just the same.

"Please, call me Michael. If we're going to break bread together, we should do so as friends." The man grinned, a feral expression. "You seem surprised by my drinking the wine, Mr. Jude. Is there a reason?"

"Please, call me Jude. Mister is too formal for friends."

"Jude it is."

"Yeah, Michael, I was a bit surprised. You're the first bloodsucker I ever met who could stomach more than blood."

"A good friend of mine convinced me that eating was a good way to discourage too many worries about my dietary habits. Blood alone will make people talk after a while. Oh, and please . . . let's not get off on the wrong foot, Jude. We prefer the term 'vampire,' or even 'Cainite' to 'bloodsucker.'"

Hell-Storm

Jude smiled, nodded his head. "*Touché*, Michael. My apologies for the insult."

"Nonsense. No offense taken and no harm done."

Jude was about to respond when the waiter returned with the bean and pasta soup. The two ate in silence for several minutes, finally pushing away the empty bowls and drinking more wine before the conversation continued.

"Michael, I doubt very seriously that you wanted to meet me for dinner. Would you like to discuss what's on your mind?"

"An excellent countermove, by the way. No one's ever quite had the balls to meet me in the restaurant before. Of course, no one's ever taken ten million dollars from me before, either."

"Nonsense. You popped Benjamin Siegel for just over that amount."

"Bugsy? Money had nothing to do with Bugsy. He was an asshole. Also, he was making moves on my grandniece, even after I warned him."

"Hey, I understand." He eyed the man and was eyed in return: two contenders squaring off before the fight actually began. "So let's cut to the chase. What's on your mind, Michael?"

Giovanni leaned back in his seat, then reached into his jacket for his cigar case. He offered one to Jude, who politely declined. "I want to know why you've decided to take me on, Jude. To my knowledge we've never met before, but this smells like a vendetta."

"Take a guess. I'll let you know if you're right."

"You working for the boys in New York?"

"Not even close."

"Lost a parent or sibling to the gambling bug and decided I was a good candidate?"

"Nope."

"Needed quick money and just happened to pick my place? Twice?"

"Sorry. Still cold." He smiled. "Should I give you a clue?"

"Please. I've used up all of the standard answers."

"Due west of here. About twenty miles or so. That's why I'm here."

Michael eyed Jude, puzzled for a moment. Then he nodded his understanding. "What? You want to take me on for a bunch of losers? C'mon. You really expect me to believe that shit?" The man actually managed to look indignant.

"Yes. They told me what you did. What you had done to them for the love of money. I don't think blackmail's a very good reason to kill so many people." He shrugged. "I'm funny that way."

"No. You're stupid that way. I'm willing to make you a deal. You keep the money and get out of town. We'll call it even."

"Have you ever been out there, Michael? Have you ever listened to them? Heard their screams? They can't rest."

"Yeah? Shit happens. If they'd stayed out of my business, I'd never have bothered them." He shrugged, washing his hands of the matter. "What does this matter to you, anyway?"

"If they'd all deserved it, I might even let that fly. But you killed babies, Michael. You killed little children, and you killed the wives and husbands of the greedy ones. All because you were afraid they might tell somebody something about you."

"People die all the time, Jude. They die horribly. Diseases, poverty, war . . . even senseless crimes. For every one of them that dies, there are two more waiting to be born. It's sad."

"You had them dig their own graves, Mike. You had some of them buried alive. You're a very twisted man. You need therapy."

Giovanni's fist slammed into the table with

enough force to lift the settings into the air. "You need to learn the meaning of respect!" His voice was boiling with rage. "You need to remember that you are alive because I choose to let you live!"

There was silence again for a few moments. Jude watched the man as he visibly reined in his emotions. Then he smiled. "I do respect you, Michael. That's why you're still alive. That's why you still have money. What I did to your slot machines was nothing. I could do that to every single machine in every single casino I even think you're connected to. I could do that same thing to all the decks of cards in all your dealer's hands. Your roulette wheels . . . Everything you own. I could destroy you in a matter of hours. I choose not to."

Jude stood up, stretching his hands toward the sky. "Not yet at least. I like to see my victims suffer, too. Good-bye, Michael. I'll be watching you."

Jude walked to the door of the private room and willed himself elsewhere before his hand even reached the knob. He stepped from the luxuriously decorated restaurant into the place where he was most comfortable. The streets where good people didn't walk.

His new suit drew a few eyes. Obvious displays of wealth can do that in bad places. One look at the owner of the suit was enough to stop the thoughts of quick cash which came with viewing the outfit. It was good to be home again. He knew he should move on. He knew there would definitely be a price to pay for his flamboyant act. But he did not care.

Jude was feeling restless, and the idea of a good fight might help him forget the memories which were trying so hard to surface.

Some things are best left in the past. Dead and buried, as it were.

VI

The Wyrm's minion rejoiced. So far nothing it had encountered was capable of stopping its growth. This was as it should be. It remained cautious just the same. There was no benefit in arrogance. That sort of zeal it saved for its enemies.

The tactics used were simple enough: Wait patiently and someone would come along. Every victim simply meant another mind to absorb. Another body to imitate. Still, the humans were unusual. Some of them could almost sense that something was wrong with the impostors sent out from the main body to bring forth enlightenment. Perhaps they responded on an instinctive level, as the memories of Father RipThroat suggested. A form of the Delirium. Perhaps, as suggested by Padre Montoya, the humans could feel the presence of the devil. The colony-mind contemplated this dilemma, even as it joined all of its parts again, taking the time to assimilate the information granted by the latest converts.

The Meeting Place was ideal. Beneath the subbasements of the Platinum Palace, a narrow crack trailed far into the earth, leading to a deep, dank place where nothing grew save the familiar decay left behind by the Great Corrupter's trail. Here, kindred beings moved in places where the barrier between the realms of the physical and the spiritual was thin. Some were long forgotten by man and beast alike, driven away from the physical world by the defenders of a dying planet. Others still moved freely, unhindered by the restraints nature tried to impose. And others still, like the group-mind entity, simply drifted for countless millennia before finding a way into the Gaia-Realm.

Having found this place by accident, it wanted to stay. The curiosities it encountered were endless. The concepts of thought and deliberate motion had never occurred before it came here. That these two experiences could combine was an even more exhilarating idea.

The ideas of Good and Evil remained unknown until the thing had expanded in size and awareness. Each new form absorbed and converted became a thousand new experiences and memories to savor. Like a junkie seeking another fix, the entity simply could not get enough of the sensations.

It had developed a new fascination of late. It liked words. Words were like power, the ability to express itself if it so desired. Again, the concept was new and thrilling. It had even come up with a name, one that made perfect sense in lieu of Padre Montoya's memories. The hive-mind called itself Legion. For truly, the word fit well.

Legion slumbered, the endless thoughts moving through its brain sending shivers of pleasure across its massive form.

Since Mexico City, Legion had consumed over three hundred human minds and more other forms of life than even it could truly comprehend. And, oh, there was so much more to learn . . .

6

I

The Dead were restless. For what seemed like an eternity, they'd been forced to stay in the ground twenty miles west of Las Vegas. Brooding, angry, they tried to break the hold their burial ground had on them. From time to time others of the Dead would wander through the area. Most were lost or seeking the answers that would let them find peace and move on to the next realm, if such a place truly existed. When the strangers passed into the area, they, too, were trapped. There was a barrier here—a wall of powerful energies that would not permit them to leave.

So instead they stayed together, forced by circumstances to work as a unit. They learned to survive against the endless tempestuous winds that tore at their very beings, trying to force them past the unnatural prison holding them in the place where they died. Some wept as they worked; others paused from time to time, to roar their frustrations to gods unable or unwilling to help them. A few simply grew quietly insane.

The crazy ones were the first to discover a few secrets about being dead. Like: If you tried very, very hard, you could affect the world of the living in small ways. You could make the wind blow, or push the sand of the desert floor across the ground. The lunatics also discovered that you could unite forces and move even more air or soil. Sadly, they also discovered that the barrier held their powers at bay.

They knew instinctively that the barrier existed because *he* wanted it to. Giovanni. The destroyer of lives and stealer of souls. Even more than they prayed for release from their bonds, the Dead wanted to make him suffer. His screams of agony would be reward enough for what they'd endured.

Then Jude came to visit them. Jude, who was just mad enough to hear them when they screamed, just kind enough to want to help and, perhaps, just powerful enough to help them escape the walls created by Michael Giovanni.

The Dead had no doubt that Jude would return. When he did, they would ask him for his aid in destroying their prison. Having been in his mind, they knew he would aid them in any way he could. His feelings of guilt over past crimes would see to that.

So they waited as patiently as they could for Mad Jude's return. They waited and they practiced their special tricks. They grabbed the wind and forced it to do their bidding, reveling in the fierce cold they generated. They heaved the arid soil into the air, watching as their two tricks worked together to make something new, something especially dangerous. When they finished their practice, the cacti in the area were dead. Not only were the plants torn from the ground, they were frozen solid as well. They shattered when they landed on the rocky soil.

Oh, yes. They waited. They could wait as long as necessary. Jude would come. He would free them, and Don Michael Giovanni of Clan Giovanni would know what a horrible mistake he'd made. He held power over them, true, but his power could not hope to stand against them all.

They would not make the same mistake that he did. They would not leave him intact. The Dead planned to tear his withered soul into a thousand pieces and scatter most of those pieces to the winds of the Tempest.

All save a small fragment for each of them to hold on to. The small pieces could suffer as well as the large—they'd learned that, too. They'd had a long time to learn about being dead. Long enough to know what could best hurt a tortured soul.

II

Gabriel and Shaun spent the night walking the streets of Las Vegas. They covered everything, from the center of the city, where money endlessly cycled through countless hands, to the worst corners of the suburbs, where trailer parks held the hopeless and destitute. The search was as maddening as it was fruitless. Though they often encountered the spoor of their prey, they could find no physical manifestations.

They did encounter other minions of the Wyrm, however. Gabriel learned a truth he'd just as soon have done without: The wolf does not hide in sheep's clothing, that was left for the Wyrm.

They were moving through a neighborhood where everything seemed in place when they met the fomori. Shaun was silent, as he had been for some time, and Gabriel was content to remain silent as well. The memories of what he'd seen earlier continued to haunt him. No matter where he went or what he saw, he could not escape the image of Paisley's ruined body. *No*, he said to himself. *Her name was Angie. I think I want to remember her that way instead.*

Everything seemed okay with the neighborhood. The lawns were green; the houses were well kept and pleasant to see, even if they did look an awful lot alike. But something about the place bothered Shaun. He kept looking around and shaking his head, even mumbling to himself.

"What's the matter, Shaun?" Gabriel whispered, because speaking aloud seemed improper in a vague way. He suspected Shaun would be angry if his voice carried.

"I don't know yet. But something's wrong." He looked around, feeling his hackles rising even before his mentor continued. "There're no dogs."

"What?"

"No dogs. No cats or insects either. Do you even hear a cricket?"

Gabriel listened to the sounds of the night. Nothing moved or made a sound, save for the gentle breeze playing in the leaves of a few olive trees. He felt like he was watching a movie where someone had forgotten to add in the sound track. He sniffed the air, noticing for the first time that there was no scent of any animal but man in the area. His nerve endings flashed with a thousand tickling pinpricks as his skin developed goose bumps. "Shit. Nothing at all. Even the air smells wrong."

Shaun tapped him on the shoulder, using his chin to indicate a house just down the way. "There. I can sense them."

He looked at the building. Like all of the others, the lawn was perfectly maintained. *Everyone keeping up with the Joneses. That's what Dad called it.* His eyes told him he'd walked into a picture-perfect neighborhood and was now looking at a home right out of "Father Knows Best." Every other sense told him a very different story. The grass in the front yard was wrong somehow. The blades looked just slightly out of place. The Big Wheel sitting on its side in front of the garage was just as off kilter, though he could point to no one aspect that made it so. The entire place simply felt *evil*.

He studied the windows, where cheerful light nonetheless left a leprous taint as it spilled onto a postcard lawn, and shivered again. "This place is bad, Shaun. I don't like this at all."

"That's two of us. Be prepared. It's time to pay these fine people a little visit."

"What? What are we going to say to them? 'Hi, pardon us, but have you seen any monsters around here?'"

Shaun smiled tightly and nodded. "Something like that." The short man sprang over the lawn and landed carefully on the walkway leading to the front door. Without missing a beat, he reached into his light jacket and pulled out two pamphlets. The stress lines faded from his face and an almost-mystical serenity came over him, unlike any Gabriel had seen before.

He rapped politely on the brass knocker, smiling and waiting. A few moments later, a chunky individual with little hair and too many chins answered. The man had gray eyes and gray hair, with a dark tan and a peeling bald spot. "Yes? May I help you?"

he asked. The man's voice was normal enough. Once again, Gabriel's other senses told a very different story. Where Shaun bore a fairly strong scent of the Wyrm, the harmless-looking man nearly overwhelmed his senses.

Shaun smiled politely. "Good evening, sir." Shaun's voice sounded entirely wrong. Smarmy and slicker than spilled oil. "I'm very sorry to bother you, but I was wondering if you are familiar with the words of the Lord."

The man slammed the door in Shaun's face. Shaun calmly slipped the copies of *The Watchtower* back into his jacket and turned away. When he was back on the street, the pleasant expression faded, replaced by a burning hatred. "There are four of them that I could see. Two adults and two children." Gabriel stepped back, shaking his head. Before he could speak, Shaun continued. "I know what you're thinking. You can get that notion out of your head right now. They may look like kids, but they're not even human anymore. They're related to whatever killed the Bone Gnawers earlier."

"But—"

"No. Don't let yourself think. Not right now. Now you've got to trust in your instincts and remember everything I've taught you about fighting. Trust me, we're outnumbered and likely to get ourselves very hurt if we don't move quickly. You can take the larger ones first if it will make you feel better."

Gabriel stared into his mentor's eyes and wished he was anywhere else. Still, he accepted what the man said.

"Okay, Gabe?"

Gabriel nodded. "Let's just do this."

"Aye, that'd be for the best."

As with every transformation, the change made

him more confident. His already-enhanced senses grew even sharper; he could hear the sounds of the family become clear even over the noise from their television. A rancid odor he'd missed before became evident: a smell like dog shit on a hot, humid day, mixed with the sharp tang of rising yeast.

Eight feet tall, Shaun cleared the wooden fence into the backyard without making a sound. Gabriel followed suit, feeling like a clumsy elephant in comparison. The backyard was dark, but hid nothing. A solitary beam of light painted the lawn here as well, but this time the light came not from a window, but from the sliding glass doors. Shaun plowed through the glass without even flinching. Gabriel had to think about it first.

The family—looking all too much like the sort Norman Rockwell liked to paint, thanks so much for the guilt trip—sat watching their television until Shaun made his entrance. The transformation occurred nearly instantaneously. One of the children stared in stark terror at the sight of them entering. Gabriel could smell his urine as it stained his toddler-sized Oshkosh overalls. His bright blue eyes, under a crown of baby-fine blond curls, grew wide. The little girl sitting next to him—*Jesus, help me, she can't be over ten years old*—sprang from her sitting position and screamed at the top of her lungs. Her pretty face began to stretch wider and wider, impossibly large. She leaped toward them— and, as she moved through the air, her skin peeled away like so much bloody toilet paper. The meaty mass under her skin glistened wetly, but sharp protrusions grew out of her body. Her teeth tripled in size and sprouted wicked barbs, as did her fingernails.

By the time Gabriel overcame his shock, she was all over him. He never even had a chance to see what the mother of the household looked like; the daughter hit him harder than he'd ever been hit before, and the momentum of the impact sent them both out into the backyard. Something inside him made a muted snapping noise, more felt than heard, and a wash of hot pain flooded his back. Before he could even try to stand, the little monster was gnawing on his shoulder and scrabbling at his stomach with the talons on her feet. Liquid fire burned a line across his stomach, and then something cold spilled into the muscles of his shoulder.

And for the first time since his change, Gabriel White allowed himself to drown in his rage. The little feral thing—his mind flashed on images of a pissed-off cat in a Chuck Jones cartoon: an endless blur with teeth and talons trying to shred the fur off his body and doing a damned good job of it, too—moved and weaved and cut and sliced at him for about three more seconds, and then he swatted it across its head with one paw. Despite the monster's ferocity, its skull exploded like an overripe tomato. The high-pitched shriek coming from the once-human mouth stopped very abruptly. Maybe it was dead and maybe it wasn't. Either way, he slammed his other fist into its body and felt a savage joy as more of the thing fell away like so much bloodred mud. Just for extra measure, he separated the remaining parts of the thing by grabbing an arm and a leg and making a wish. The remaining chunks quivered and flexed, but did not attack.

Something very large and heavy slammed into the interior wall of the house. He saw boards crack and heard the booming impact even as he jumped back into the madness. A stream of putrid black sludge flew through the air, spraying across his chest and across Shaun, where he was trying to stand up again. Where the stuff hit him, his fur began to smoke and then to burn. A bloated black mass wearing Daddy's pants sucked in a great breath of air and then vomited more of the toxic stew at his face. This time, Gabriel ducked to the side. The fire burning a hole into his torso only made him angrier, and he moved to strike the flabby coal-colored body with both of his paws. Just to make his point clear, he roared at the thing. Once again his hands sank deep into a freakish form. Only this time, they got stuck. The creature grinned with its toothless maw and started laughing. "You like that, B'rer Rabbit? You like how that feels?" The thing's voice sounded phlegmy and seemed to come from within the bloated creature's abdomen.

Gabriel roared in response, pulling with all of his strength and stretching the gooey matter. He heaved the entire weight of the tar baby into the air. Still he could not break free. The thing expelled another stream from its mouth and Gabriel ducked, feeling the burning pain drip down his back.

He looked around the room, seeking a weapon to aid him. Shaun was fighting the other big thing and faring better against it. A small part of Gabriel's mind wanted to panic, but raw anger overwhelmed the cowardly voice that begged him to run. His captured hands felt as though they were stuck in a food processor.

Frustrated and in pain, Gabriel slammed the sticky blob into the hardwood floors. It spread over the ground in a sluggish wave, releasing his hands as it thinned out. Then one of the beefy arms reached up and hit him square in the nose. Something in his muzzle snapped loose and ground into his cheek. Pain eclipsed everything else. He fell backward, blinking at the hot tears streaming from his eyes and trying to remember who he was. He remembered around the same time the tar-monster planted a massive foot into his stomach. The air left his body in a whoosh, and his eyes tried to climb out of their sockets. Two enormous black hands wrapped around his shattered snout and face, blocking his eyes and mouth. He tore at the mass with his teeth, but only managed to force the glue-like muck toward the back of his throat. He closed his eyes tightly, praying the fire wouldn't catch there as well.

Unbidden, thoughts of Teri came to him. Thoughts of how soft her lips were, how magical her smile was. With the images, a renewed vigor swept over him. Fury boiled out from his body in the only way it could. He started thrashing wildly, clawing with hands and feet and heaving his entire body upward in an effort to escape. His hands became stuck again. But rather than trying to pull back, he forced them forward until they emerged on the other side of the Jell-O–man's body. He managed to gain some purchase with his legs, and literally shoved himself entirely through the thing's rubbery form. His fur still burned in places, but he could breathe again as soon as he coughed the foul goop from his mouth.

He reached out blindly and grabbed at a piece of furniture even as he rubbed the paste from his eyes. He managed to grab the coffee table. His eyes felt hot and gritty, but he could see, albeit through a reddish black veil. Gabriel used the table like a snow plow, slamming it into the re-forming pudding-thing before it could gather itself together again. He pinned it to the wall, vaguely aware of the Sheetrock cracking under the impact. It thrashed madly, sending waves of agony through every burn mark on his body. He was still trying to figure out how to really hurt the monster when Shaun came to his aid. Holding a large piece of broken glass, Shaun drove it through the blubbery face of the creature, carving away a large chunk of pseudoflesh. When he was done and had tossed the section away, he repeated the process on another part of the blob. He made sure the parts landed in different areas.

It took over five minutes to kill the thing. Luckily, it stopped screaming after only two.

They sat for a moment, winded and wounded, and Gabriel felt the muscles in his body vibrating frantically as the excess adrenaline in him tried to escape. Not far away, a creature that once upon a time had been a small boy stared at the two Garou with an expression of abject horror. The Cupid's bow mouth gaped in a silent scream, and a thick white mucus fell from the pudgy bottom lip and spilled across its lap.

Gabriel stared back, remembering to bring the creature to Shaun's attention. Shaun nodded, speaking in that warped slur he always used when he tried to talk in the Crinos form. "Aye. He's no threat to us, not for now at least."

"What happened to it?"

"The Delirium. His mind couldn't accept us, so it shut itself off." Shaun shook his head. "Perhaps he's still too human. We have to kill him just the same."

Gabriel looked at the gray, fungoid thing still looking very much like a young boy despite the change in flesh tone, and shook his head. "Isn't there some way we could just . . . "

"Change it back?" Shaun finished the question for him and Gabriel nodded. "No, lad, there isn't. Some might have that ability, but I most surely do not. And it's a fair bet that you don't either. Believe me, if there's anything left of the boy inside that beast, he'll be grateful."

He turned away from the older man, trying in vain to find something *unblemished* by their battle on

Hell-Storm 127

which he could focus his attention. Shaun's bloodstained paw rested for a second on his shoulder. He winced from the pain, but forgave the accidental slight immediately. For just now he'd had quite enough of violence. "Go on. I'll handle this. Some other time, perhaps you'll understand the necessity." Gabriel nodded and stood. "Go be human again, if only for a while. The last thing we need is anyone seeing two werewolves stomping away from here, and I'll wager the police are already on their way."

Gabriel allowed himself to change again, feeling an itching pain as fur thinned out and became adolescent hair again. He felt his height fade away, and with it the anger he'd sustained through the combat.

He stepped away from the house, stumbling through the remains of the glass door and onto the lawn. The pulped remains of his first kill glistened in the night-dark grass, shriveling away as he watched. It melted into nothingness much like dry ice melts, but no fog of cool air formed around the evaporating puddles. Instead there was a stench that must surely have come from the pits of Hell and a faint hissing sound. Gabriel moved around the mess, thinking of the pretty little girl who'd been sitting in the living room of her house before they broke through the glass doors. *Did we cause them to change, or would they have become like that anyway?* All the powerful, feral emotion that had possessed him only moments ago dispersed as surely as her mortal remains. In their place came an overwhelming numbness, which stole the energy from him.

In the house behind him, an infant began to cry in a ragged voice. The sound stopped abruptly. His view of the perfect family's clean backyard faded away, replaced by a blurred mockery as faulty as the people who'd owned it. He heard a harsh moan escape from his mouth, but could not comprehend that it came from him.

In Garou society, anyone born under the full moon as he was became a warrior. "Ahroun" was the term Shaun kept pushing at him. He did not feel like a warrior just then. He felt like a little boy who had realized far too late the magnitude of his sins. In all his life, he'd never wanted to become a killer.

A part of him died that night, though years would pass before he realized what it was. Innocence can only be lost once.

III

Jude woke up around the same time he felt the gun pressed to his temple. He awoke fully aware of his situation: one assailant, one BIG barrel to the side of his head, and a very serious need to pee making his bladder hurt.

He came to the conclusion that moving even an inch would be a mistake. The shadowy figure confirmed his decision even as he fully reached the thought. "Evenin'. I'll make you a deal right here and now. You don't move, and I won't blow your head clean off'n your shoulders. How's that grab ya?" The voice coming from the shadowed figure sounded cheerful.

"S-sounds like a fine bargain, indeed."

"Then my guess is we're gonna get along just about as right as rain." The Texas drawl annoyed Jude in a vague sort of way, but he chose wisely again, and decided not to mention the problem to his uninvited guest.

"So. Is there some way in which I can help you, Mister . . . ?"

"Jack Dawson, at your service. You can call me Jack, or you can call me Dawson. Don't much matter either way."

"What can I do for you, Jack?"

"Well, sir. A mutual acquaintance of ours, and my guess is you know who I'm talking about, wanted me to make a point for him." He heard a rustling of paper, and then Dawson cleared his throat and continued. "And I'm quoting here, so please don't take the language personally, leastways not as far as I'm concerned. 'Mr. Jude. I enjoyed our conversation and meal tonight. Pleasant company and witty conversation always make my nights more enjoyable. Now that the formalities are out of the way I have asked this fine gentleman'—I'm assuming he means me at that part—'to make clear my position on your earlier statement. If I ever see your face in one of my establishments again, I will do all within my power to make you suffer as no man or mage has suffered before. I will crush your weaselly ass into pulp and serve your fucking head to the next son of a bitch who looks at me crosseyed. I will find any member of your magickal tradition who comes into this town and see that person skinned alive before I do so much as take two steps. I will gleefully spend a fortune tracking down anyone who has associated with you in the past and see them tortured to death over a span of months. I will capture their souls and continue the tortures for the remainder of my unnatural life. This I promise.

"'Again I thank you for an interesting evening. Sincerely, Michael Giovanni.' End quote."

The two of them remained where they were for a

long, timeless span. Finally Jack Dawson spoke again. "I'm not often one to speak ill of Mike, seein' as we go back a good eighty years or so, but I have to say that's just plain one of the meanest letters he's ever had me deliver." The man's voice still radiated with good and apparently genuine cheer, and Jude decided he rather liked Dawson in an odd way. Despite his annoying twang and apparent occupation, the man seemed genuinely friendly.

"Why would someone like you associate with someone like him?"

"Hey, business is business." The shadow-man leaned back, withdrawing the gun from its frightening position. "For what it's worth, I don't plan on killin' you unless you make me. I'm just passing on the message. I'm very selective about who I kill."

Jude sat up, looking at the man in front of him. "Why don't I doubt that?"

"Why lie? If I wanted you dead, you'd be there already."

"What if I offered you ten million dollars to kill your employer?"

"I'd be flattered, maybe even tempted, but I guess I'd have to say no in the long run."

"Would you kill me if he offered you the same?"

"Like as not."

"I could probably turn you into a frog, y'know."

"Yeah. Mike said you were a wizard, an' seein' as he comes from a long line of 'em, I'm inclined to believe him."

"He said I was a wizard?"

"He said you were a mage. Same thing, different term, least as far as I can tell."

"Well, that explains a lot."

"Like what?"

"Like how I can do magic."

"You mean you didn't know you're a mage?"

"Not by any terms." Jude thought about it for a second and frowned. "I think he'd have a tough time with that whole hunting down my tradition thing. I don't think I have one."

Dawson reached over and flicked on the light switch. Jude squinted until his eyes finally adjusted to the sudden brightness. He looked at his visitor and saw beyond the illusions covering his body. Jack Dawson looked like a long stretch of bad highway. His skin hung loosely on bones and flesh that had long ago turned into leather. The creature speaking with him bore a strong resemblance to any number of mummified corpses lying around in countless museums around the country. An unexpected memory flashed through Jude's mind, of a trip with a group of schoolchildren when he was only a child himself. The body of a woman who'd died in a cave in Arizona was on display behind a glass case. Her lips were bared to reveal a mouthful of bad teeth and her eye sockets showed clearly behind closed lids. Her joints looked horribly arthritic beyond the gray, stretched skin, and her ribs seemed out of proportion to the parts of her body where the organs had atrophied into so much dust. Jack Dawson looked much the same, but he wore nice clothes and his eyes were visible within the sockets. His lips moved freely as well, but his gums were just as black and receded as the desert mummy's.

"Yeah. Ain't I just a pretty sight? You're good. Most people never get to see what I really am."

"What are you?"

"A vampire. Only I ain't as pretty as most of 'em. I look my age."

"You look dead. No offense."

"None taken, Jude."

Jude looked at Jack Dawson for a long time.

Neither of them spoke. When Jude started talking again, he almost frightened himself. The silence was very prolonged and the sudden noise caught him off guard. "Have you ever seen the graveyard your friend Mike made?"

"Can't say as I have. Why?"

"I think I've heard of your kind before. You can actually speak with the Dead, can't you?"

He shrugged. "When they feel like talkin' to me."

"So can I. The ones Michael Giovanni murdered like to talk, too."

"That a fact?"

"Yes. They like it very much. They are angry with him for what he's done." Jude started remembering the way they'd made him feel, and a shiver slashed hotly through him. "They're suffering, and it's all his fault."

"Well, I reckon he must have had his reasons . . . ."

Dawson sounded doubtful, though, and Jude made his proposal. "Why don't you come with me? Out into the desert. Why don't you listen to what they have to say?"

"Now why would I want to do a fool thing like that?"

"Because I think you're bothered by the pain the Dead feel. I think you don't like it when they suffer."

Jack Dawson rose from his seat in the chair he'd somehow managed to slide beside the bed without making a single sound. He walked over to the front door of the cheap dive Jude called home. "You plannin' on messin' with Mike's casinos tomorrow?"

"No. Not really. I just wanted to make a point."

Dawson made a "hmm" noise and nodded. "Then I guess I can spare a few hours tomorrow night." He opened the door and slid into the hallway. "I'll meet you here, after sunset. We can talk about what Mike's been up to." The door closed. Dawson was gone. Jude lay still for a few minutes, then turned off the light and made himself comfortable. He was asleep in minutes.

7

I

Gabriel needed time away from the madness. Everything around him seemed out of focus. Shaun tried to calm him down, but the man's presence only made the situation worse. His mom was off with her new friend, and Gabriel could not fault her for that, but did so anyway. With no other options available, he did the only thing he could do. He walked.

This time he stayed away from the darker parts of the city. He walked along the Strip, straying only a few blocks from the major casinos when he actually decided to take side roads.

And he thought of Teri. Calling her home was completely out of the question. Her old man made the monstrous thing he'd battled tonight seem tame in comparison, at least as far as tempers were concerned. But he longed to hear her voice. Teri made his life saner, helped him keep his balance in a time when his entire world insisted on shaking down to its very foundations. He desperately wanted that strength now.

Instead, he got Jack Dawson. The man was just there, leaning against the wall of a convenience store and watching the people go by. At least that was how it appeared at first. A few seconds later, Gabriel realized he was actually talking to himself. But as soon as he saw Gabe, he stopped the chatting and waved. "How they hangin', little buddy?" He stared at the man for several seconds, unable to think of a single thing to say. Dawson studied him and finally came closer. "Don't look like they're hangin' too good at all. Wanna talk about it?"

"I-I don't know if I can."

"Mmmm. That makes it a bit harder to get the problem fixed, now don't it?"

"How do you mean?"

Dawson leaned back against the wall and crossed his arms. His face seemed both amused and solemn. "You remind me of another kid I know. Too busy feeling bad to notice when the answer's right in front of your face." Gabriel waited for him to continue, ignoring the insult. "You ever know someone who was walkin' 'round with a chip on his shoulder? The kind of person who just begged to have that chip knocked away so he'd have a good excuse to start swingin'?"

He thought about it. "Yeah. Yeah, I guess I have."

"You ever see a person after a really bad car wreck or an accident? Someone who just can't quite cope with what they've seen?"

"Mm-hmm."

"Well, Gabe, you look a little like a pissed-off badass with a bad case of shell shock. On top of that, you look like you're about ready to start squirtin' tears like a two-year-old baby." Dawson paused and spit a wad of brown juice from his mouth. His head turned to lob the tobacco, but his eyes never left Gabriel's face. "I figure you're either about as crazy as a man can get, or you've had a shit-poor day. Either way, you ought to talk with someone, before the situation drags you down into the shadows."

"What do you mean 'into the shadows'?"

"I mean if you stay this way for too long, you're gonna find it damn hard to get on with your life. Depression sucks. But it's addictive, too. So whatever your problem is, you need to spit it out now, not wait for it to just go away."

"I don't know who to talk to."

"You could try your luck with me if you wanted. I've been known to keep my mouth shut when it comes to the bad stuff."

"I hardly know you, Dawson. I mean, no offense, but what would you know about my problems?"

"Sometimes a fresh perspective is the best one to have. And when it comes to problems . . . Son, I've got about a hundred years of experience over you. That don't necessarily make me wise, but I bet I've dealt with most anything you could come up with."

Gabriel tilted his head and pointed toward the less populated areas. The ones where the shadows were darkest. Dawson nodded and followed along with him. Dawson was the first man he'd ever actually seen saunter instead of walk. Just the same, he noticed the man's hands stayed near the holsters on his hips—well concealed, but Gabe knew they were there—and while he had no doubt the man was listening to him, his eyes seemed to look everywhere.

Hell-Storm

Gabriel spoke, in broken, fragmented strings, of all he'd been through in the last day. He also spoke of the pain and confusion he'd felt since becoming a werewolf. The man's easy silence and friendly demeanor soothed him. That Dawson never accused or condemned him, either with his eyes or with words, also helped him finish his tale. The constant tok-tok-tok of his bootheels striking the concrete lent an almost-mesmeric rhythm to his story. By the time his tale was told, the well-paved roads had disappeared, replaced by sun-cracked tarmac and desert sand. As far as the eye could see, the Mojave spread out in silent waves of gray.

"You don't like being a werewolf, do you?"

"No. Sometimes. I dunno."

Dawson's throaty chuckle filled the air between them. His easy smile seemed brighter out here than it ever could under the neon lights. "Yeah. You like it. You're just ashamed to admit it." He spit his chewing tobacco into the sand, covering the remains with the toe of his boot. "I got the same problem sometimes. I enjoy what I do until I let myself think about it."

Gabriel nodded. "I love being able to change. I love running through the desert on all fours and smelling the air and seeing so much that I never knew existed before. But I hate the anger I feel when I'm in the man-wolf state. I hate the things I did tonight."

"You hate that you killed a little baby girl. You probably know a dozen that age."

Gabriel started crying. The tears fell, and he was simply too tired to care. Almost twenty-four hours he'd been without sleep, and he had more hours to go. Dawson set a gentle hand on his shoulder. "You go ahead and cry. You've earned it. The little ones always make you feel bad. I know. I've been there."

Gabriel sobbed, embarrassed by the tears in his eyes and the mucus hanging from his nose; comforted by the man who held him, despite the dead smell he exuded. After a time, the pain in his soul lessened and the waterworks shut themselves off. Dawson gave him an old bandanna to use as a snot rag and he took it gratefully.

With the crying jag over, he felt cold and spent.

When Dawson spoke again, the words came as something of a surprise. "You're girlfriend . . . Teri, isn't it . . . ? Would you have felt differently if it was her?"

"Hunh?"

"If your girlfriend Teri became one of them Fumery thingies, would you want her to be like that?"

"No. No, I don't think she'd be very happy as a fomor."

"So maybe the little girl wasn't very happy either. You've got to look at things from the perspective of your enemy. If you can do that, it won't hurt as much when you have to kill them."

"Have you killed very many people, Dawson?"

The gunslinger looked out into the darkness. His eyes seemed far away. "Oh, yes. More than my fair share."

"How many?"

"I lost count a long time ago. They died, I lived. That's all that really matters. But, you want to hear something strange?" Gabriel nodded, not really certain if he wanted to hear it or not. "I can see every last one of them. I can remember the names of all of my victims, too." He looked at Gabriel White with haunted, lonely eyes. "Sometimes, they even come back to remind me."

II

Laughs-Too-Much meandered through the desert with little concern for her safety. She trotted past rattlesnakes who did not seem to care if she was near and paused once to watch a fat, black tarantula skittering up the side of the sand-blasted cliffs. Few things in the Mojave kept her attention for more than a few seconds, so she moved on. A distant coyote howled mournfully to Luna far above in the night sky. Understanding his pain, she joined him in the lament before seeking something of interest to break the monotony.

The cool breeze rustled through her fur, bringing with it a scent that finally held her attention. Wyrm-stink danced with vulgar abandon on that wind. Wyrm-stink and the smell of Garou as well. She panted a moment, wagging her tail furiously with amusement. Finally, a little sport to make her night more entertaining.

Despite the potential fun, she remained careful as she searched for the source of the great stench. Being downwind from the cause helped substantially. After only a few minutes, she located the Wyrm-stinkers. They were indeed Garou, but they were Garou of the Black Spiral. Her hackles rose and her lips peeled back from her teeth. Also, her tail wagged even more frantically than before. This, she decided, would be fun.

Their home was a mess. Not surprising when one considered the source. She remembered the tricks taught her by the Trickster, and made herself fade from view. Odorless and scentless, she proceeded into the haven of her enemies.

If nothing else could be said for the Black Spiral

Dancers, they could still be called filthy. Every good animal knew not to shit where you sleep. The Dancers had forgotten that rule.

The caves were damp, despite the arid desert outside. They were also filled to capacity with the slumbering forms of the mutant Garou. Metis for the most part, bred of two Garou and thus deformed and sterile. Virtually all werecreatures reverted to their natural shapes when they slept. Only two of the Dancers had shed the man-wolf form. She crept past a creature that far more resembled a furry toad than any wolf, and sniffed at the smallest human among the group.

She was wrong. Only one was not a metis. One wasn't even a Garou.

The human did not look well. Her skin was hot and feverish, her lips chapped and dry. Even in sleep the girl was restless. She moaned and turned her body in an endless effort to find comfort while leaning against a harsh rock wall. Humans, she decided, were far too fragile for their own good. The Delirium was working on this one. Soon her mind would snap beyond repair, unless she was removed from the sight of so many werewolves.

If the Dancers were leaving the human unmarked, there had to be a reason. Either she was meant for use as bait, or she was being saved for someone special. Laughs-Too-Much knew she was right. She'd seen what the Dancers left of anything they did not wish to save for something special.

If the girl-human was important to them, for whatever reason, they could not be allowed to keep her. She moved away from the cave to contemplate this problem. Never once did she touch one of the foul things. That would come later. After a short time spent watching the cave, Laughs-Too-Much came up with an idea. Her tail wagged with such energy that she scared away a scorpion considering how best to sting her. She was lucky that way.

III

They were fighting again. The bad things that had taken her from her home. Despite the often brutal way her father beat her, Teri wished he were here to help her now. The thought of her five-foot-ten-inch dad taking on the bat-faced leader of the monsters started her giggling. *Hey, what's an extra yard or so of height when it comes to saving damsels in distress anyway?* The strangest part was that she knew in her heart he'd do his best to save her, even against such impossible odds. Her father was simply overprotective. That little lie had helped her keep her sanity for years already, and she saw no reason to change her beliefs now.

The tears came again, but quietly this time. If he hadn't been drinking that night, she'd have left the White residence much earlier, maybe even early enough to avoid this little version of hell.

Yes, he was overprotective and that was a good thing. Sometimes, however, he was also overindulgent. She'd toyed more than once with the idea of reporting him to someone in one of the many family counseling services. Now she wished she had. God, didn't she just.

The bat-thing came over to where she was sitting, forcing the pleasant thoughts of her father away. He had food with him. Some odd piece of meat that he'd tossed into the fire. Despite her fear of the thing and even her fear of what sort of meat he'd prepared, her stomach growled in anticipation of the coming meal. Right before her eyes, the creature changed. It shifted from big and hairy monster to far more human monster. Edward McTyre. Gabriel's father.

"Hello, Teri. How are you feeling today?" His voice was a purr of sadistic delight.

"Why are you doing this? Why are you keeping me locked away?"

"Why? Because you belong to Gabriel. He'll be very happy to see you, too. I'm certain of it." He ran one hand through her filthy hair and she flinched back despite herself. "Relax, Teri. I won't hurt you. You belong to another."

"Please . . . please let me go. I won't tell anyone about you. I just want to go home." She hated the whining sound in her voice. She was almost seventeen, far too old to sound like a little girl any longer.

He smiled, not unkindly, and shook his head. "No, Teri. Home is where the heart is. Your heart belongs to Gabriel. I can tell by the way your pulse increases whenever I mention his name. You'll be with him tomorrow, or the day after that at the latest." He stared at her for a moment, licking his lips. "But first we have to get you all cleaned up. A new dress, maybe some nice shoes and makeup. And we most definitely have to get you a shower."

He stood up after patting her affectionately on the head, and called out in a language she did not understand. One of the others came forward. Jet black fur and eyes a shocking hazel color. This one looked more like she imagined a werewolf should look. If the breasts were any indication, this one was also female, and Teri supposed she should be grateful.

"This is Aglamush. She is also called Christie. Christie's going to keep you company for a while, and the rest of us are going to find a nice new place to stay and a pretty new dress for you." The female changed shape until she, too, was human. Her hair was just as dark and her eyes were the same, but otherwise she bore no resemblance to the monster standing where she was, only seconds before. She was shorter than Teri, with wider hips and a heavier chest. She was also rather homely.

The girl smiled at Teri and sat down next to her with uncanny grace. "Hi."

Teri nodded her hello back, still focusing most of her attention on Edward McTyre. "Now, Teri. Behave yourself while we're gone. Don't try running away or anything foolish like that." He grinned and did a slow, lazy wink at her. "Christie's been known to eat people when they tried to run."

Teri looked at the girl and Christie smiled, revealing a terrifying number of sharp teeth. "Don't worry, Teri. I'm on a diet."

McTyre seemed to find that notion vastly amusing. He roared with laughter, and Christie joined in. Teri did not laugh. Somehow she suspected the girl might be willing to make an exception regarding her weight loss plans.

IV

Laughs-Too-Much peeked around a stunted cactus and watched as the vast majority of the Dancers left their dwelling. One, two, three, four, five . . . Five. That left only one behind with the human girl. She waited while they gathered together and moved off to a gathering of rocks, tumbleweeds, and manmade netting. They moved things around until their actions revealed two large ... The word escaped her for a moment; she'd been a long time without using human speech. Automobiles, that's what they were called. After a few more minutes, the group climbed into the metallic beasts and drove away. Still, Laughs-Too-Much waited.

She stared at her collection of weapons and frowned briefly. The rescue would hardly be as much fun with only one enemy, but one took what one could get. After thinking carefully about her choices, she grabbed the small hatchet and a four-foot-long wooden jo stick. The hatchet she placed in the back of her belt. The short staff she carried in one arm. Laughs-Too-Much smiled at the sun far above and then moved toward the cave entrance. Finally, a little action.

V

Christie was getting a little weird. Just a minute ago she'd seemed almost normal, almost human. Now she was talking about the best ways to prepare stolen infants. Worst of all, she seemed extremely sincere about her recipes and about how wonderful they tasted.

"Oo'Rock shouldn't have started me thinking about them. Now I'm gonna have to go out and steal one." Teri stared openly as a line of spittle fell from the girl's soft mouth and dripped to the floor. *Jesus, help me. She's actually drooling over the thought ...*

Aside from being a monster and eating children, Christie seemed like an okay sort. Which, by her way of thinking, only showed how far Teri had

Hell-Storm 145

slipped away from sanity. She thought Brad Pitt was a doll; Pearl Jam and Nine Inch Nails were her favorite bands, though she confessed to a secret desire to see Barry Manilow in concert. *Okay, now she's scaring me.* Most of all, she, too, hated "Melrose Place" and "Beverly Hills 90210." Somehow the thought that Christie and the others actually lived in the city made their temporary cave-dwelling habits almost tolerable. Almost, but not really.

She just wished the girl would stop going on about how tasty human brains were.

"So why are you guys after Gabriel?"

Christie's eyes refocused, and she realized she'd been salivating. "Sorry," she said sheepishly as she wiped her mouth and chin. She paused a moment longer to contemplate Teri's question before answering. "It's because most of us can't have babies."

"Why not?"

"Well, most of us had parents who were werewolves. When two Garou have kids, the kids are almost always deformed, crazy, and sterile."

"Geez. That must suck."

Christie smiled and giggled. "It makes for a lot less action on Saturday nights, if you catch my drift."

Teri caught it and blushed. "But what's Gabriel got to do with all of this?"

Christie's smile grew even broader. "You're a virgin, aren't you?" Teri nodded and the girl cackled. "I thought so. I haven't seen anyone blush that hard in a long time. Gabriel's not a metis. He was born of Garou and woman. So he can actually produce more children. That's something to be proud of."

"So can a lot of guys. Lots of guys can get a girl pregnant." She didn't ask the question on her mind. She was afraid of the answer.

She got a reply just the same, one that confirmed her fears. "Yeah, but not all of them are werewolves."

"Bullshit! Gabriel is not a werewolf. I'm his girlfriend, I'd know." But she knew she was lying even as she spoke. Gabriel had changed since his father's death. There was simply no denying that. He spent a lot of time out at night when she herself was stuck at home. They'd even argued about it once, before Gabe pointed out that he spent that time with Shaun Ingram, "learning how to fight" as he so quaintly put it.

"Bullshit, nothing. I've seen him change. He's a werewolf."

"When did you see him change?"

"About six months ago. We've been watching him for a long time."

"Why? Why didn't you just grab him and take him instead of involving me?"

"Because Oo'Rock wasn't healed yet."

"Healed from what?" The man Christie indicated looked skinny enough to have suffered from cancer, but she somehow doubted that was the case.

"The Skinner." Christie spoke in a whisper, suddenly a child telling stories around a campfire late at night. "The Skinner peeled his hide right off and threw him in the ocean. He spent over a year reteaching himself to walk and fight, 'cause the Skinner cut the tendons in his arms and legs, too."

Teri shivered at the thought of anything mean enough to cut the hide on that monster. The concept chilled her. "What's the Skinner, anyway?"

"His name is Samuel Haight. He hunts werewolves and takes their skins so he can make more werewolves like himself."

"Samuel Haight? But that's Diane White's boyfriend."

Christie nodded. "That's the other reason Oo'Rock wants Gabriel. He says he's good bait for the Skinner. He wants the Skinner real bad." Christie licked her lips, even as her lips spread into another smile. Teri felt another chill rush along her spine. "So bad he can taste him."

"That's disgusting." She just couldn't hold back anymore. She forgot herself and spoke her mind even as she realized she was making a big mistake.

"What is?"

"Eating human flesh." Yep. There it was: an awkward statement almost certain to piss Christie off. She did her best to prepare for having her head torn from her shoulders. To her credit, she managed not to wet her pants again.

Christie simply shrugged. "Some people like chocolate. I like humans."

"Chocolate doesn't have feelings."

"Plants do. Cows do, too. You eat them, don't you?"

"You show me a head of lettuce that has composed music, or a cow who's directed a movie, and I'll agree with you." The girl seemed completely stunned by the concept. As if somewhere along the way she'd simply forgotten that people could do more than eat and sleep and mate. "For all you know, the last baby you fricasseed could have been the next Eddie Vedder."

"Oh. I'd never eat Eddie. I want to marry him."

"Yeah? Show me an article where he's into cannibalism. Show me where he's said that kidnapping and murder were okay in his book. You're talking about the man who won't deal with Ticketmaster because he thinks they're ripping off people."

"Geez. You make it sound like I'm a bad person. Well, I'm not, you know. I happen to be a very nice person once you get to know me."

"Yeah. You just have this thing about sautéed baby parts."

"Oh yeah? Well, you snore! You're not exactly perfect yourself."

"Christie, there's no comparison. Snoring never killed anyone."

"That's what you think. Oo'Rock's been known to kill a few people for snoring too loud, I'll have you know. You should just be glad he's saving you for Gabriel."

Teri was still working on an appropriate retort when someone threw a wet rag into Christie's face. The change was instantaneous. Christie rose from the ground and swelled in size simultaneously. This time, Teri just watched with a sort of detached amusement. "Piss!" she screeched, waving the wet cloth. "Some fucker pissed on this!" Christie's voice was deeper than most men's and growing deeper by the second. She changed into her monster-self, snarling and looking every bit like someone who'd steal a baby and cook it on the grill. Her muscles rippled under a sleek, glossy hide, and the rumble coming from her throat sounded like an avalanche on a late-night movie. "I'll kill 'em!"

Teri finally managed to look in the direction the rag came from, and saw another amazing sight. Another werewolf stood there, but smaller and obviously cleaner. It was obviously female—there were breasts under that thick pelt of fur, fairly small, but breasts just the same—and shorter than the Christie-thing by a good eighteen inches. The creature's pelt was deep red, highlighted with lighter red and almost-golden hints. She was beautiful and strange, a vision that should not exist but refuses to go away when you rub at your eyes. She was also smiling, eyes wide and tongue lolling insolently. Her very being seemed infused with good humor, and her tail wagged ferociously.

Christie looked at the creature and snarled. Then she leaped forward with her massive fangs bared and both taloned hands ready to grab fur and rend flesh. The other werecreature moved, and somehow Christie wound up with her tail in the air and her face mashed against the stone wall of the cave. The other one yipped out loud, repeatedly, never once losing the goofy expression on her face. Christie was back up in a flash and ready for more.

She roared another challenge and started forward, only to land across the room a second time. The yip that escaped the smaller one's mouth this time was not a slight. Christie's right paw dripped blood. The newcomer was bleeding from a nasty gash across her rib cage. The smile was still on its face, but now it had a nasty edge. It crouched low and waited for the Christie-monster to attack again. Even as the Black Spiral Dancer was moving forward to do so, a short, vicious-looking ax appeared in the wounded thing's hands, flashing from claw to claw as it was juggled.

Christie didn't seem to care. She charged again, screaming with a surprisingly human expletive on her lips. The two made contact, and a second later Christie's arm landed next to Teri, twitching and bleeding. Christie let out another scream, this one much higher in pitch. The little one moved again, and the side of Christie's skull disappeared in a torrent of red. The girl who'd spoken of eating babies and wanting to date Eddie Vedder fell to the ground with a dull boom, twitching but lifeless.

Teri looked at the mutilated corpse, and something finally clicked in her head. The screams came back again, with a throat-rending fury. They lasted for a very long time.

VI

Diane White did not sleep alone on her fourth night in Las Vegas. Andrew Montgomery was a wonderful lover—far more interested in pleasing her than in anything else.

So why did she feel cheapened by the experience? This handsome man slept next to her, looking as innocent as a newborn baby, and she tossed fitfully on the edge of sleep, fading for a few seconds at a time before waking again with a burning heat nestled between her eyes.

Damn. This was just too much. She felt guilty. That was the problem. Guilty because she'd enjoyed herself more in their lovemaking session than she'd been able to enjoy sex at any other point in her life. Guilty because her son was only one room away—assuming that he'd actually bothered to come home this time—and she was in bed with a man who'd been a friendly acquaintance at best when they arrived a few days earlier.

A few days? Sometimes it seemed like only hours, other times it seemed like years. Nothing made sense anymore. She'd truly hoped to regain her equilibrium during this little vacation, but instead her life just kept spinning farther into orbit. She felt dirty when she knew she should not. She could hold no anger for Gabriel staying out all night, when she knew that she should be scolding him for leaving the hotel without her permission. She could not even be angry with Shaun—sweet, kind Shaun, who'd unwittingly stolen her son's affection—for letting the boy out of his sight.

Every time she thought about how she should feel, her emotions refused to respond in the right way. Damn it, she deserved better than this. She'd fought hard to get her life into some semblance of order, but everywhere she turned chaos bloomed like wildflowers.

She looked at Andrew and thought of Sam, doing her best to ignore the guilty voice that demanded a little more respect for dear, departed John. A tired, bitter anger bloomed in her chest: not enough to make her feel overly bad, but just enough to make her wonder when everything had gone so horribly wrong.

Just enough to keep sleep at bay for another night. Long after Andrew kissed her good morning and left to prepare for the grand opening of the Palace in two days, she sprawled across the bed. Sleep would not come to give her comfort and shelter. Only the nightmares again. More nightmares than any one soul should have to suffer alone.

VII

Shaun Ingram sat in his room and watched the television without really seeing any of the shows running. He felt cold to the very bottom of his soul.

What in the name of heaven and earth made me push the boy into a Wyrm-hunt this early on? True, he'd been training Gabriel for over a year, but that was no excuse. He'd also been training Gabriel in increments too small to measure properly. He couldn't rush Gabe, not if he wanted a sane Garou on his hands. Gabriel was far too messed up already. He was alone as few of the Garou could ever be alone. He was the last of his tribe, a tribe long thought dead.

Worse still, he was already suffering from the Great Corrupter's influence. Most werewolves were more aggressive in the Crinos form, but Gabriel was just plain vicious. He seldom thought things through—though Shaun had only himself to blame for that one—and he attacked with a wild abandon few could hope to maintain if they wanted to live.

And where do I get off even thinking I'm qualified to teach the boy? I'm an outcast of the Black Spiral Dancers. I've been down the path that leads to the Wyrm. So where in the name of Jesus do I get off thinking I can teach the boy the ways of Gaia? The thoughts came unbidden, unwelcome. Sadly, they were also unavoidable. Shaun knew enough to see the Wyrm's influence in his own actions as well. It was only a matter of time before he led the boy into the mouth of the monster they both loathed and allowed the foul creature to sup on his innocent soul.

TBS was playing one of the endless *Howling* movies, this one set in Australia. He flicked the remote control's power button and shut the damned TV off. Despite himself, he liked the stupid movies, bad special effects and lack of plot notwithstanding. Right now he needed a clear mind. He needed to think of a way to save the boy and maybe even himself—if it wasn't already too late.

The silence didn't help, not that he really expected it to. Shaun stared at his distorted reflection in the picture tube. Ugly. Ugly and foolish. What he needed was proper advice, and there was only one place to turn for the knowledge, much as he wished there were other options.

Ah, sweet Luna. I'm afraid. I don't want to go there. The Umbra. There—it was out and done with. He had to journey into the spirit realms before it was too late. If luck decided to favor him, he'd find the answers he needed in the Umbra. *And if I don't like the answers? What then? There'll be no turning back, I'm certain of that. Once I've committed, I'll have to go all the way with this madness.*

He'd been listening to rumors for as long as he could remember. One of the more common rumors about the spiritual shadow-realm of Gaia spoke of places where a Garou could have the Wyrm-taint removed from him. A place of purification. A place so beautiful and perfect that the very sight was enough to drive the truly deranged to their deaths. Alas, the same rumors also warned that the process was costly. Sometimes even the most well intentioned Garou suffering from the Wyrm's taint supposedly wound up dead or crippled.

I'll not lie about it. I'm scared. I've rather grown fond of living. He'd heard a hundred different names for the place he sought. Only one ever more than twice. Erebus. The place of the silver lake.

Shaun Ingram stared at nothing for a very long time. He stared blankly and wondered if he'd finally lost his mind. *Aye. But it's the only way. The boy will be redeemed and cleansed, or he'll die. That's all there is to it.*

Feeling the weight of his responsibilities as surely as a man far past his prime feels the weight of his years, Shaun Ingram stood before the mirror in his plush hotel room and stared deeply into the eyes of his reflection. Anyone watching would have been shocked to notice that his reflection seemed to stare back with equal ferocity. There were secrets held by the Garou and known to very few others. The Garou were of a dual nature in more ways than one. They were of wolf and human. They were of nature and civilization. And they were of this world and the one beyond.

Using the mirror as a gateway, Shaun stepped sideways from the world of the physical, vanishing completely. Even as he moved into the Umbra, he felt another duality. He was glad once again to see the truth of Gaia's beauty, and he was terrified of what lay ahead. In the spirit world, even dreams could kill.

8

I

Gabe and Dawson walked slowly back toward the Platinum Palace. Neither of them really wanted the conversation to end, but both had reasons for getting home before the first rays of the dawn's light hit the streets. For Gabriel's part, he was feeling far more human now than he had when he first ran across the vampire almost four hours earlier. The gunslinger was right. Talking through the problems helped.

"You feelin' a little better, Gabe?" Dawson's voice was subdued, but jovial nonetheless.

"Yeah. Thanks for listening." He almost felt embarrassed by his earlier confessions, but only almost. The easy manner of his new friend quelled such worries.

"Good. You just remember what we talked about the next time you get to feelin' low, and you'll be fine."

"Jack?"

"Yeah?"

"Can I ask you a personal question?"

"Don't see why not." The man shoved a wad of tobacco into his mouth as he spoke, and the words were a little muffled.

"How did you become a vampire?"

"I was sorta waitin' for that one." The man looked to the sky off to the east and shrugged. "Not much time, so I'll give you the abbreviated version. Back a ways, when I was feelin' pretty damned low myself, I decided I was gonna have to get rich fast, or I was gonna have to just call it quits and get myself killed." He looked over at Gabriel with a sly smile. "I wasn't havin' much luck with the ladies, so I figured on having a lot of money to please 'em, or just plain stealing away a little girl name of Elizabeth Owens Halloway. She was a fine-lookin' girl, and sweet as could be, but she was also from a wealthy family. My pappy was a freed slave, and my momma was just about the prettiest half-Injun woman ever to live. I'm afraid my pedigree wasn't much to write home about, though. Now, I could pass myself off as a Latino if I had to, and I could speak damn good Spanish too, so my color wasn't really an obstacle. But I only had about a nickel to my name, and her daddy was something of a very rich type. He'd sooner shoot my eyes out than have me set them on his daughter.

"I didn't quite manage to get rich. So I decided I'd just have to steal my bride." He paused again, tapping one temple with his index finger and winking. "I wasn't too bright back then, but I reckon I got better as time went on. Her daddy caught on about the same time I was sneakin' into Lizzie's room. So, bein' as he was a cattle baron and hired lots of men, he had extra help when it came to getting me out of the way.

"Well, sir, they didn't really mean to hurt me as bad as they did, I suppose, but the boys on that farm beat the sin out of me, and then they hit me a few more times for any sins I might be thinking about committing.

"They left me in bad shape and dropped me off about halfway to town. Town in this case bein' a little place in Texas called Waco. No sooner had I managed to stand, than Lizzie's dad showed up and decided to finish the job for his boys. He rolled me off the main road and shot me in the back twice, just to make certain I wouldn't hurt his daughter's virtue any.

"I spent the next day too tired and hurt to move. I just watched the blood oozin' out of my body and cookin' itself in the heat. I cooked pretty well myself. I had a little strength and a lot of fight left in me, though. I lay there and did my best to keep a couple a buzzards from peckin' at me, but they got in a few good licks before decidin' there was easier pickin's elsewhere, I guess. By the time night came around again, I couldn't even speak. I was feverish and just about finished with living.

"Then the man who made me a vampire came along. He was like I am now, sorta dead-looking, but able to hide it when he wanted to. He showed up looking just fine, and when he saw I was alone, he took away the illusions and showed me what he really looked like. If I could've screamed, I would have. He was—well, he was an ugly sight. Sorta like someone took a perfectly good man and then stuck him in a smokehouse for a few months. He looked like six foot of beef jerky with a bad attitude.

"When I started crying—I was too weak to scream or fight, so that seemed like my only option—he asked me my name. I told him, 'cause it seemed a safe bet he wouldn't eat me while I was answering questions. One look at his teeth and I knew chompin' down on my skin was a likelihood.

"'Who did this to you? Who left you mostly dead?' he asked, and I told him my story." Dawson looked off to the right, passing by a series of unlit windows. Gabriel sneaked a view as well, and saw the shadowy remains of a man under the hat Dawson wore. Mirrors, it seemed, refused to lie about how he looked. Small wonder the man always wore a big cowpuncher's hat.

Despite the death mask the man wore for a face, Gabe could see emotions warring very clearly in his friend's reflection. "The man sorta hunkered down over me and smiled. He said, 'Would you have the peace of the grave, or would you have revenge against your attackers?' I guess maybe I should have chosen peace, but I said I thought revenge would be a sweet thing.

"Pretty as you please, the man slashed his own wrist with a knife and dropped some of his blood in my mouth—That's how you get to be a vampire, Gabriel. They suck out your blood and give a little of their own. Only by that time, there wasn't a whole lot of mine that wasn't cooked into pudding on the ground around me, so I got to miss that part of the trip—and then I just sort of died. Not permanent like, but for a little while.

"When I come to, the man had me slung over the back of his horse and was leadin' me back toward Waco. The moon was way up in the sky, and I figured I'd been away for a while . . . ."

"What did you see when you died?"

"Nothin' like I expect you'll see. Leastways I hope you won't see it." He spit tobacco juice on the sidewalk again, and kept quiet until a group of late-night revelers had passed them by. "Let me finish this one up, Gabe. Keep the questions for later.

"When we got back to the town, he took me over to the funeral home and dragged me into a cellar with him. He left me lying down there, just getting hungrier and hungrier, and when he came back, he had a corpse with him. I drank the blood out of that corpse, and it filled me with energy enough to heal a few of the wounds on my body.

"I'd lived in Waco most of my life, and I knew every soul living there. The place was sorta small, and only about fifty families lived in the vicinity all told. Well, after I'd finished my meal, I saw who it was I'd fed on. He was a big old fellah, and he'd been a friend to my father. I felt about as sick to the soul as a man can feel, but there weren't nothin' I could do about that at the time.

"I stayed down there for fully a month, feeding on what the man brought me and learning the secrets that'd help me live among the people who weren't quite as nasty-lookin' as me. During that time, my body started to rot and my nerve endings felt a whole lot of pain. For a while I got about as bloated as a hot-air balloon, and then all the extra moisture left my body. But I learned what I needed to, and I learned how to listen to the Dead. I learned that the Dead suffer even after life is over, and I learned that some of them deserve to suffer and some of them don't.

"At the end of my month in the cellar, the man who made me what I am said he was leavin' and told me his name. I thanked him for his trouble and he went on his way. He never told me what to do or how I should do it, he said that was for me to figure out. But when I asked him questions, he answered them. When I asked him if he'd kill old Silas Halloway if he were me, he said he rather thought not. 'Cause then he'd be as bad as old Silas. I guess I should have listened to the tone of his voice instead of just hearin' the words. He sounded like a man who'd been haunted for a long, long time.

"I blew a few holes in Silas that same night, and in about ten of his men as well. Every bullet they fired in return just went through my body and left a hole I healed a few seconds later. Bein' a vampire does have a few advantages, same as bein' a werewolf, I suppose.

"That's how I found out that the Dead can take bein' murdered real personal. I've been hearin' old Silas and his men ever since. They don't come around too often, but they come around just the same."

"They still haunt you?"

"Not all of 'em, just the real ornery ones. Most of 'em gave up on me a long time back. I explained my side of the story and they listened. But I've been making amends ever since."

Dawson stopped speaking and nodded toward the closest building. "This here's your stop."

Gabriel was shocked to realize they'd traveled the full distance to the Platinum Palace while the man told his tale.

"I reckon I'll see you around, Gabriel."

"Yeah. I guess you will. One more question?"

"Sure, but make it fast, son. The day's about to break and I'm sort of partial to staying out of the sunlight."

"Why are you in Las Vegas, Jack?"

"Straight truth?"

"Yeah. Straight truth."

"I'm here to make sure this here buildin' don't ever open. You'd do well not to be here around ten tomorrow night." Dawson pinned him to the wall with a look. That look said the whole place was in deep shit, and Gabe figured he could get the family out before anything went down. Dawson continued.

"I don't aim to hurt anyone, just to make sure this place don't get opened. I like you, Gabriel. So I'll say this to you, and I want you to know I don't mean you no harm when I say it. Don't cross my path and don't warn anyone. If I get into a bad situation with security or with you, I'll defend myself."

Gabriel frowned. "No worries there. I don't want to hurt you, and I've seen how good you are with your guns. Just do me one big favor, please?"

"If it's in my power to do so."

"Give me two extra nights. One last night for my mom's sake. This whole place was designed by my father. He's dead now, and I want her to put him to rest. She hasn't been able to, but I think this trip will do it."

"I don't know, Gabe. That's askin' a lot when you consider what it'll cost me."

"Please, Jack. Two nights and she'll be gone. She'll have done what she came to do. Maybe then she can get on with her life." The man still seemed unconvinced. "Haven't you ever lost someone? Haven't you ever needed to remember them one last time?"

Dawson turned away, a scowl on his face. When he looked back, he nodded. "Two nights. I'll lose my bonus, but that's okay. Hell, I got somethin' to do tomorrow anyway, and money ain't everything. But you owe me for this one, and I always collect my debts. Do we understand each other?"

"Yeah. Thanks, Jack."

Dawson looked at him and he stared back. An understanding passed between them on a very primal level. "You were planning to sack this place yourself, weren't you?"

Gabriel smiled and winked. "Let's just say I didn't expect this place to make a big profit."

He waved as he pushed past the heavy, reflective glass door. Dawson nodded before moving on.

Gabriel entered his hotel room just before the sun rose. He felt tired and drained. Sleep came over him almost as soon as he hit the bed. Slumber held no mercy—only screams and pain, and the face of a little girl who became a monster and a bloated gray thing that cried just like a real baby.

He whimpered in his sleep and tears flowed from his eyes. Not that he ever noticed.

II

Jude opened his eyes, stifling a scream which desperately wanted to escape his numb lips. *Too close . . . Too goddamned close.* Too close to what?

(The memories. The past . . .) A part of him tried to say. He stifled that small fragment of himself with a mental shaking.

What was closing in on him? He hadn't any idea, but whatever it was sent shivers rippling through his sweat-painted body.

The sun was up, and even through the window he could feel the heat of the desert baking into the pavement. The day was going to be merciless. He climbed from his bed and walked over to the bathroom. A shower was what he needed, no doubt about that. The stench of fear mingled with his sweat was potent. Fear, he decided, was something he preferred to live without. Thanks just the same and have a nice damn day.

He turned on the hot water and waited until a cloud of scalding steam rose from the mildewed tiles before stepping into the stream. Burning needles danced across his skin, threatening blisters but not quite managing to accomplish the feat. When his skin started turning pink from the assault, he turned the hot water off with his left hand and simultaneously cranked on the cold water. The shock was invigorating. When the gooseflesh started creeping across his skin some minutes later, he reversed the process all over again. Half an hour passed before his skin began wrinkling, looking like a prune, and he wondered why he could remember clearly when it hadn't taken but a few minutes for that to happen.

The answers are in the past, my friend. You have but to look.

He shoved the thoughts aside with an angry desperation and trudged into the single room of his cheap flat. He ignored the bed and walked over to the curtain which hid his closet and his clothes. Jeans today, and an I HEART LAS VEGAS T-shirt. He put on his ratty sneakers, ignoring his usual boots. Something in the air seemed to whisper that he'd need speed today. The shitkickers just wouldn't do. He never argued with his intuition. It had never let him down yet.

The bag of oranges he'd picked up a few days earlier contained only one fruit, and a rotten one at that. He'd just have to go shopping today, little as he wanted to. Something in the air—

(They want to kill me. They're going to make their move today. There will be blood, so very much blood.)

—had him feeling nervous. He hated that feeling. The sensation that he was no longer in control of his own destiny.

Without any conscious thought, he pushed past his blanket-*cum*-closet door and groped around the trim above the interior of the entrance. There was a hole in the wall there—just how it got there he could not for the life of him remember. From the small entrance he pulled out two sheaths, and swiftly concealed the knives against the interior seam of his jeans with well-practiced moves.

He gave the blades no thought, but was comforted by them just the same. A button-up shirt worn like a jacket concealed the part of the handles resting above his belt. He counted the wad of twenty-dollar bills rolled up in his pants pocket and satisfied himself that there was enough for a good meal.

It was time to go. Time to do a little—

(Killing. Gonna break some bones and maybe even take a few trophies. For old times' sake.)

—shopping. More oranges. Vitamin C was good for the body. Maybe even a few donuts, because he deserved a treat. Hell, he might even go over to the Coffee Clutch and have a real breakfast for a change of pace.

Jude opened the door and stepped into the hallway leading down to the main road. Not far away, a dog was yipping up a storm. He could smell exhaust, oil, fear, and sun-baked dog shit on the wind. He could hear the dog and the television of the fat slob in the next apartment. Geraldo was talking to Women Who Sell Their Bodies for Money and the Men Who Love Them.

He walked out of the building. And there they were. Tony's friends. He counted quickly, eyes fluidly around the area. Fifteen all told, and most were carrying what his new Giovanni's messenger boy, Dawson, would have referred to as "heavy artillery." They'd brought in a few reinforcements from LA. Their head honcho—

(Smoothie. He calls himself Smoothie and he hates you. He hates you a lot!)

—was standing front and center with a long-barreled handgun. A .38 Special to be exact.

Smoothie tried for a sneer, but it came out looking like a nervous tic instead. "Tony's dead, man. He was my second. Now you gonna die, too."

Jude closed his eyes for a second, trying to keep his calm. He failed.

When his eyes opened again, the world had taken on a red haze. He heard laughter coming from somewhere nearby and was only mildly surprised to realize it came from him.

III

Malcolm "Smoothie" Williams looked at the man responsible for the deaths of three of his friends and could not decide if he was angry or afraid. The creepy bastard was laughing at them. They had guns trained on him, and the sick motherfucker was *laughing*. Man, that just wasn't the way these things went down. Smoothie was twenty-five years old and had killed a dozen men already. None of them ever laughed, not even Scratch Lopez, and he was hopped on angel dust when Smoothie wasted him.

Jude was looking a little crazy. The dude just grinned away and spoke in a barely audible voice. "Come on, then. Let's do this deed so I can go get breakfast. I want an omelet today."

Jomo Smothers was looking right at him, waiting for the signal to attack. He was the lead attacker here, much as the idea scared him. Smoothie nodded, and all hell broke loose. The brothers opened fire, and Jude started moving faster than he should. It was sort of funny, but not in a laughing way. Smoothie saw the way Jude was moving, saw the spots where bullets were hitting the guy, but he never saw any blood. Jude ran over to where Nino was standing. Nino fired point-blank, and even with his little .22, the bastard should have been capped, only he wasn't. Darwin fired at the man, but missed and popped Nino in the shoulder. Nino screamed like his ass was on fire and did a crazy sort of spinning dance, hopping from foot to foot, before he fell to the ground. His shoulder was gone and a red hole took its place. Nino's gun went off three more times, punching wounds in Jomo's El Camino. Jomo made a funky noise and fired at Jude again.

Somewhere along the way, Jude's clothes started gathering new holes, but still there was no blood. Jude did that fast move again, and two of the guys in from Los Angeles dropped to the ground. One of them was screaming as loud as Nino, but the other one just fell down like a rag doll, only this rag doll was bleeding from a big cut along his neck and chest.

Smoothie took aim and fired. He just kept the trigger pulled back and sprayed the crazy man with bullets. He knew they were hitting, could actually see Jude's body slam forward with every impact, but he still wasn't getting anywhere. The dude just looked his way, those funky blue eyes of his gleaming with twisted good humor, and suddenly the gun in his hands jammed. At least that was what he figured out later. The gun made a funky noise and hummed and clicked for a second or two. Then the barrel expanded and exploded. White-hot pain lanced across Smoothie's face and his left eye blacked out as something cut across it. His hands felt like they'd been stuck in a meat grinder. Somebody fired at Jude and missed. Smoothie felt a hammerblow in his stomach and one on the right side of his chest. Next thing he knew he was on the ground, looking on with his right eye while Jude made a mess of everything again.

He felt numb. He felt numb and tired and very confused. He watched on while the fools he'd brought with him kept shooting, only their shots kept getting wilder and wilder and the goddamned bullets cut into concrete and broke windows and smashed into the boys and bounced off Jude and a few more sank into his own body, making things wet and slicked up with hot moisture. The smell of cordite and blood and piss was everywhere.

And when it was done, the only person standing was the bastard they'd come to teach a lesson. Now that he was standing still, Smoothie could see the bruises and scrapes all over his body.

Smoothie rolled his good eye around, looking over his army and wanting to cry. His right eye was all for that; it'd been weeping something fierce for the last few minutes. His left eye didn't seem capable. Jomo, his blood brother since the age of twelve, was looking right at him. But his body was lying all wrong, and the eyes staring his way were beyond seeing. Jomo's mouth was frozen in a big "O" of surprise. Doobie Moss was sitting against the wall of Jude's apartment. Only, his head wasn't where it was supposed to be. All that remained above his shoulders was a bloody mass that looked a lot like a loaf of bread soaked in Heinz ketchup. Smoothie's stomach made hungry noises, and he felt sick at the notion.

Albert Michaels, called Hand Jive because of the way he was always giving everybody the finger, looked like he'd been folded over on himself. One of Al's arms was missing from the elbow down, but Smoothie could see where it lay in the street, still twitching. His middle finger pointed right at Smoothie, making a silent accusation while Hand Jive moaned deep in his chest.

Everyone else was out of his line of sight, 'cept for Nino, who looked pretty good in comparison to the others. Smoothie was kind of glad he couldn't see them. He wasn't very happy about Jude, though. Jude was looking down at him, smiling and covered almost from head to toe in blood. His face was splattered with angry red droplets, especially around his mouth. His teeth were crimson and bared in a feral grin. His maddened, glazed eyes formed a shocking contrast to all the deep red covering his body and face.

Jude squatted next to him, leaning down so they were face-to-face. Smoothie tried to move, but only his head and neck got anywhere. The rest of him was numb, right below the fire burning in his upper chest.

Jude reached out and touched his face with a gentleness that sent wild echoes of terror screaming through his brain. "Smoothie." The man's voice sounded malignant. "You need to remember that when you're facing one opponent, it's best to use your hands. I never even touched but half of your guys. The rest were shot down by your own people."

"Muh fuh. Mmonnuh kll yuu." Damn, but his mouth wouldn't work either.

"Pretty hollow threat under the circumstances. And I never touched my mother, not in that way at least." The twisted joy left Jude's face. For a second he lost all expression, and then a friendly, cheerful smile spread across his features. The blood smears around his mouth made Smoothie think of a clown. "So, listen. I'm gonna go clean up now. This was fun and all, but I've got to do my shopping. You guys gonna be okay?"

Smoothie didn't know whether to laugh or cry, and either way it hurt too much to try his luck. "Oh huu hell, somitch."

"Great. Let's get together and do lunch. Have your girl call my girl. Later, tater." Jude walked back into his building, gingerly stepping over something lying on the ground next to Doobie Moss. Smoothie wasn't sure, but he thought the bruises under the blood looked smaller. From where he was on the street, Smoothie couldn't decide if it was a nose or an ear.

A dog came over to him, wagging its tail. After a few seconds, it started licking his face. He closed his one good eye as he heard the first distant wails of sirens. Then the world went dark.

IV

While Jude took his second shower of the day, Gabriel White took his first. Despite having slept only a few hours, he was wide-awake and refreshed as soon as he rolled out of bed. He felt good. Better than he had in some time, actually. His mind was in working gear for a change, and his body felt invigorated.

As soon as he'd finished with the shower, he slipped out of his room and went down to the Golden Cup for breakfast with his mother and Shaun. They also seemed in good order, but Shaun appeared distracted, despite the smile on his face.

His mother chatted away as she seldom had in a long time. Her complexion was better; her appetite was almost superhuman in comparison to the norm. She ate and talked and looked around the place with gusto. Maybe the change of scenery was finally doing her some good.

Gabriel was glad to be alive and even happier to see his mother in such a fine mood. If she seemed a little nervous, that was all right, too. She almost always seemed a little nervous.

They spent the day together. Just the three of them. They shopped in the stores throughout the massive, air-conditioned interior of the Palace, buying T-shirts with a dozen slogans about Las Vegas and a dozen knickknacks they'd never have any use for.

They had fun. For a while, Gabe felt like a kid again, instead of a murderer.

They enjoyed themselves through lunch and later went swimming in the massive pool atop the Platinum Palace. Despite the almost-abandoned feel of the building, a large crew of employees worked around the clock to make certain everything was perfect for the grand opening the next day. The Muzak system was running smoothly and the air was filled with lighthearted music. But less than a thousand guests occupied the entire place. Big as it was, just about everyone felt as though they were standing alone inside an abandoned church—everyone seemed to have a great time.

The whole merry crew stayed together all the way through dinner, basking in each other's company. Then Diane excused herself. There was a formal banquet (no food for Diane, thanks, she was stuffed to the gills) that she felt obliged to attend. Before either of the men could think of an appropriate excuse for not attending, Diane made clear that they should find some other way to amuse themselves, as the affair would likely bore them to tears.

They ran off like kids given a pardon from a full term of summer school.

When next Gabriel and Shaun met with Diane, the circumstances were far less pleasant.

V

Around the same time Jude was tearing through a small army of urban warriors, the amoeboid thing lairing beneath the Platinum Palace divided its vast pool of flesh into its separate human components again. They shared one mind, but each had separate memories as well.

Maria Davillar stepped away from the mass and headed toward the Sands Casino. Today she was scheduled to work a double shift as a cocktail waitress. Maria was one of Legion's best collectors; her job required a surprising amount of physical contact and her outfit almost guaranteed a few minutes of private conversation with any number of men and women. Whether she liked it or not. She liked it these days. Anything to add to the memories and experiences of Legion.

Legion kept her warm and safe. Though there was a time when she'd have argued that point. Maria had always valued her privacy. She slipped through the sewer system, flowing effortlessly past the barriers which could have stopped her if she were still human. Along the way she absorbed three rats and the remains of a small cat they'd dragged to their haven earlier. When she'd reached the appropriate location, she poured herself out of a manhole cover and resumed her original shape. No odors betrayed her noxious abode; she had learned how to mask the foul stench of the sewers mere seconds after she'd been converted. Her auburn hair blew in the desert wind just as it was supposed to, but each strand reveled in the sensation.

Once inside the Sands, she clocked in and went about her daily chores. Before the day was finished, she'd absorbed and regurgitated seven people. She'd have tried for an eighth, but worried about being seen. She'd almost been spotted on number five, one Victor Humes. He'd taken longer than the rest of them, primarily because there was so much of him to transform. She shared his memories now, just as she shared the memories of all her converts. The rest of Legion would be pleased. He had so very much information for them to share.

On her way back to the nest Legion had created—she walked the streets this time, because Legion always enjoyed the memories and there was a decent chance of catching another one or two new additions—she saw a familiar face. Not familiar to her, but rather to Legion as a whole.

Legion had last seen the face's owner in the city of Tijuana. This one had resisted, fought back against Legion, and even wounded Legion before it could flee. Even badly injured, this one had managed to fight off the contagion-factor which made Legion almost unstoppable. Maria almost didn't recognize the enemy; he had scars where none had existed the first time they met.

Maria grew afraid. This one was an unknown quantity. It could not be assimilated into the beautiful whole. Worse still, it knew Legion for what Legion was. Perhaps matters would have ended differently if she'd only managed not to panic. But the sight of the enemy so startled her that she lost cohesion for a second, half-reverting to Legion's natural state.

The enemy noticed.

VI

Joe Hill saw the girl walking his way and smiled. She was a fine-looking girl, more than suitable for a night of fun and feeding. He put on his best smile, forgetting for just a second that the scars on his face were not pleasant to see. She looked his way and took a step back, eyes wide and mouth open in a gasp of obvious shock. Then her body quivered for a second, wiggling like Jell-O in an earthquake.

Joe could appreciate a few wiggles in all the right places, but her face damn near split in half before resolidifying. Her skin changed colors briefly, shifting to a much paler shade and erupting in one spot with a violent red streak. "Fuck me," Joe muttered. "Lookit what I found."

The creature turned and started running, moving with inhuman speed. Joe followed as soon as he'd recovered his wits.

Las Vegas truly never sleeps. Despite the late hour, large groups milled and moseyed along the sidewalks, making it hard for Joe to keep his quarry in sight and damn near impossible for him to catch up with her. Joe normally tried to be polite, especially when infiltrating enemy territory and trying to avoid trouble with Camarilla elders. But there were limits to his patience. When it finally became clear that he would lose his prey if he continued being civil, he started bulling his way through the crowd.

He tried just pushing past people at first, but when that failed, he started shoving the idiots out of his way. Some fell down, some were even knocked over. In one case, a woman in her eighties, who was justifiably excited about winning eighty thousand dollars at the craps table, didn't move fast enough and got slammed hard enough to send her skidding into the street. The oncoming cabby simply wasn't expecting anyone to land in front of his Yellow Cab and could not stop in time. She never cashed the check she'd received for her winnings.

Oh, how he ran. He shoved people aside like so many sacks of wheat flour; abandoning all pretense of mortality, Joe propelled himself across the sidewalks at speeds that simply weren't possible for mortals. He violated the Masquerade followed by the Camarilla on at least seven different occasions during that chase. When he came to an intersection where the light had just changed and noticed that his quarry was on the other side of the road, he took a running leap and used the cars in his way as stepping-stones to reach the other concrete shore surrounding the river of traffic. The resulting collisions took almost two hours to unsnarl.

When the girl bolted down an alley, he increased his pace, moving with the grace and speed of a cheetah in pursuit of a meal. He made the corner so fast that he literally had to run halfway up the far wall of the alley to avoid smashing into the obstacle.

And as soon as his feet hit the pavement again, the thing calling itself Legion attacked. This was smaller than the one in Tijuana, but it had learned a few things since then. He came around that last corner expecting to see a girl just over the edge into womanhood, or maybe even a slimy puddle of ooze with more teeth than a chain saw. What he hadn't expected was what hit him square in the chest and knocked him right back out of that alley. He hadn't expected a Lupine.

The werewolf hit him so hard that his chest partially wrapped around the massive fist. Several bones broke on impact, a testament to how strong the beast was and how fast he'd been moving. Joe was so shocked by the monster's sudden appearance that he simply lay in the street for a few seconds before trying to move. Bad mistake. The monster struck again. Even as it moved forward, the creature thickened and elongated. The huge paws grew even bigger, even as the torso swelled. The creature changed shape radically, its apelike arms splitting twice and sprouting wicked-looking hooks and barbs. The new limbs bore a strong resemblance to the rending claws on a praying mantis as they wrapped around him and started pulling. The bladelike edges of the insect appendages sank into his flesh, pulling meat away from bone. Joe screamed, and his mind went blank for a second, overwhelmed by pain like nothing he'd ever felt before. Two of the scythe-arms tore at his shoulders and two at his thighs. The enemies locked together in a sickening parody of sex, and Legion's mouth grew wider and wider. Its face took on grotesque proportions, expanding to accommodate a maw large enough to bite Joe in half.

And then things got really messy.

VII

Dawson kept his word and met with Jude just after sunset. But not before he spoke to the spiritual remains of twelve punks who'd thought they could take the mage with nothing but a few handguns. As was almost always the case, the wraiths' silent screams half deafened him. They wailed and raged, refusing to accept their fate and find their way on to a better world. Their anger, fear, and pain trapped them just as surely as chains would have.

Yellow tape surrounded a good portion of Anderson Avenue near Jude's apartment. Streamers of the stuff ran like a web spun by drunken arachnids. Inside the larger and more deliberate strands, chalk figures painted a grim picture of what had occurred earlier that day. 'CRIME SCENE NO TRESPASSING' was the warning written on the tape. *No shit*, Dawson thought. *It sure as hell don't look like Christmas decorations from where I'm standing.* Blood still smeared sections of the road and even the building walls where more chalk-circled holes had only recently been added to the decor.

He listened to their dilemma as he looked over the scene, nodding sympathetically. Still, he offered no help. They'd done this to themselves with their petty need for revenge against one man. One extremely powerful and potentially dangerous man, granted, but one man just the same.

After he'd heard what he needed to from the wraiths, he walked over to the front door of Jude's apartment, knocking this time instead of picking the lock. Jude opened the door a few moments later, dressed in jeans and a shirt with an illustration of the Golden Gate Bridge across the front. His eyes looked feverish, and his mouth was drawn into a tight, thin line.

"Hi, Dawson. Glad you remembered. I'd almost forgotten about our meeting."

"Howdy, Jude. Nice shirt. Been to San Francisco lately?"

"Not that I can remember, no."

"Hmm. Y'all've got some mighty pissed-off ghosts hangin' 'round on the street. Looks like most of 'em are pretty new here, too, if the chalk bodies littering everything are any indication."

Jude nodded, apparently missing the sarcasm in Jack's voice. Somehow, he just wasn't surprised by the idea. When the silence between them had stretched to an uncomfortable pause, Dawson continued. "Any idea what happened outside?"

Jude's grin was a nasty thing, a promise of pain and suffering. "I had a run-in with some old friends, who decided to stop me from shopping. Gee, you're almost as curious as those cops were earlier."

"What happened to the cops?"

"Nothing. I just made sure they forgot about me."

"Mmm-hmm. You ready to show me this little graveyard you were talkin' about last night?"

"Oh. Sure. Do you mind walking? I don't have a car." He actually sounded embarrassed about the idea.

"Luckily I do. Why don't I drive, and you can show me the way. I've got a lot to do before the night is over."

"Hey, sounds like a winner to me." Jude paused, staring at him with an unsettling intensity. Jack had the nasty suspicion that Jude wouldn't mind killing him. Not even a little. "Does it hurt being dead, Dawson?"

"Can't say as I know, seein' as I ain't dead yet."

"Oh. I just figured with your skin like that you'd know about that sort of thing."

"It hurt when it started, but it stopped after a couple of years. Just took me a while to stretch out the skin is all."

They climbed into Jack's truck, and Jude pointed the way. For a while he was completely coherent, and more *there* than Dawson would've thought possible. Seeing him that way was almost scarier than the dream quality which normally made Jude look so innocent and so damned crazy at the same time.

He could not deny it. Jack Dawson did not like being around this particular bundle of joy.

They made the grave scene in no time, and Dawson sat Indian-style for a while, listening to what the Dead had to say. As little as he liked the man next to him, he liked what the victims of Michael Giovanni told him even less. Compared to the sounds the imprisoned spirits made in the silent desert, the ghosts outside of Jude's place barely even managed a whisper.

9

I

Michael Giovanni paced his office. He ignored the people anxiously waiting for him to speak, instead looking at another sheaf of papers he'd angrily yanked from his desk. Thirteen punks dead, two more critically injured. Not in a nice, quiet hit. Oh no, these stupid assholes had to get themselves mangled and popped in the middle of the day with, no doubt, numerous witnesses. It would take all of his clout in the city to keep the presses quiet on this one. Gangland violence. Stupid, wet-behind-the-ears punks making a mess of everything he'd managed to accomplish by getting themselves in over their heads.

He walked over to his notepad and scribbled a coded note to himself about getting the LA gangs the hell out of Vegas by any means necessary. Enough was enough.

After making his lieutenants sweat in silence for

a few more minutes, Giovanni sat down behind his desk and looked each of them over. His face was a study in disgust. Not that he actually felt disgusted with any of them.

Raphaela Giovanni was as lovely as the day he'd brought her over. Had it not been for her need to stay out of the sunlight, she'd have made a perfect fashion model. The green in her eyes offset the black of her hair wonderfully. She was also so loyal it almost hurt to be around her. She handled the money-laundering aspects of their business in Vegas, and he knew there were no problems with her work.

Francis Giovanni stood next to her. Frank was a good worker, responsible for the media's silence when it came to the affairs of Clan Giovanni, and he, too, was not a problem. That he was a perfect double for Michael himself was only a bonus.

Antonio Giovanni was Michael's only son—though Mike had his doubts about that; Sofia had tended to flirt too much, God rest her soul—and something of a moron. But he, too, was loyal.

His eyes shot right past Victor Humes; there was no reason to suspect Vic of being incompetent. He knew better.

That just left Angelo. Thirty-seven years as a member of the clan and still he had a bad attitude. One of the five was going to answer for what was happening in town. Mike just hadn't decided which one as yet.

"Seems like we're losing a little ground around here," Mike purred. "Every time I turn around something else is going wrong in my city. Two nights ago we had a tenement burn down. Not a big problem if we lose a few bums, but bad press just the same. One night ago we get a line on a family getting cut to ribbons by—get this—trained bears.

Hell-Storm

Then, this morning, while I'm getting a little sleep, somebody tears up Anderson Avenue and a gang trying to move in from Los Angeles, with some big guns."

He leaned over the desk, lifting his body back out of the seat. His voice dropped two octaves, and he pinned each one of his seconds with a baleful glare. "Is it just me?" he demanded. "Or is this shit getting a little out of hand?"

No one answered his question, which was probably for the best. But Angelo was too dense for his own good. He made a suggestion. "Maybe you should tell us what you want done, Don Michael. Your word is law." The sarcasm in his voice was faint, but it was evident just the same.

"What do I want done? I want you to find out who's responsible for this shit and I want you to hang the fuckers out to dry! That's what I want done! I want you to get me some answers! I want the blood of whoever is mucking up the waters around here!"

Everyone but Vic and Angelo flinched. Angelo held himself in check, and Vic was too used to this sort of outburst.

"I want reports by this time tomorrow night. I want reports that explain what happened and who made these things happen. If I do not have those reports, I'll expect very good excuses. Do I make myself clear?" They nodded in unison, a small army of marionettes controlled by one set of strings. "Good. Excellent. Now get the hell out of here and get to work." He watched as they left, all but Vic.

"Boss."

"Yeah, Vic?"

"We gotta talk."

The tone of Vic's voice caught his attention: Vic did not sound himself. "What's the matter? You feelin' okay? You look like you ain't feelin' so good." The giant leaned a little to the right, like a man on a ship in turbulent waters. "Sit. Make yourself comfortable and tell me what's wrong." For the first time in half a decade, Mike Giovanni felt something akin to genuine concern for another living being.

"I—"

"What is it, Victor? You can tell me?"

The man was sweating profusely, his whole body shaking and twitching. Mike walked around the desk and placed a hand on his shoulder, concerned about his friend.

"I'm sorry about this, Mike."

"Sorry about what?" He was confused for a second, and then the pain erupted in his palm where he touched Vic's wool suit. He tried to pull back, but the hand would not move. He yanked furiously, but the fabric simply stretched to accommodate him. Michael Giovanni looked at his traitorous hand just in time to watch the charcoal gray fabric of Vic's jacket blossom around his hand and then contract until it covered his entire forearm.

"Jesus Christ! Vic! What're you doin' to me?" For the second time in one day, Michael Giovanni felt genuine emotion. This time, it was fear.

He looked wildly about the room for a weapon but could find nothing. Instead he attacked with his other arm and tried to break away from the demon-possessed wool. When his free hand struck across Vic's shoulder, the fabric opened up in greeting.

Victor Humes stared at him with eyes both feverishly excited and monumentally sad. "I'm sorry, Mike. You deserved better."

The fabric had teeth. Many, many teeth. And it knew how to use them.

II

Jude heard the sounds before Dawson did. They were wet sounds, full of violence and fading screams. They brought back a thousand flash-image memories that Jude could have lived without. He'd done many bad things before, things he fully intended to forget. But the sounds and sights before him evoked the past with a blaring scream of pain.

Just what he was seeing was difficult to say. The shadows could hide nothing from him. But the entwined figures defied easy identification just the same. Long brown hair framed a feral but lovely face, wrapped around a broken arm which seemed to grow longer as he watched. Another face appeared, far more masculine and pale white in comparison to the rich brown skin of the feminine counterpart. The whole mass was screaming, a wailing cacophony of almost-words that set Jude's teeth on edge. A muscular leg clad in the remains of a leather boot pushed harshly against a breast growing teeth and half a face. Two arms of very different proportions struggled against each other in a tug-of-war in which the frailer-seeming arm quite literally swallowed the heavier.

Beside him, Dawson drew his pistols with machinelike precision. He seemed at a loss as to exactly which part he should shoot. Jude watched the odd battle, mesmerized by the way the female aspects overwhelmed and engulfed the male extremities in a sickening parody of lust. The masculine face growing from the center of the entire mass looked toward him and then shifted slightly to stare at Jack Dawson beside him.

"Dawsssonn . . . Help me . . ." The voice was

distorted and broken nearly beyond recognition. A heavy gurgling sound came from the mouth, which was pulled back into the living sculpture like something out of Salvador Dali's worst nightmares.

Dawson stood perfectly still, his eyes fixed on the submerging face and his mouth open and as slack as an idiot's. "Damn. That almost sounded like Joe Hill...."

"You know him?"

"Might be. I might know him at that." The man's voice was almost wistful, almost incredulous. Something in his tone sent Jude into action. Jude stormed the massive, swirling lump and grabbed a handful of the most masculine-looking part he could find. He grabbed and pulled with all of his considerable might.

The bloated mountain of flesh let loose with a shriek that sent his teeth rattling in their sockets, but still he pulled. Concentrating on pulling the male free, he heaved for all he was worth. He was only vaguely aware of his shirt splitting at the shoulders. A massive rupturing sound erupted from the creature in front of him. Two very distinct screams came from the thing, and cold, black blood splattered across his eyes, blinding him momentarily.

He had no conscious knowledge of what he was doing. Had you asked Jude what he knew of genetic matter and forced separation of DNA, he'd have told you he knew nothing. Every wave of power he sent from his body into his hands was triggered by some primal instinct beyond his ability to understand. Without forethought, he separated the separate genetic forms on a submolecular level even as he forced the struggling bodies apart. As he blinked the slimy residue from his eyes, he forced his arms into the creature in front of him and pushed desperately to tear it asunder. Behind him, Dawson was saying something that he could not comprehend. Something about an old comrade. It didn't matter; he was far too busy to bother with the noise.

The bones in his right arm tried to soften, but he refused to let them. A mouth overflowing with teeth tried to sink into his left leg, but he willed the daggerlike fangs to grow brittle and shatter instead. He opened his own mouth and roared defiantly. Summoning strength he never suspected he had, Jude heaved the two struggling forms away from each other, throwing them in opposite directions.

A few seconds of silence passed. In that time he assessed the damage to himself and to the thing he'd split in half. One male figure, broken and bleeding. One female figure, already struggling to her feet. The male kept trying to stand despite his massive injuries. Jude watched them both from the periphery of his vision, smiling absently.

The woman looked up and pinned him with her stare. Beyond her broad face and classical features, a light bloomed deep within the liquid brown of her eyes, holding him enthralled even as the woman moved forward. That light promised salvation and damnation in equal measures: a thousand fevered kisses and an endless stream of obscenities. Jude stared back with longing and revulsion, feeling himself move toward the woman even as he struggled to resist her siren's call.

So beautiful. Had any woman ever been so amazingly perfect? Of course not. How could any mere mortal hope to compare to the glorious light in this goddess's eyes? He felt himself responding to her in ways he'd forgotten about. He lusted after all that she was and all that she promised. Perfect lips parted in a secretive, promising smile, and he started forward. *So beautiful. Surely she was as beautiful as . . .*

Something shot past his right shoulder in a blur,

striking out and marring the angelic face before him. The magnificent light faded, replaced by a darkness deeper than any he'd ever thought possible. The flesh began to blacken and swell, cracking like a rotted jack-o'-lantern. The sensuous curve of her mouth split wide open, revealing teeth designed only for rending and tearing. Instinct drove Jude backward just before the rotting arms of his almost-lover could wrap around him in an assuredly fatal embrace.

As Jude watched in horror, the woman-goddess before him decomposed where she stood. Her body erupted with weeping sores and blood flowed from the wounds, clotting in midair, even as it fell away from her devastated beauty. She did not scream as she died. She whimpered once and fell to the ground. In a matter of a few seconds, the body putrefied into little more than a puddle. Even that started evaporating almost immediately.

Beside him, Dawson spoke. "I don't know what the hell that was, but it sure looked like it wanted to do a number on you."

Jude nodded. "I think you're right, Dawson." To himself alone he added: *And I think I wanted it to. I think I wanted to be with it in heaven or hell.*

III

Jack Dawson stared at the man on the ground, feeling the urge to wipe nervous sweat from his mouth despite his lack of perspiration. He had short brown hair over an angular face. Angry red scars covered older, long-healed wounds on what was otherwise a handsome set of features. The last time he'd seen Joe Hill, the man was a new member of the Sabbat. Dawson had been there for his recruitment into the fanatical sect. That he was still alive at all said a great deal about his success in the radical cult.

The man—vampire, actually—was broken in a dozen ways, most of which would have been fatal to a living human, but were only painful to a Cainite. Even as he watched, Hill began healing himself, reknitting his bones and flesh. Dawson grabbed Jude's arm and pulled him back. "He's gonna be a mite on the thirsty side when he's done fixin' himself. That sort of trauma takes a lot out of a vampire. It'd be best if you weren't standing too close when he stands up."

Jude nodded and backed away, still looking a bit dazed, but obviously able to comprehend what was going on around him. Dawson looked on as Hill righted himself, a hideous need obvious in his awkward posture. The man was a sight, with his shredded clothing and gaping wounds still unhealed. "Good to see you, Joe. Why don't you go find some food. I'll be here when you get back." The lean, angry-looking man stared at Jack for several seconds, nodding, and then moved into the night.

"What will he feed on?"

"Don't much matter to him. He'll take as much as he needs, and then he'll be back."

"What if he grabs some poor soul off the street?"

"Then some poor soul's gonna die in a bad way. But I don't think getting in his way right now would be very wise." He stared hard at Jude, adding emphasis to his words with a dark look. "I know what you're thinking, but don't get any stupid ideas. You're good in a fight, but I can bet money he's better. Right now he's so damn hungry he'd wrestle a grizzly to the ground to get rid of his thirst." He looked around and finally spotted the man's firearms. He knew Boot well enough to know he'd never go far without his pistols. They looked all right, but the holsters were in hideous shape, mangled and stretched.

"I—"

"Don't. I mean it. I've seen him in a bad mood. He'll be back soon. Then you can try reasoning with him. But for right now that'd be begging for more grief than you want to deal with."

Jude nodded reluctantly. The two stood around for almost half an hour, staring at desert fauna and thinking their own thoughts. Finally the man showed up again, looking far healthier and dressed in casual slacks and a *My Folks went to Las Vegas and all I got was this Lousy Tee Shirt* T-shirt. The clothes fit him well enough but made him look like a tourist out for an evening of fun. His boots were gone, replaced by tacky tennis shoes that lit up every time he moved.

"Ain't you looking a sight, Boot."

The man nodded, a slight curl of his lips the only indication that he was in a good mood. His eyes tried to look everywhere, and Dawson guessed the man was feeling a touch paranoid. Finally, he spoke. "I didn't think you were even alive anymore, Dawson. Haven't seen you in almost eighty years."

Dawson handed him his guns and he smiled gratefully.

"Hell yes, I'm alive. No thanks to you, you bastard." Despite the bitter words, Dawson felt no resentment.

"Yeah. Well, you shouldn'ta stole my horse. Nothin' pisses me off faster."

"Wasn't yer horse. You stole it."

"What's yer point, son?"

"Can't say it was your horse is all."

"Yeah. Well, you're still alive, ain't ya? You think you would be if I'd wanted revenge?"

Dawson opened his mouth to respond, but Jude took that moment to interject. "Would you like to introduce me to your friend, Jack?"

"Hunh? Oh. Sure. Jude, this is Joe Hill. Boot, this is a new friend of mine, Jude. He ain't got a last name as far as I can tell."

The two shook hands, but Hill seemed a little leery of contact—not that Jack could blame him.

"Why does he call you 'Boot,' Mr. Hill?"

"Actually, that ain't a name I've heard in a while." Hill smiled wistfully. "I guess it's cause I used to leave a lot of empty boots behind."

"I don't get what you mean."

Dawson broke in. "It's cause Joe here used to be a right mean gunslinger. He left a lot of men dead, and back then you marked the graves of strangers with their boots, 'specially iffn ya didn't know their names."

"Used to be?" Joe Hill smiled, and the toothy grin he delivered was chillingly cheerful. "I'm better now than I was back then."

"Why don't that surprise me?"

The three stood in silence for a few seconds, until Jack brought up what was on all of their minds. "What the hell was that thing, Boot?"

"Don't rightly know, but I followed it from Mexico City and I mean to bring an end to it one way or another." The man reached to his side, and when his fingers encountered only air he cursed. "Either of you boys got a cigarette?" Neither of them did. "Damn. I could use one."

"Excuse me? Didn't we just kill the thing?" Jude was as direct as a child, and Dawson found himself wondering just how much of the man's mind was off in the Twilight Zone.

"Nope," replied Hill. "We just killed a part of it. But I think I know where the rest of it is."

"Why you so all fired set on killin' that thing, Joe? It ain't much yer style to care one way or the other about anything didn't affect you directly, last I saw." Boot Hill looked back at Dawson with a cold, expressionless face.

"Killed a few of my people down in Mexico City. That, and 'cause Galbraith wants it dead. She says it's too damn big a threat to let it go around doin' its own thing."

"You're serious, ain't ya?"

"Yup."

Jack smiled. "Some things never change."

IV

Teri Johannsen stared at the creature across from her, still rather amused by the strange being's attitude. She'd been half-carried, half-dragged away from the cave of her kidnappers, and now she was being served slightly overcooked rabbit by the oddly delicate creature. She felt safe enough—certainly the thing had not tried to attack her—but she was not permitted to leave the hillside where they sat near a low-burning fire.

"Can you speak?" She'd already asked the question several times, and each time the creature nodded an affirmative and stared at her with twinkling amusement in its eyes. It did so again. "Well then, say something, dammit!"

As the silence progressed, Teri grabbed up the still-hot rabbit's leg and gnawed on the stringy meat. Her stomach grumbled its gratitude.

"Something, dammit." The voice so startled her that she dropped the meat on the ground. The thing across the fire grinned like an idiot and wagged its tail.

"Oh. You're very funny. How's about you tell me your name."

"Laughs-Too-Much." The voice was oddly husky, and the words were slow and labored, but clear. "My name is Laughs-Too-Much. But you may call me Loki."

"Loki?"

"Yes."

"What are you? Are you like the things in the cave?"

Its muzzle wrinkled back in a grimace. For all the world it looked like it had tasted something foul. "No. I am Nuwisha. They are Garou. I am Coyote. They are Wolf."

Teri thought about this. The creature's answer certainly explained the difference in size. Wolves were substantially larger than coyotes on the average, at least if her schoolbooks could be considered accurate. She'd never actually seen either in person before now.

"My name's Teri. Teri Johannsen."

"Teri. You have a good name. It will bring you much joy in life." The creature nodded, smiling that dog-smile again. "Why do the Garou chase you so?"

"I—" She honestly had to think about just why. She'd been so confused by most of what occurred during her time in the cave that little made sense. Much as she wanted to remember everything, her mind seemed determined to forget. "I think they wanted to use me to get my boyfriend. I don't really remember very well."

"Hmm. I thought maybe a thing like this." Loki

scratched herself under the chin, and Teri wondered if the Nuwisha had fleas. "Where is your life mate?"

"My what?" The very thought. They'd never even gotten past heavy petting.

"Your 'boyfriend.'"

"Oh. He's in Las Vegas. He and his mom went off to Las Vegas to get away for a little while. Then his father showed up and decided to take me along to go find him and—"

Loki listened intently as she started her tale, asking numerous questions along the way. Before too long, she'd spilled her entire life story to the furry thing. Then, just to make life even more interesting, Loki changed shape. She grew smaller and her fur disappeared. In a matter of a few seconds, a very attractive and completely naked woman stood in front of her. Teri judged her mentally and decided she wanted to have as nice a body when she was fully grown. The woman's hair hung down past her waist, and was as wild and ungroomed as it would be if she'd never been to a hairdresser in her entire life. Which, now that she thought about it, was a very likely possibility.

"You're human?"

"No. I am Nuwisha. But I can look human if I choose to."

"Then why were you that monster thing?"

"I did not choose to be otherwise until now." Even now, Loki had a broad grin on her handsome face. "I am not comfortable with this form. It is . . . awk-ward." She struggled with the last word, apparently not used to speaking English despite the lack of any noticeable accent. "We must go now. I will take you to others who can help you and your boyfriend."

"Who?"

"I do not know the word in Man-speak. They are

like the ones who held you, but they are not like them."

"Uh-huh. Do I have any choice in this?"

"You may stay here. The ones I took you from will be searching for you. They will find this place soon." That damned grin again.

"Um. Okay. Let's go."

"There are many hours of walking. Should I carry you?"

"No. That's okay. I can use the exercise."

The woman jumped nimbly from the rocks, landing in the hard-packed dirt below the hill where they'd dined. From the base of the hill, she gathered a collection of sticks, knives, and bones, which she wrapped in a small, crudely woven blanket. Teri took the hill with a great deal less finesse.

A few minutes later, they started on their way across the desert. After a couple of hours, Teri started wondering whether or not the offer to be carried was still open, but did not ask. They were still walking long after the sun began to rise.

V

Diane White moved easily among the friends of her late husband. For one night, if never again, she allowed herself the luxury of being someone important. As much as this night was meant as a celebration of the grand opening the following day, it was also meant as a celebration of her deceased husband's achievements. The Platinum Palace was his design, his crowning glory. And everyone present knew it. She was hugged, congratulated, and revered for her association with the late Jonathan Avery White. Her only sorrow was that he could not be here himself.

Andrew was there, however, and he made a wonderful stand-in, as well as a perfect escort. Andrew had worked closely with John. Was, in fact, the primary reason that John's last design had undergone no major changes from his original concepts.

Through the tinted glass of the massive windows, she could see the skyline of Las Vegas. Not all that far away, the Luxor sent a powerful beam of light far into the heavens where, she had no doubt, John could look down and see his vision made a reality at last. For the first time, the lights outside the Palace were lit. Chrome trim reflected back the glorious beacons of color that cut through the night air. For this one night, she'd let herself believe in magic. Tomorrow was soon enough for reality.

Throughout the evening, a dozen or more people who looked familiar but whom she could not call by name stood and spoke of John's ambitions and his realized dreams. She smiled graciously, accepting the words of praise in the spirit in which they were given. She was Mrs. Jonathan Avery White one last time. And if she cried a few times, no one seemed bothered by her quiet tears.

Despite his faults, John had been a good man. She only now understood how much she truly missed him. After a truly fabulous meal—which Diane somehow found room for—she and Andrew danced again, gliding among the other participants in the night's festivities. As the moon reached its zenith outside, they retired to his room.

They kissed; they made soft, sweet love. And then what had once been Andrew Montgomery raped her mind, body, and soul.

VI

Gabriel and Shaun explored the depths of the Platinum Palace. They did so cautiously; being discovered in a Wyrm-lair would almost certainly result in a painful death if they were caught by surprise. They skulked around in the darkness, trying to find any clue to the origin of the foul stench neither could ignore. What had started as a faint taint seemed to have grown to a massive infected wound under the entirety of the building.

"I can't even sense it anymore. The damned thing's disappeared, whatever the hell it is." Shaun was all but snarling, and the sound set Gabe's nerves on edge. He did his best to contain the anger building inside him, but it was getting harder to ignore.

"Well then, we must be looking in the wrong damn place, Shaun. We've been over every level of the goddamn building, and we haven't seen so much as a rat."

Shaun stood perfectly still, his eyes wide and his mouth hanging open. "Sweet mother of God. You're right. You're absolutely right. Nothing. Not a single damned thing."

Shaun's expression and voice matched perfectly. They both reflected genuine fear. "What? What's the matter now?"

"Gabriel. We're in the subbasement of a very large building. Look around and tell me what you see."

"Walls and a few boxes. So what?"

"Now look again, and tell me what you don't see. Sniff the air and tell me what's missing."

He focused, studying every detail as carefully as

he could. Concrete foundation walls; a solid concrete floor with several drainage holes; several boxes carefully labeled and set against one wall; seemingly endless rows of fluorescent lights. Pipes ran across the ceiling in an endless array of mechanical spiderwebs. He sniffed the air, catching only the sweaty scents of himself and his companion. Scents of corrugated paper and metal along with concrete. He sniffed again, and the hackles on the back of his neck rose in a bristling lump.

"It's too sterile. There's no scent of life down here. Not even a whiff of dust."

"Aye. No living thing, nor anything dead. There's not even a cobweb. We're standing on acres of ground where there aren't even spiders on the walls. There's not a particle of dust or dirt on the ground."

"It's like something cleaned it all away...."

"Hmm. Or perhaps something ate it all."

"What could eat every single speck of dust. Hell, what would want to?"

"The Wyrm has many names, Gabriel. Not the least of which is the Great Devourer."

"Let's get the hell out of here. We've gotta get Mom away from this place, Shaun. We should have done that first, when you sniffed the taint in this place."

"Yes. We should have. So why didn't we?"

Gabriel gave no answer. Instead he moved back the way they'd come, ignoring the potential threat of discovery. He never looked behind him to see if Shaun was following. Instead he simply started to run. Faster, faster still. Somewhere above him, his mother was preparing for a special meeting with the most influential people in the building. The thought sent spasms of fear coursing through his veins.

VII

As the sun crested the desert floor to the east, Michael Giovanni joined for the first time with Legion in its entirety. The fleshy pool of almost-liquid barely rippled as he stepped into its depths. Instead it simply absorbed him and assimilated all of his knowledge.

For the first time in his 483 years, he did not feel alone. He was, instead, overwhelmed with a tidal wave of emotions and experiences the likes of which he'd never experienced in over four centuries.

There was fear, to be sure. But there was also an amazing sense of release. His pent-up fury faded, replaced by a calm, soothing tide of pleasant memories from the minds of Legion.

Others within the collective spoke to him, exchanging memories faster than light from a powerful bulb can fill the darkness of a windowless room. One in particular called out and was answered. The voice, now a part of the endless tide of memories, belonged to a man he'd called an enemy only days before. Andrew Montgomery. He who lorded over the Platinum Palace. Perhaps there is truth in the old saying: *Like calls to like*. Certainly that was the case between Giovanni and Montgomery. They could accomplish so much more by working in unison than they ever could separately . . . .

10

I

Gone.

Diane White was gone, and so was the lousy bastard she'd been with, Andrew Whatsisface. Gabriel dwelled on that thought as morning slowly broke in his room. There were no signs that she'd been back to her room, and despite following her scent all the way to Montgomery's room, no clues to her whereabouts were available there either.

Oh, there was evidence that she'd been there, but she was not present herself. Her underthings were on the ground; the sheets were covered with her scent and mingled with the rat-bastard's as well, but she was not there. The scent did not seem to leave the room, either.

Shaun had gone away, off to see if he could track her down. Gabriel, however, held on to no real hope that she was well. The room where she'd vanished stank of the Wyrm's foul presence.

After a few minutes, he finally noticed the light flashing on his phone. He had a message waiting for him. After three failed attempts to follow the proper pattern for punching numbers, he managed, at last, to make the message play back for him. What he heard set his heart afire and chilled him to the marrow at the same time. He heard the voice of his father, clear as crystal.

Not John White. His real father.

"Good evening, Gabriel. This is Edward McTyre. You can call me daddy." Even on a message, the man sounded smarmy and self-assured. Gabriel hated hearing him speak. "I just wanted to let you know I'm coming to pay you a visit. You should do your best to be there when I arrive. I have a friend of yours who desperately wants to see you again. I want to see you, too. And if I don't get the opportunity, neither will she. She'll be too dead to care. Expect me by noon." The sudden click of the phone and a recorded dial tone echoed through his mind. He managed not to scream his rage. Instead he simply sat still.

He rocked on the bed, staring at the blank white wall before him and seeing only red.

II

While Gabriel White listened to a message left for him the day before, his biological father was starting a methodical search of the desert near where his packmate and sometime lover, Christie, had met her maker.

He supposed he'd miss her. She'd been a delightfully

twisted lover, despite being a mere metis. Useless as breeding stock, but fun just the same.

Her death wouldn't really make a difference in the long run, just as long as he could get the little blond bitch back into his hands. Without her, his chances of getting Gabriel White without a serious struggle were slim. He wanted the boy undamaged. What good was a breeder if he wasn't in decent shape for fighting as well?

It took quite a while to find the girl's trail. She'd done a fine job of hiding her scent. Or rather, whoever was with her had done a fine job. They were traveling on foot, and that was a bonus. In a car they might have stood a chance of escaping. The odor was unfamiliar—definitely one of the changing breeds, but also most certainly not Garou. While that didn't leave a lot of options, Oo'Rock had never run across any of the other shapechangers in all his years. They were quite rare.

He sighed. It was almost going to be a shame to tear the creature into little pieces, but he'd manage somehow. He howled a summons to his companions. The time had come for a hunt. After so much inactivity, they were all a little wired. They could all use the break.

The ground was dry and hard, with only a small amount of vegetation and a lot of sand to hinder their progress. Edward McTyre knew there would be little difficulty in catching up with his prey. They were on foot, and the girl was only human. Whatever had taken her would be hindered by the difficulties of traveling with the girl. They were so limited in what they could achieve.

Werewolves, on the other hand, had the stamina to run at full tilt with little or no worries about exhaustion. A definite advantage when chasing down your next meal.

III

Teri was worn-out. Her legs and the blisters on her feet throbbed with every beat of her heart. Loki added insult to injury by moving on with casual ease. And, frankly, Teri's position—slung over the shoulders of her companion in a fireman's hold—was uncomfortable.

Loki was singing something, a chant in a language which sounded vaguely Native American, but only vaguely. The woman seemed annoyingly cheerful. Every step the Nuwisha took carried them closer to where they needed to be, and annoyed Teri just that much more. Perhaps some part of her mind acknowledged that the frustration she felt came from the fact that a creature which should not exist was carrying her, but it certainly wasn't her conscious mind. Indeed, her conscious mind refused to accept that the Nuwisha was anything more than a strong woman in a fur coat.

"How much farther, Loki?" Her voice rattled with every step Loki took. The woman seemed to find that amusing, and she laughed.

She laughed at damn near everything, and Teri began to understand why she was named the way she was.

"Not far, Snow-Cap. Only until we pass the next hill." Another point of annoyance; Loki insisted on calling her "Snow-Cap" instead of using her name. She looked at the hill, a mercifully small one, and judged the trip would be over in around another hour.

"Who are we going to see?"

"The Uktena. They will aid us if they feel your story is worthy."

"Worthy of what?"

"Their help. They can grant you assistance against the Black Spiral Dancers. They can help you find your life mate."

"I told you, he's my boyfriend, not my life mate."

"If you say so, Snow-Cap."

"My name is Teri."

"Yes. I know this already."

"Then why do you call me Snow-Cap?"

"Because your fur is white from the sun and you need a good name."

"What's wrong with Teri?"

"That is a human name. I prefer to think of you as other than human."

"Why?"

"Because humans are silly, and you are not silly."

"I guess that makes sense. Okay, you can call me Snow-Cap if you want."

"I know this. I would call you Snow-Cap anyway. It is the name I have chosen for you."

"Whatever."

They continued on in relative silence, the only sound being Loki's singing, until they passed the hill she'd spoken of. Teri's skin was an angry red from her time trekking across the desert. Despite a solid tan from being outdoors in San Francisco, the heat and light of the Mojave were taking a serious toll. Directly after they reached the other side of the stone barrier—the side which was mercifully well shaded—Loki set her gently down on the cool sand.

They sat for a few minutes. Teri shivered with what she knew from past experience had to be at least a minor case of sun-fever. Too much burning and not enough time for her body to absorb or expel the excess radiation.

Loki breathed heavily and, for the first time, Teri

realized the exertion of carrying her must have been fairly severe. She watched as the woman shifted from one form to another, refusing to acknowledge that anything at all had changed. All bestial elements were gone, and her rescuer was once again a naked woman with a very athletic body. *Just took off her fur coat, that's all. No monsters for me, thanks just the same.*

"We will wait here."

"What are we waiting for?"

"The Uktena. They will come to us."

"Why don't we just go to them?"

"We are at the edge of their territory. If we go farther without their permission, they will kill us."

"Why would they do that? Can't they see we need help?"

"They will see this. But they will not care. To enter without their permission is to die. They are very secretive about all that occurs within the bawn of their caern."

"The what of their what?"

"Within the area that is sacred to them." Loki had that silly grin back.

"Oh, you mean like an Indian burial ground?"

"That is close enough for you. It is much like a burial ground. Only more so."

"I don't understand what you mean."

"I know. But that is all right. Sleep now. You need rest. I will watch over you."

Teri didn't argue. Within moments, she was snoring softly. She did not see the people who approached from seemingly out of nowhere, nor did she hear the words they exchanged with Laughs-Too-Much.

IV

Joe Hill couldn't honestly say he dreamed very often. Mostly he had days of catatonic slumber where rest was the only thing that mattered and anything else was a waste of time. If he did dream, he almost never remembered.

But when he awoke the following night, he did so with a scream fighting to get past his lips and a sheen of blood-sweat matting his hair in place. The room where he awoke was dark, but he could still see the shape of Jack Dawson sitting in a chair not far away. Dawson's ability to sleep in an upright position used to fascinate Joe, but after all he'd seen in Mexico, little fazed him anymore. At least damn little that he'd admit to.

Despite the fact that the sun had just set—even through the walls he could sense the faint light still radiating from the western horizon—Dawson was awake and alert. "Evenin', Dawson."

"Howdy, Boot. Y'all looked like you weren't sleeping so good. Everything all right?"

"Course it is. What the hell sort of question is that?"

"Kind of question I ask when I see someone breakin' a sweat in their sleep and I hear 'em pissin' and moanin' to themselves. You made enough noise to wake the Dead."

"Yeah. Well if anyone'd know . . ."

"It'd be me." Dawson smiled at the old joke, and then grew serious. "Listen, what you got planned for tonight?"

"Was thinkin' about hunting that booger-man of mine down and getting its sorry ass messed up. Why? You needin' some help?"

"Might be. Make you a deal? You help me an' I'll help you?"

"I reckon we could work that out." He paused to light a cigarette, looking over the lighter's flame to stare at the walking corpse asking him for favors. "What are you needin' help with?"

Dawson looked at his hands, found some little flake that bothered him, and began toying with a loose patch of his own flesh before answering. "Damn. Left my hand lotion in the car. This weather's just hell on rot, let me tell ya. I need a little backup for when I go see the prince of the city."

"Giovanni? I thought all a' you Samedi-types were on good terms with them Eyetalians."

"We are. 'Cept maybe for this case. Seems ol' Mike's made a few hunnert enemies out in the desert. Lotta dead folk out there are hankerin' for a chance to tear him a few new assholes."

"Why would they care what he does?"

"'Cause he's the one had 'em killed, ya idjit." Jack finally lost his patience with his little flap of skin and just tore the whole chunk of rotting epidermis from his hand. "He had 'em all killed off and then he locked their spirits in a small area of the desert." He looked up and stared at Joe. Joe met his stare with a mild curiosity. "The stupid son of a bitch has kept them from their final rest, and they're a mite sore about the whole thing."

"So what? What the hell can they do about it?"

"It ain't what they'll do that's got me worried. It's what Jude'll do that makes me think this wasn't his best move." The man tried to sound nonchalant about the situation, but Joe knew him from way back. He could tell there was some sort of personal investment in all of this. Something about the situation just plain chapped at Dawson like a rock under a saddle blanket bothers a horse with a three-hundred-pound rider.

"What's all this got to do with you and me, Jack?"

"It's like you and your horses. It bothers me when the Dead are mistreated."

"That why you called it quits in the Sabbat?"

"You know about that, huh?"

"Yeah. There's still a bounty on yer head. Melinda Galbraith don't take it well when one of her personal advisers defects."

Dawson's voice grew cold. "You plannin' on tryin' to collect?"

"If I was, would I tell you?"

"Yeah. I think you would. You're a little funny in the head about that whole honor thing. You always have been."

Joe laughed. "Yeah. I would. An' the answer is no. I don't hunt down friends. Just like I don't kill 'em for stealin' my stolen horses, ya damn thief."

When Dawson spoke again, his voice was warmer, but distracted. "I figured as much. If it counts, I think of you as a friend, too, Boot. That's why I ain't reported yer presence here. I could. Mike'd listen if I told him about the price on yer head."

"What? There's a price on my head, too?"

"Joe, you're the leader of the Black Hand in Mexico City. You've been hunting and killing Camarilla spies in your territory for years. Hell, I thought they'd got you down and dead a long time ago, just for the money you're worth to whoever takes you down. Yer about as outlawed as they come, son. It's just a surprise to me that they ain't got yer picture on 'America's Most Wanted.'"

"Yeah. Well, there's more to it than you might suspect, Jack."

"I used to hear stories about how good you were at torture, Boot. I heard you could make a man scream until his voice box exploded and never let him slip into unconsciousness. That don't exactly tell me yer being a nice guy to the folks you meet."

"I'll tell you about it sometime, but not just yet. Deal?"

"Deal. Now, will you help me with Giovanni?"

"Yeah, but you gotta help me with the snot-monster in exchange." He paused a moment, then continued. "And ya gotta tell me why you're so all fired set on swattin' this Jude fella."

"Hell, that's easy." Dawson stood up, holstering his pistols as he went. "The boy's a crazy mage. He's just as likely to wipe out the whole city as he is to go whup up on Mike."

"Yeah, I figured he was a mage. How the hell else could he o' got me out of that mess last night?"

"You hungry?"

"I could go for a bite."

"Fine, you do your stuff and then meet me at the morgue on Harmon Avenue, okay?"

"You can't still be drinkin' dead folks, can ya?"

Dawson opened his mouth in a big, shit-eating grin. "Ain't nothin' finer, Boot."

"That's just nasty, *hombre*. If it ain't warm, I don't want it."

"Naw, it's like drinking fine wine, my man. Better when it's aged some."

"I don't like wine. I like whiskey."

"That's 'cause you ain't as cultured as my own fine self."

"Shit. Cheese is more cultured than you, boy."

Dawson left, and Joe stayed for a few extra minutes. It was nice just talking to a friend again, instead of worrying about how afraid everyone was whenever you came around. Sometimes, having a reputation as a badass had its downsides.

V

Shaun came into the room just about the same time Gabriel was thinking about tearing the whole place apart. Not because the building had done him any harm, simply because he was pissed.

Pissed and worried. The bastard hadn't shown. There was no telling what sort of tortures the Black Spiral Dancers were even now inflicting on his mother.

Much as the idea scared him, Gabriel knew he'd join with them if his mother's life were held as ransom.

He was still contemplating what his next move should be when Shaun entered his room. But Shaun did not come in through the door, he came in through the mirror. Gabriel stared slack-jawed as the man slipped into the room as if he'd stepped through an invisible door. He did not appear from nowhere, exactly, but the transition from nothingness to transparent figure to solid form was so fast it almost seemed that way.

Gabe, already as tense as a coiled spring, fairly flew off the bed, a scream of shock erupting past his lips. His eyes flew wide and, if asked later, he'd have stated matter-of-factly that his heart didn't just skip a beat, it actually stopped and then cranked into overdrive.

"Geaagh!"

"Hi, Gabe." Shaun smiled, and Gabriel snarled instinctively.

"What the hell are you trying to do to me? Give me a stroke?" He clutched both hands to his chest, trying to reach through his own chest and calm his speeding heart down to a normal pace. No luck—

the ribs and flesh stopped his attempt. "How did you do that?"

Shaun smiled again, an eerily serene expression that seemed out of place on him. He did not look so much like a leprechaun as he did a religious convert who'd seen the face of Jesus Christ Himself.

"I've been to the Umbra. I've been looking for something, and I believe I've found it."

"Looking for what?"

"I'll tell you later. Right now we have to discuss what to do about your mother."

"Edward McTyre has her." He couldn't have shocked his mentor more if he'd pulled a taser from his pocket and fired straight into the man's chest. The serenity on Shaun's face disappeared, replaced by a wretched look of fear.

"Sweet Jesus. Tell me you're lying to me." The voice of his teacher was as shaken as the man.

"No. I'll play the message for you if you'd like." When he got no response he did just that, and watched as Shaun's face grew paler and paler.

Shaun started mumbling, his face a fevered study in fear. No, not fear. Panic. "How could that be? I saw him killed. I saw him go over the side of the bridge; his skin was gone and he was bleeding everywhere. Bleeding and screaming, and I heard him hit the water and I looked for a body and he was gone and, omigod, he's still alive. Jesus, help me. The bastard's still alive." The words grew faster and louder until Gabe could barely even manage to understand him. The man held himself, wrapped his arms around his body, and pulled slowly into a fetal position. He watched Shaun Ingram curl into a protective ball, feeling a new dread cool the anger in his body. He felt the skin on his hands break a sweat—

If McTyre can scare Shaun that badly, what's he doing to my mother?

—and felt himself start breathing faster.

He looked down on his mentor and felt a twisted glee; here was the smug bastard who always knew the answers, stumped by an old enemy being alive.

What did he do to you, Shaun? What could make you so scared?

Along with the perverse joy came anger and contempt. No thought went into his action as he kicked the man in the ribs hard enough to roll him over and send the air whooshing out of his lungs.

"Get up, goddamn you. You get up right now." He hardly recognized his own voice. The satisfied quality in that sinister tone could not have come from him, could it? "Get off your ass right now or I swear I'll tear your fucking heart out."

Shaun looked at him, perplexed by the violent action. He looked too damn stupid to live.

"Get up! Get up now!" Gabriel lashed out again, planting a solid blow in his mentor's shoulder. It felt so good he did it again, only remotely aware of the grin spreading across his numb face. "Get up, you coward! Get up, or I swear to God I'll kill you myself!" He watched from a great distance as his foot smashed into Shaun's stomach. He noticed the size of his foot, which had split his shoe at the seams, the heavy white fur covering the top of his naked foot and the near-claws thrusting outward from where his toenails used to be.

He failed to notice that Shaun was bigger too, an error which almost proved fatal.

Just as his foot was preparing to crash down on the man's head, a deep growl erupted from Ingram's mouth and a fist as large as a ham slammed into Gabriel's testicles. The pain was so intense that he could not even manage a gasp before he fell to the ground.

In all his sixteen years, Gabriel White had never

been struck in his privates. Certainly, he'd never been hit there by a man trained in hand-to-hand combat. He found himself mimicking the very position Shaun had taken a few moments earlier—curled into a ball with his arms wrapped around his head and his legs drawn in close to prevent any more damage to his bruised privates. Try as he might, he could not draw a breath.

He looked up just in time to see the bared fangs of his mentor moving toward his face. The massive jaw parted, and teeth as large as a grown man's thumb and sharp enough to cut into bone closed around his throat. He felt the points just start to break the skin on his neck, and closed his eyes in preparation for the pain to come.

After several seconds of waiting, he grew impatient and opened his eyes. As he allowed himself to breathe, the pressure eased around his throat. The maddened eyes of Shaun's wolf face glittered coldly and he could feel the furnace-breath of the monster atop him as it snorted with rage.

Gabriel felt himself heaved from the ground and thrown across the room. He hit the wall hard enough to crack the plaster behind the wallpaper. Despite the pain running through his balls, he tried to climb to his feet. Just in time to get a furry knee in his face. His head snapped back and slammed the wall again, sending black sparks dancing across his vision.

"You miserable little whelp! I'll tear your heart out!" The sheer volume of Shaun's voice was nearly deafening, even past the ringing in his ears.

He wanted to apologize, to beg for mercy: anything and everything it took to save his life. Everything kind was gone from Shaun's face, every speck of humanity faded and replaced by raw hatred. Shaun hit him one more time, a savage backhand that sent him to the ground before he could even blink.

The whole world went gray, leaving only vague images drifting in a fog. He tried to move again, and the heavy mist overwhelmed him. In its place a deep, frightening black came along and buried him. From deep inside his mind, something dark hissed and pulled back from the pain.

VI

In the Mojave Desert, roughly twenty miles from the Las Vegas city limits, the angry Dead grew suddenly quiet. He was coming back. Jude, their savior and their only living hope for revenge.

They sensed him before they saw him; his power was like a beacon in the night. He seemed different somehow, changed in a way they could not comprehend. His power was as real and as tangible as ever, but his demeanor was more commanding.

They drew together in a group, forcing themselves to remain calm, even as the instrument of their freedom stopped just at the edge of their prison.

"Hi." His voice was the same, but the tone was wrong, bitter and angry instead of the blended confusion and hope they'd come to expect. "I've given some thought to your predicament." He paused, searching for the words he wanted. "I'm going to help you get free. But there's a catch. I'm only going to let you free if you swear not to hurt anyone but Michael Giovanni. What you do to him is your concern, but everyone else is mine."

The demand was unexpected. They'd hoped he would

help them, if only to stop the sound of their screams. Their revenge would not be as sweet if they had to limit themselves . . . .

"I know this isn't exactly what you want, but there it is. Take it or leave it."

Jude sat down, managing to look at each of them separately. "I'll wait here for your answer."

The Dead conferred among themselves. Some were angry, some disappointed, and others indifferent. In the long run, there was really only one decision they could make.

Jude walked the desert at a slow, casual pace. Each step he took covered forty times the distance it should have. In less than an hour, he was back in Las Vegas.

VII

The Platinum Palace was a wild storm of activity. News crews and photographers gathered in clusters, filming the ever-growing tide of people entering the massive structure. Every person who entered the Palace received one hundred dollars' worth of coins and tokens, compliments of the house. Most of them spent the money in less than an hour, gambling their gift away in futile attempts to win a bundle at the craps tables or in a hand of blackjack. Virgin slot machines lost their chastity, often giving nothing in return, but occasionally spitting out a tidy sum of coins.

For every person who spent their hundred in free tokens, another dozen came to get the same chance at an instant fortune. The vast majority delved into their own pockets to continue playing their games of chance.

Pentex made its finest investment ever. It gave away millions in tokens and got back twice as much in return. Many commented on the efficiency of the staff: how quickly they managed to send people to the rooms reserved months ago, how flawlessly they handled the occasional situation which could have exploded into violence.

None commented on the odd fervor with which most of the gamblers tried again and again to beat the odds. In any other city the frantic, desperate attempts to win the battle against Lady Luck would have been suspicious. But this was Las Vegas. Greedy behavior was a common occurrence here: not just a daily event but an hourly occasion.

The Palace was filled to capacity long before the midnight hour tolled. Efficient, polite security guards pulled people aside from time to time, leading them into areas where the masses could not observe what occurred. They were never gone for long and the people who joined them always came out with them a few minutes later, happy and smiling. But they stopped gambling. Indeed, they left the place within moments of returning to the main areas. The same event occurred in the area where the amusement park operated smoothly, sending happy, screaming crowds on rides meant to thrill. When the people came back from talking with the courteous staff members, they also left the Platinum Palace.

Their leaving meant more people could come in. More people who could spend their money and ride the rides. More people for Legion to convert.

Legion feasted as never before. Soon the time would come to send out minions to other places. Minions who could expand the area owned by

Legion, who could allow the experiences to grow more numerous and more intense.

The colony-mind of Legion thrilled at the concept. Finally, Legion's addiction could be satisfied.

VIII

Gabriel woke up only a few minutes after Shaun finished beating the shit out of him. He'd reverted to his human form, but his wounds had healed. Being a Garou did have a few distinct advantages.

Shaun had moved him to the bed and sat in one of the plush chairs situated around the small table near his window. The man still looked ready to kill him, though he, too, was in his human form.

Gabe thought back on how he'd reacted to Shaun's momentary panic and wondered if he might be losing his mind. Not that he could blame himself if he was. The last few days and nights had not been very relaxing. Still, he could think of no excuse for how he'd reacted.

Shaun, on the other hand, seemed ready with an explanation. "The Wyrm's hold on you is growing stronger. If we don't get you taken care of, and soon, you'll go over to the Corrupter with or without your father's help." His voice was deep and filled with frustration.

"I'm sorry, Shaun. I didn't mean to do that to you." He meant what he said, but a part of him felt anger for the apology even as he said it.

"I know. That's why you're still alive. I take poorly to being attacked for no reason." Shaun sighed. "I'm too old and too tired for this foolishness. We will deal with your mother's situation, and then we will deal with burning the Wyrm's taint from our bodies and souls."

"How can we do that? I didn't think it was possible." Gabe focused all of his attention on Shaun, wondering what magic the man would perform to stop the insanity from taking him over completely.

"There is a way. Maybe." Shaun looked him in the eyes, and Gabriel could see the madness dancing in his mentor's soul. He was also falling to the Great Corrupter. "Provided we can survive the cure."

The man stood up, looking away from him to stare out the window. Below them the festivities continued, at least if the searchlights and fireworks were any indication. The grand opening of the Platinum Palace. A week ago the idea seemed like a wonderful chance to get away from all of his problems. Now? Now he knew better. He'd rather still be at home, spending time with Teri and dreaming of regaining his old life.

He wanted nothing to do with being a werewolf. It was all a load of crap. Let others fight for the world; he just wanted the right to live his life as he pleased.

He walked over to the window, standing beside the man who was his friend and teacher both. The glass reflected them; both of their images looked drawn and bitter.

Outside, the festivities continued and the celebrants moved on the ground like drunken ants at the world's biggest picnic. Somewhere beyond the crowds, a pack of werewolves held his mother hostage, looking to trade her life for his sanity.

The only catch now was to find them.

"Are we going to wait for them, Shaun? Or are we going to hunt them down?"

"I'm thinking a proper hunt would be a pleasure right about now, Gabriel. I'm thinking they should die, and this time stay dead."

Gabriel's reflection smiled, a feral grimace that bordered on the maniacal. "I'm thinking the same thing. Right now the taste of blood in my mouth is sounding better and better."

"Then you're worse off than I'd hoped. You're starting to sound like me."

Though a fragment of his mind panicked at the thoughts running in his head, he spoke them out loud just the same. "Great minds think alike, Shaun." He fisted both hands, feeling the tendons in his arms straining and the flesh of his palms rupture as his nails bit deeply. "I think it's time my father learned what it means to mess with what's mine."

"What sort of lesson were you thinking of, Gabriel?"

"Mom's boyfriend, Sam, taught me a trick or two, and you've taught me plenty. I'm sure I can come up with something."

The dark, coiled thing in his mind hissed aloud. This time, Gabriel welcomed the noise only he could hear.

11

I

Jack Dawson and Joseph Hill made quite a sight as they entered the Palisades Casino. Both were dressed like cowboys—not surprising when one considered their history—and both looked twice as grim as the Reaper. Jack was intimidating enough, but Joe stood a full six inches taller, and the scars on his face made people nervous. They stormed through the pit, heading directly to the concealed entrance of Don Michael Giovanni's office. The guards did not stop them. This time it was another of the Giovanni who barred their way.

Antonio Giovanni looked enough like his father to make most people hesitate, but the thick black mustache he sported broke the illusion with ease. "Hi, Jack." His voice was softer than his father's, but it, too, bore a familiarity with being in power. "I need to speak with you before you see my father."

"Good to see you, Tony. Let's go talk."

"Who's your friend?" Tony's eyes barely even flickered in acknowledgment of Boot.

"This is Joe. Joe, this is Tony. He's an associate of Mike's." Both men nodded to each other. "It's okay to talk in front of Joe. He knows how to keep his mouth shut."

Giovanni nodded, then moved off toward another part of the casino. The people playing the games ignored all three of them. After a few minutes of walking through the quieter sections of the building, they reached another well-concealed door.

Tony opened the vaultlike entrance with an old-fashioned key and ushered them both inside. Unlike his father's office, this one was decorated in a style which reflected his true age—Early Tudor, though the New York accent made him sound like a punk from the fifties. Several paintings of funeral scenes from every imaginable era stood out from the rest of the decor. Jack chose to make no comment.

"What's the situation, Tony?"

"I thought you should know. He ain't behaving like himself. He's got a bad case of the mean attitudes and I don't think he's going to get any better." Tony's New York accent stuck out like a drop of blood on a new blanket of snow, but the words were still intelligible. "I don't think you should go in there with an attitude, not if you want to live."

"How's he actin' strange? I've known your dad for a long time, but I've never known him to misbehave with guests."

"Yeah? Well, he keeps calling people into his office and locking the door afterward. So far he's called about half the Cainites in the city to come see him. That ain't a lot of vampires, but it's enough to keep him busy. You know how it goes when the prince calls on someone. Especially when the prince in question has a rep for blowing away anyone who gets disrespectful."

"Yeah? Go on . . . ."

"Yeah. Well, he's askin' them all in there, one at a time, and every time someone comes out, they ain't acting normal anymore, if you get what I'm saying."

"Clue me in, Tony. I need to hear the straight shit."

"They're all coming out of there like they just left a date with triplet nymphomaniacs. I've never seen so many happy vampires in one night. But they're also looking at the decorations in this dive like they've never seen them before. It ain't right, Jack. It just ain't right."

"I'll be careful, and I'll see what I can find out, Tony."

"You'd best be careful, Jack. He ain't asked to see any of the Family yet. Halfway through the night, and he ain't asked to see anyone but the lowliest in the city. Something's gone bad. Really bad."

"Listen. You just get us in to see him, we'll find out what's what."

"Deal. You find out, there's a bonus waiting for you."

"Fuck yer bonus, Tony. I don't need no bonus to check on a friend."

Tony grinned. "Sorry. Old habits die hard."

"Tell me about it. I still can't break myself of looking at the girls, and my equipment ain't worked in over nine decades." Boot laughed. Tony only winced. Tony still liked to do things the old-fashioned way, despite the inability to assist in the creation of human life.

They made their way back through the casino, ignoring the crowds and being ignored in return. Jack looked around the area, trying to decide if anyone standing in front of a slot machine or placing bets at one of the tables was a potential threat. Caution became a way of unlife after a few years, and he'd been cautious long before he became a vampire.

Tony cleared his throat when they reached the door to his father's office. "Listen, maybe I should check first, see if he wants to meet with you."

"I don't think that's necessary." Jack smiled as he spoke, doing his best to look friendly and stern at the same time. "Your daddy 'n' me go back a ways. Besides, I'm supposed to be on assignment for him. I reckon it's about time for a progress report."

Tony nodded quickly, then scurried away. Jack liked the kid well enough, but Tony always struck him as the sort who just couldn't stand genuine conflict. He thought about the fact that the "kid" was almost three hundred years older than he and sighed. Why they'd ever made Antonio Giovanni a vampire was one of life's little mysteries.

Jack and Joe opened the door and headed down the long corridor leading to Giovanni's office. As soon as the first barrier closed again, Joe spoke up in his soft, easy voice. "Boy's kind of a sissy, ain't he?"

"Yup. 'Course he's a sissy with enough money to buy every politician in this country and enough influence to make sure we never see the outside of this building again if he so desires. So I wouldn't be callin' him that too loud iffn I were you, Boot." He thumped the taller man on the chest, a smile plastered to his face. "You been too long in the wilds of Mexico to remember your manners, son."

"Wilds of Mexico, my ass. Only thing wild down that way is me. All them others down there are just like Chihuahuas. They bark a lot, but they can't bite worth a spit."

"Yeah? Well, just you remember that up here yer ass belongs to the man we're about to meet. If you want something nasty said, you make your point through me. We got a history, me and Mike."

"Whatever. But I ain't never run from a fight yet."

"Yeah, I know. One look at your face is all it takes."

"You ain't exactly looking like you won a lot of fights, either, you asshole."

"Shut up. We're here."

Jack knocked on the final door, waiting politely for a response. After a few moments, Michael Giovanni opened the door and told them to come inside.

"Where have you been hiding, Jack?" The man's face was wrinkled with good cheer, and despite the fact that he looked Joe Hill over, he never said a word about the addition to their usual meetings.

"I been scopin' out the scene at the Platinum Palace. Place was built well, but I don't foresee too much trouble in breaking it down."

"Yeah. Well I've been meaning to talk to you about that. I had a discussion this morning with the manager of the Palace. We've reached an understanding. Forget about taking the building apart and forget about causing the employees any harm."

Jack froze for just a second, then nodded. "I can do that, Mike. Hell, consider it done. Normally I'd insist on my fee—"

"Of course, Jack. Consider the matter handled."

"But in this case I'm gonna waive it, 'cause I need to talk with you about something."

Mike moved behind his desk and sat down, attentive and ready for whatever Jack had to say. Dawson could have screamed. "So talk to me, Jack. What's on your mind?"

"Well, Mike. You ain't gonna like this much, but there's a little problem brewing outside of town, and I think you need to fix it before it gets out of hand."

Mike Giovanni's face lost its friendly expression the second he heard the words. "What sort of problem?"

"Mike. Damn, this is hard. It's about your graveyard."

"What, the place where I put busybodies?"

Damn, the man sounded awfully casual about the matter. "Yeah. Mike, I know we've been friends for a long time. You know I have all the respect for you in the world. But you've got to fix the mess you made out there."

"What are you talking about?" There it was, that edge in Giovanni's voice that told Dawson he was treading on thin ice. "Let's get this straight. I do not make messes, Jack Dawson. I clean up the messes other people make."

"Mike. The Dead out there are sorely pissed at you. You've got 'em locked up tighter than a gold miner's purse. They're damn angry with you for holding them like you have."

Giovanni slammed a fist into the desk in front of him, his stony exterior cracking to reveal a nasty-looking set of canines. "What the hell is it to you what I do, Jack? We've had an understanding for a long time. Our clans have had an understanding. You and yours don't mess with me and mine. We return the favor. Now you want to tell me how to run my business? So a few spirits are pissed off. Big fucking deal. I don't like to hear them moan and bitch about how cruel I am. I don't like the idea of some moron who meddled in my affairs coming back from the dead to bitch at me because I put him in his place. So I lock 'em up. Who the hell cares?"

"They do. I do. It ain't right."

Giovanni stood up, his hands balled into fists at

his sides. "Who the hell are you to tell me what's right? You need to remember who you're talking to, Dawson. If we were not friends, I would have you killed for speaking to me in this way." The man's accent grew thicker as he spoke and his words grew strained and formal.

"It's because I'm your friend that I feel I have to talk to you this way. Dammit, Mike, I didn't just stumble across that graveyard, I was led to it. Your little buddy, the crazy boy? Jude? He's the one who showed me where they are. He wanted me to understand why he's been giving you so much shit."

"So what? You're taking his side of this?"

"No. I'm giving you a warning. That boy plans to set 'em free. And the only thing any of 'em care about anymore is tearing you apart. I've seen 'em. They might just be able to do it." Dawson stood up, gesturing for Joe to follow him. Boot stood up as well, glaring quietly at Giovanni. "I didn't come here to give you any grief, old son. I came here to let you know you're in a heap of shit and there's a storm coming to shake it up. You do what you want with the knowledge."

They turned and walked away, leaving Giovanni in his seat behind his desk. The man said nothing at all as they left.

Ten minutes later, after a very curt good-bye to Tony, they were outside again, walking through the night air and intimidating the humans with every step they took. The humans had a right to be nervous: They were both predators, and the mortals could sense their ability to hunt and kill on a primal level, even if they could not recognize in a conscious way what it was that set them apart.

They walked in relative silence for several minutes, the only conversation being a stream of muttered curses under Jack's breath.

Then Joe finally spoke up. "That wasn't your friend Giovanni."

"What the hell are you talkin' 'bout, Boot?" Dawson looked toward the big man, shoving a wad of tobacco leaves in his mouth and chewing for a second before continuing. "I've known the bastard for close to eighty years. Don't you think I ought to be able to tell when I'm talking to him?" But even as he said the words he felt a niggling little doubt trying to worm into his mind. Something Mike said just—

"I had a discussion this morning with the manager of the Palace."

—didn't sound right. A minor detail, but one that stuck just the same.

"First time I met that booger-monster, it messed up my face." Joe touched the heavy, dark scars that seemed to almost completely cover over the ones he'd had since Jack first met him. His finger traced the tanned flesh that so contrasted his normal pallor. "I can't get rid of the scars. They're permanent. I can reshape my own skin if I feel like it, Jack. But I can't touch these. They resist every attempt to alter them. Believe me, I've tried." This time it was Joe's turn to pause. He moved his fingers deftly, pulling a paper and loose tobacco from his poke and rolling a cigarette. He struck a match off the heel of his boot and started puffing before he spoke again. "When I met up with that thing last night, the scars on my face sort of heated up, like they were near an open flame, but not close enough to really leave any burns."

"What are you saying, Joe?"

Boot placed a hand on his shoulder. The cigarette in his mouth bobbed up and down with his words. "They ain't never burned before then, Jack. But they burned again when I was near your buddy. I think he's been taken over by that oversize slug."

"No. That's bullshit. Mike's way too tough for that sorta crap."

"I had a discussion this morning with the manager of the Palace."

"I'm a pretty tough *hombre* myself, Jack. But that sucker almost got me. Would have, too, if you and your friend Jude hadn't shown up."

"Yeah, but you put up a helluva fight, Boot. You said yourself you'd been at it for a long time. You said you'd managed to escape it before."

"Yeah. But I also said I didn't know how I escaped the first time. But I think I have an idea about that."

"What? What makes you so sure Mike couldn't have fought it off, too?" And there was that thought again, floating through his mind like—

"I had a discussion this morning with the manager of the Palace."

—an echo that just wouldn't fade.

"Jack, I can change the shape of my body. I can alter my face if I want to. It's one of the powers I was taught by the Black Hand. It's a dangerous trick, but I know how to do it. I think that's what saved me. I could pull away from it almost as good as it could grab me." To illustrate his point, Joe held one hand before his face. He flexed the hand and Jack Dawson watched while the fingers first grew longer and then thicker. Then they reverted to their normal shape and size. "Can Michael Giovanni do that? Can he, Jack?"

"No. He can't. Leastways not that I ever heard of." Jack's thoughts went back to what Giovanni said earlier, and finally realized what was wrong. "Oh shit. I think you're right."

"I know I'm right. But what changed your mind?"

"He said he'd talked with the manager of the Platinum Palace this morning."

"Yeah? So what?"

"Boot, I've known Mike Giovanni for eighty years. In all that time he's never said anything about morning. He's over three hundred years old. For him it's always 'night' or 'evening.'" Dawson spit a stream of tobacco juice against the corner of a convenience store they were passing. "He don't think of morning as anything except the time when the sun is up. I know he don't, because we've actually had talks about it. He'd have said he talked with the manager last night. Not this morning."

"Are you sure about that?"

"As sure as I am about my name being Jack Dawson. That man ain't Mike Giovanni. He's an impostor."

II

Gabriel White learned an important lesson about money: If you have enough and are willing to spend it, you can learn just about anything. Even stuff that should be kept confidential. For example, the location from which a phone call came the day before. Armagosa Valley was their destination. Shaun's money and unusual charm went a long way toward finding out that little gem of information.

Armagosa Valley was a small town, barely worthy of being on the map. The call came from a pay phone located directly in front of the Cactus Needle, a combination bar and motel set just at the edge of the city limits. Long ribbons of yellow tape warned people that a police investigation was under way in the Cactus Needle. Apparently the tape was used as a warning, just in case the police cars and chalk bodies on the ground weren't quite enough to keep the citizens of Armagosa Valley away.

Judging by the three unbathed youths hanging around the building and smoking generic cigarettes, the good townspeople had little else to do in the middle of the night. Gabriel watched while Shaun worked his magic with the local constabulary. Money exchanged hands, and apparently words of wisdom were traded as well. Shaun came back over to the truck. "This happened yesterday. According to the fine officer over there, four people were torn to shreds by what appeared to be a pack of wild animals." Shaun snorted. "Officer Dermott believes it may have been rabid coyotes or maybe even a red wolf."

"Swift, isn't he?"

"At least he had the decency to point us in the proper direction. Northeast of here. The trail leads toward the Valley of Fire State Park."

Gabe pulled out the map of Nevada and started looking, using his finger to guide his eyes. It took him a while to find the place. "Shit. All the way on the other side of Vegas. That's a good ways off, Shaun."

"Aye. At least it would be if we had to go that far. But I don't think we will."

"Why not?"

I think we'll find them long before we reach Lake Mead and the park. I think they're around here." He jabbed his finger at a shaded area with the legend: DESERT NATIONAL WILDLIFE RANGE. "Unless I'm remembering wrong, there's a lovely little spot out there where the US government took to hiding a few of their earlier accidents involving nuclear waste. That's the sort of place Oo'Rock will seek."

"What the hell for?"

Hell-Storm   229

"The waste depot is pure poison, a sure place of power for the Wyrm and for our kind."

He thought about that for a moment. The Wyrm defiled nature whenever possible, destroying life and reveling in entropy. It made sense. "So where is this place? Do you know the way?"

"Aye. Stayed there once before, when we'd done a bad spot of losing to a tribe of Uktena in the very same park." He shook his head, looking lost again. "Lord, Gabriel. Pray we don't run across that lot. They've a solid base of power. They'll tear us apart if they catch wind of what we are."

"Couldn't we just tell them what we're looking for?"

"Certainly. They'll likely even listen for a few minutes before tearing out our throats. They're much more polite than their cousins the Wendigo."

"What if you're wrong? What's to stop them from going for the Valley of Fire?"

"Oo'Rock's sense of self-preservation is far too refined. The Valley of Fire is sacred to the Uktena and the Nuwisha alike. Nothing of the Wyrm would dare go to that place if it wanted to live."

"But the Uktena are in the state park, too. What's the difference?"

"The difference is that the Anasazi lived near the Valley of Fire. When they left, they put a curse down to crush anyone who would destroy what was theirs. The other difference is the ghosts of the Nuwisha who once thrived there. They'll destroy anything they can, and they'll laugh all the way through it."

"What are the Nuwisha?"

"Werecoyotes. I've heard they have the power to drive their enemies insane." Shaun shivered despite the heat. "I believe it, too. I've heard tales of the Nuwisha. I've heard they are a very vengeful lot."

Shaun started the truck. "Let's get on the way. We've your mother to save, don't we?"

They moved on, driving in a northerly direction. Within an hour and a half, they were at the site of the hidden toxic dump. Finding the cave where the Black Spiral Dancers had camped was not difficult. After ten more minutes of Shaun's looking around the area, they were on their way again.

"Do you know where they are?"

"I've a suspicion."

Gabe looked at the man, studied the tension lines on his face and the jerky way he was moving. "What's the matter?"

"What do you mean?"

"I mean you're not acting right. You're too jumpy."

"It's worse than I thought." The man's sigh was deep and heavy. "I don't think they have your mother, Gabriel."

"But he said he had someone important to me."

"Aye, and he does at that."

"Who?" Gabriel knew the answer before the words were free from his mouth.

"I checked their hive three times over. I smelled the taint of the Dancers and I smelled the perfume of your girlfriend. They have Teri Johannsen with them." Gabriel grew numb, felt a frosty finger dance down the length of his spine. "Or at least they did."

"You mean she got away?"

"I can't tell for sure. It could be she got away, or that something else captured her." He shrugged, steering around a large collection of rocks blocking the only spot where a vehicle could get by with ease. A lesser vehicle would never make it past the obstacles running alongside the rocks.

Gabriel's mind worked furiously, trying to calculate what the Dancers would have done to Teri. His soul shrank away from the idea. What they'd done to his father, what they'd tried to do to his mother, these things held him in thrall. "Shit, Shaun. She's got to be okay. She's just got to be."

Shaun stopped the truck. The engine idled as he looked over his shoulder and back toward the rocks they passed. "Oh, Jesus."

"What? What's wrong?"

Shaun pointed toward the rocks. "Look back over your shoulder and tell me what you see, Gabriel."

He turned and studied the pile for long minutes. He could see nothing at first; his eyes had long adjusted to looking into the reflected glare of the headlights. After a few moments of blinking, he could see the stone barrier. He could make out the individual lumps of earth at the top and the base, but the slabs of earth toward the center seemed blurred. He stared hard, finally realizing that they were not so much blurred as hidden. They were covered by a heavy mesh of rope and netting.

"What the hell . . . ?"

"Vehicles. Judging by the tracks we were following, I'd say they belonged to the Alcatraz Hive. They belong to Oo'Rock and his lot."

A loud scream of metal assaulted their ears, grinding steel and crushing aluminum. The truck bucked violently and then the engine stuttered to a stop. Both of them turned toward the front of the truck, where a black-furred brute stood holding a large metal rod. The monster grinned past a set of teeth like those of a vampire bat. A short snout led to a pair of glowing eyes reflecting back the glare of the truck's headlamps. Other shapes moved in the periphery, spreading out to surround the truck.

Oo'Rock lifted the makeshift spear above his head with one arm, slamming the other down on the top of the truck's hood with enough force to shift the whole vehicle and drop the engine from its already-tortured anchors. His howl of triumph was deafening.

"Welcome." The single word was filled with loathing and insane glee. "It's so nice to see you both again."

III

Jude ran across the cowboy corpse and his friend after only a few minutes of looking for them. The walk back to town had been shorter than usual, so he felt he should give the cowboy who called himself Dawson ample warning to stay away from Michael Giovanni.

The two men seemed overly excited, talking to each other in redneckese and spouting profanities at a mile a minute. Jude listened in for a few minutes before interrupting.

"Hi. What's up?"

Boot Hill looked over at him with an expression of mild relief. Jack Dawson bore a similar look, only far more magnified. "Jude! Hey there, buddy. Damn, am I glad to see you." Jude smiled.

"Why's that?" He winked. "I know you didn't miss my sparkling personality."

"Because we've got a damn big problem brewing, that's why."

Jude contemplated that for a second, decided he really wasn't in the mood for any more problems. He had more than enough of them already. Still, Jack had been nice enough not to kill him when he had the chance, so it seemed only fair to at least hear the man out.

Hell-Storm 233

"Why don't we just scoot on away from the prying ears around here and talk about it, Jack. Then I can give you my warning, and we can all go on our merry way."

"Give me what warning?" Dawson replied. The man was trying to sound friendly, but the stress in his voice gave him away.

"The Dead are coming for Michael Giovanni. They intend to exact their revenge on him."

"Well, that's sorta what we have to talk about, Jude." They walked on, moving toward a coffee shop with exactly one cook, one bored-looking waitress, and no business to speak of. All three ordered coffee, and Jude ordered a BLT. The waitress—her name was Nancy according to the name tag on her pale pink uniform—slapped down the coffee cups and wandered off to talk with the cook for a while. Jude and Dawson slurped at the viscous liquid; Boot just looked at them both with mild disgust.

"So what's the problem, Jack?" Jude added seven more sugars to his coffee while waiting for the man to answer.

"Well, it's sorta hard to explain, Jude. But here it is in a nutshell. Mike Giovanni's been eat up by the thing that was munchin' on Boot yesterday. There's a thing that looks like him and acts like him in his office, but I don't think it's really Mike anymore."

The conversation stopped when the waitress brought over the sandwich Jude ordered. The sandwich explained without words why they were the only people in the place. The lettuce was browner than the bacon and the tomato looked as though its best days were a few weeks in the past. Jude handed over a hundred-dollar bill and told the woman she could keep the change if she left the coffeepot behind and brought refills later. Her whole face lit up when old Ben Franklin landed in her hand.

"So why is that a problem? I'd say it saves a lot of grief." He frowned for a second, trying to remember what Dawson had said earlier on in their relationship. "Though I'm sorry for you. I know you were friends."

"We were and we are, but that's beside the point. Whatever bone the Dead have to pick with Mike is their affair and none of mine. But there's still a problem. Me and Joe did a little brainstorming, and we think maybe this thing's bigger than anyone thought." Jude munched on his soggy sandwich, nodding for Jack to continue. "We think this thing's taken over most of that new casino down the road, the Platinum Palace."

"There are too many casinos anyway." Well, that was true enough, but by the look on Dawson's face he expected he was supposed to ask something else. "What makes you think the Platinum Palace is that thing's home?"

"I've got a friend over there. He's a Lupine. He says the place smells of the Wyrm. Now, as I understand it, this Wyrm fella is sorta like a mix-up between Satan and Jack the Ripper, with all the charm of Adolf Hitler. Gabe told me the odor of this Wyrm is getting stronger and stronger. When I told him I was supposed to bring the place down, he said that was a good thing. He just made me promise his mom and his friend and him could leave before I did my number on the place."

"Did you say his name was Gabe?"

"Hunh? Oh, yeah. Gabriel White."

Jude was only vaguely aware that Jack was still talking. He heard the words but only half listened as the man spoke of the deal with Giovanni and the megacorporation known as Pentex. His attention returned when Dawson got to speaking of how Joe sensed the location of the monster's nest by the strange feelings he got from the scars on his face.

"Joe? Do you have anything to add?"

"Naw. I ain't much of one for talkin'."

"What did it feel like when the thing tried to eat you?"

The big man frowned, an effort that only succeeded in making him look twice as mean as he normally did. "Well, I reckon it didn't really want to eat me so much as it wanted to become me. It was already gettin' a good hold on my brain when you stopped it from chewin' me up."

"Why did it want to be you? What made you special?"

"Hell, son. I couldn't begin to guess. Wasn't nothin' special about the girl it did that to. Maybe it just likes having different faces."

No one spoke for several minutes. Dawson and Jude killed off the pot of coffee and Boot smoked a few cigarettes, but that was all. Finally Jude looked at the two cowboys and nodded. "So. Let's go see what's what at the Platinum Palace. This may put a new bend on my plans."

"I was really hopin' you'd say that, Jude. I really was." Dawson sounded relieved, and Jude marked the change in his demeanor as his good deed for the day.

"I said it may. I didn't say it would. There's a difference."

They walked down the Strip, passing a constant flow of people as they headed toward the Palace. From half a mile away, they could clearly see the colored searchlights illuminating the sky in a rainbow of colors. Jude walked quickly, and the others had trouble keeping up.

There was an enormous line to enter the building, but it moved swiftly, because large numbers of people were leaving at the same time. The sight was unusual; for all the world it looked like an assembly line in a Warner Brothers cartoon. The chrome and mirrored glass facade of the building was attractive enough, but Jude felt odd about the structure just the same. He could almost swear he'd seen the place long before now.

Yes, I saw it at her place.

But at the same time the angle was all wrong. The sense of déjà vu was intense.

"What do your scars tell you now, Mr. Hill?"

"Call me Joe. My daddy was Mr. Hill. My scars feel like they're gettin' a sunburn, that's what they tell me. That thing is here. And I mean it's here in a big way."

Jude closed his eyes, focusing his mind on the memories of the night before and what his senses had told him when he struggled to separate the two half-merged people then. Yes. He could feel the odd presence of the creature, but it was amplified a thousandfold. Whatever the beast might be, it was growing even as he sensed it.

Then the creature sensed him back. Where he felt the central focus of the thing—a massive boiling tide of thoughts: greed and lust and an insatiable craving for raw emotion—there was a sense of awareness. It knew him for what he was, and it was angry at the intrusion into its mind.

The line moved ahead and he felt gentle pressure on his back. He opened his eyes and moved forward, shaken by what he'd felt. Almost everyone ahead of him was in the building. He moved to join them and finally reached the door. The men standing at either side of the main entrance stared at him, a long hard look that made him feel guilty, though of what he could not say.

"You all right, Jude?" Dawson spoke in a whisper.

"Yes. But I don't think it wants me here."

"You think there'll be a problem?"

"No. Not yet at least. Stay out of the casino and keep away from the amusement park. If any of the staff tries to lead you away, ignore them or leave the building."

"Whatever you say."

"Good. Now then, I need to go register."

Despite the strange looks the guards gave him, or that he thought they gave him, they did not attempt to bar his entry into the building. He was handed a bag of casino chips, which he held on to as he broke from the long line leading to the gambling arena. He walked directly to the front desk.

A small group of employees waited to assist anyone who might need their help. He walked up to the most attractive woman there and smiled. "Hi. I was wondering if you have a Diane White registered here."

"One moment, sir. I'll have to check." She was a very attractive girl, with long red hair and the kind of body that screamed surgical alterations. Still, she was courteous enough. After a few seconds of typing away on the computer, she smiled a plastic smile and responded. "Yes, sir. She is listed as one of our guests."

"Could you tell me her room number?"

"I'm sorry, sir. I'm not allowed to give you that information." Her polite frown of apology was as artificial as the smile she'd flashed a few seconds before. "Would you like me to ring her room number?"

He gave back a grin just as sincere as hers. "Yes, please. Thank you."

"You'll find a house phone just over there." She pointed to a row of pay phones, several of which had the words House Phone above them on chrome-plated placards. "Who should I say is calling?"

"Gabriel White."

Jude walked over to the closest phone while the

Barbie doll behind the counter started dialing. He waited for a few seconds before the woman at the front desk nodded for him to lift the receiver. "Hello?"

"Gabriel? Honey? What's wrong with your voice?" The pit of his stomach opened wide, swallowing a large portion of his soul. His knees went all watery and for a second he was afraid he'd fall to the ground. Somehow he managed to recover before it was too late.

"I—I'm sorry, I must have the wrong number."

"You sound awfully familiar. Do I know you?" There was no suspicion in the voice, just a certain element of curiosity.

"I don't think so." He reached out with his senses again, racing his mind along the phone connection until he touched the mind of the woman on the other end of the line. Memories flash-flooded him, demanding to be acknowledged. "No. I'm so very sorry." He slammed the phone down, angry with himself for ever trying to reach her.

The turn he made away from the bank of phones would have done any military fanatic proud. He moved stiffly away, walking toward the exit to the outside world. Dawson and Hill followed behind him.

One of the guards moved forward, looking as if he meant to intervene. Jude stiff-armed the man, sending him sailing backward for ten yards. The reaction was automatic. He stormed past the startled onlookers, glaring at each one foolish enough to meet his eyes. The crowd parted before him; most of the people stared gape-jawed, but none tried to bar his way.

He walked fast, tearing up the distance between him and anyplace that was far away from the Platinum Palace. "Not fair. Not fucking fair at all.

Not playing by the rules," he muttered, barely moving his lips as he pistoned his legs forward. "I don't want it to go this way. It's not supposed to happen like this." His vision blurred, and after a second he realized he was on the verge of tears.

"Hey, Jude! What's the matter?" Dawson sounded almost concerned, but Jude didn't fall for it. The man wanted what everyone wanted. A piece of him. Another chunk of his soul to break into bloody fragments and devour.

"It's not fair, goddammit! That's what's the matter! That fucking thing took Diane, too! It took her and it ate her and it spit out the parts that don't matter!"

Dawson and Hill stepped back, surprised by his outburst. Hill recovered first. "Then I guess you better get this Diane back before you start causing any grief for the Giovanni."

Jude glared and took a step toward the man before Boot continued. "Hey, you got me out of that mess. Don't you figure you could do the same for anyone else?"

Jude stopped where he was, contemplating the gunslinger's words. "Maybe. Maybe I can, Boot." He looked past the man, staring at the Palace, where it glittered like a shiny new lie just fallen from a politician's mouth.

"The only question is how to go about it."

IV

Legion wanted to scream, to break open the building it inhabited and roar a challenge to whatever had come along and learned what it was. Secrecy was still important, for though Legion was growing powerful, it was still vulnerable.

The mad-thing had read into Legion's mind, seeking to answer questions about a part of the whole. Had even found the part it sought before storming away. Legion should have been ecstatic. The people were still coming forward, reaching into Legion's very body and being absorbed. In this night alone it had grown far more than it dreamed possible.

But now Legion learned about something new, an emotion it had not tasted firsthand before. Fear.

What if the mad entity came back with others as powerful? What if they found a way to hurt or even destroy it? The colony-mind was separated at the present time. It would not fully reunite until the morning came. From the Giovanni-cell Legion learned that operating at night was often safer.

Worse, the sections comprising Legion's memories were not functioning in perfect harmony any longer. Some held biases against others, causing a feedback of anger-hate that Legion found unsettling and exciting at the same time. Which was the proper way to feel? Legion did not know.

A part of Legion had not returned last night. Nor had it surfaced since its disappearance. This, too, worried Legion. The loss was small, but it was a noticeable loss just the same. Legion searched its memories, finally concluding that the loss was comparable to a receding hairline. Insignificant and important at the same time. Legion, much like the numerous humans it had absorbed, began to understand that life was a paradox. What should not be was; what was often should not have been.

New emotion number two: Confusion. The inability to completely rationalize and assimilate pieces of information into a logical working order. Legion began to concentrate almost exclusively on these new emotions—pleasing and unsettling as they were—trying to puzzle out just what they meant to the great colony-mind.

Eventually, it forgot about the invader who had probed deep into its thoughts, seeking answers to questions.

Bad mistake. Very bad.

V

Teri was well fed and clean for the first time in what seemed like centuries. She felt safe and comfortable. The Uktena of the Hot Winds Sept made her feel that way. With herbs and kindliness, they soothed her fractured nerves, bringing her back to something akin to her normal state. She looked at the half-human, half-wolf monstrosities around her and felt no fear of them. They were only people with extraordinary powers. And if the herbal tea she consumed also made her see streamers of colored light whenever she moved too quickly, who was she to complain?

When she'd awakened from her fitful slumber of the night before, she'd seen Loki sitting with a large gathering of humans and wolves, as well as a few of the monsters, which were somewhere in between. Loki spoke in soft tones, that same slightly amused look on her face. The Uktena listened. They did not seem at all amused. They seemed alternately angry and excited. One of them, an old woman with papery skin and what seemed like iron cords under that delicate flesh, had chastised Loki severely. Loki laughed at the admonishments, shaking her head and speaking in a tongue unknown to Teri.

Finally, when it seemed the older woman would take the wooden staff she carried and break it over Loki's skull, the argument ended. The woman sighed, gestured to several of the younger wolves and people, and pointed away from what appeared to be the central gathering point.

Afterward, Loki explained everything in her stilted English. The Uktena were not at all amused by the idea of Loki bringing a human to their gathering place, nor were they the least bit happy about the likely pursuit by the Black Spiral Dancers.

At their mention, Teri went into hysterical screaming fits, throwing a tantrum of epic proportions. That was when the old woman handed her a mug of tea and instructed her to drink all of it.

After a long debate, Dances-to-Luna, the old woman with the mean tea recipe, conceded that a gathering of young warriors might be allowed a chance to gain a victory against the wolves of the Wyrm. Loki found the whole thing very amusing, laughing most of the way through her narrative. Teri started finding the story amusing around the same time the pretty colors began spinning at the periphery of her vision.

Every last one of them referred to her as Snow-Cap. After the first few times she gave up trying to tell them her real name. Seeing as they all had weird names, she supposed it was a sign of acceptance. A couple of the younger men in the group made a point of standing near her and one even strutted like a rooster whenever she was near. She was too stoned to be flattered. She giggled instead.

When the tea started losing its potency and the werewolves started making her nervous again, they fed her more of the bitter fluids. She seemed able to rationalize what was going on around her, but she couldn't bring herself to care much one way or the other. That was just fine, thank you. *No reason to worry about little ol' Teri going bonkers for a while.* The thought made her giggle again.

Loki and a striking young man named Desert-Rain explained very carefully that she was to stay where she was until they returned. She nodded to show her understanding.

A few minutes after they walked away, she stood up and followed them.

She was pretty sure they intended to kill Gabriel's father and the others with him. She wanted to be there when it happened.

VI

Gabriel looked out the window, seeing his father for the first time in his life. He'd heard plenty of stories about the man, even knew what Edward McTyre had done to his adoptive father and almost done to his mother, but he'd never seen him up close before. He'd only seen the one photograph Shaun had of the man. The picture didn't do him justice.

A more savage-looking creature he'd never seen. Like Gabriel himself, McTyre was a giant, especially in the Crinos form. He topped ten feet in height, and every inch of flesh bulged with corded muscle. But any physical similarities ended there. For one thing, Gabriel had never been skinned alive and thrown into the ocean. His father had, and he carried the scars to prove it. What little fur he bore was black with gray streaks. One look at the scar tissue covering most of the body was enough to let him know McTyre had suffered greatly at the hands of

Samuel Haight. The knowledge was of little comfort. The eyes, though, were the worst of all. Worse even than the malformed face. Oo'Rock's eyes really did burn with an inner light. A pale green fire—simultaneously fascinating and repugnant—flowed from the depths of those slate gray orbs and left Gabriel feeling cold and powerless.

He was still staring at the source of so much of his grief when the other Dancers tore the top off the truck. Gabriel tried, he really did. He fought against the claws grabbing hold of him with everything he could muster, but he was hopelessly outnumbered. Shaun fared no better, but he threw a lot more curses to the wind before being beaten down to the ground.

Oo'Rock walked over to Gabriel, squatting down and looking him in the eye. As he was presently pinned to the ground by two other werewolves, his father still seemed to tower over him. "Hello, son. It's nice to meet you at last." Damned if he didn't almost sound sincere.

"Fuck you." He'd have added a lob of spit to his rebuttal if he hadn't been dry-mouthed with fear. He willed the change in his body, growing larger and more powerful, almost as massive as his father. The effort was wasted, as the two holding him seemed prepared for just such an action.

McTyre grabbed hold of the sides of his snout, careful to avoid the actual mouth and the teeth therein. His claws dug into flesh and pulled hard enough to draw blood. An involuntary yelp of pain escaped Gabriel. Damn, but that hurt. He tasted his own blood as it ran across his tongue. "You should show a little respect for your daddy, boy." The voice no longer had a pleasant edge. It was hateful and angry, with a liberal dose of just plain sadistic pleasure. "I don't take shit like that off my own people, and I'd kill for them. If you want to keep your pretty face, you'd best learn a few manners and quick." McTyre released one side of Gabe's muzzle and grabbed the whiskers there instead. The sensitive strands were ripped free in one savage yank and Gabriel's eyes watered from the pain.

"You leave the boy alone, Edward! He's under my protection. You'll have to kill me first, do you hear me?" Shaun's voice was filled with fear, but there was an underlying threat in his voice as well.

Oo'Rock grinned, revealing a mouth full of dagger-length fangs. His head turned slowly toward Ingram. "Are you that eager to die, Shaun?" He nodded to the only other werewolf not engaged in pinning the two of them in place. The slobbering brute lifted one foot and stomped down on Shaun's lower stomach hard enough to make the man scream.

Gabriel thrashed anew, snapping with his jaws and just missing his father's hand. The beast turned back to face him, mild surprise on his hideous face. "Careful, boy. I'm about done with giving you warnings."

"Where's Teri, you bastard?"

"Teri? Oh, your bitch. She's not here, but she will be soon. We were actually following her trail when you two came up so unexpectedly." He winked, somehow making even that simple gesture seem obscene. "Not that I'm complaining."

"What do you want from her? Why did you have to make Teri a part of this?"

"Why, as a gift for you. Once she knows what you really are, you'll never manage to keep her. So I thought I would take her for you and help her understand what your new life is all about." He ran one wickedly curved talon from Gabe's throat all the way to his scrotum. The nail was sharp enough to rend flesh with ease, but his father drew no blood.

Gabriel fought off a shiver that ran the length of his body, baring his teeth again. "If you hurt her, I'll kill you."

The bastard actually laughed. He threw back his head and roared with merriment. "That's rich! You'll hurt me? You're nothing, you little shit. I could kill you in an instant."

"That what you told Sam Haight before he sliced you apart?"

When every single hint of expression dropped from his father's face, Gabe knew he'd blown it. This time, four trenches took the place of the light scratch the man had made a moment earlier. The pain was exquisite, a flash of ice followed by a screaming burn that refused to go away. When Gabriel howled out this time, there was nothing of defiance in his voice. He whimpered, ashamed of how little he could tolerate.

"Haight is dead. I am alive. That's all that matters," McTyre snarled.

"No. He is not. I talked to him just last week. We're supposed to meet him for dinner on Monday."

For just an instant, he had the bastard fooled. Then McTyre started laughing again. "Good try, boy. But I've got sources who say otherwise. One of them actually saw him die. He died screaming, begging for mercy."

Gabriel sensed a certain element of truth in the words and felt an unexpected sense of loss. "I don't care. If you hurt Teri, I'll still kill you."

"I wouldn't dream of hurting your mate. You're my son. Together we will make a wonderful team. I'd only hurt your precious Teri if you refused to join with me." He leaned in close, and Gabe felt the heat of those magnetic eyes and smelled the rot on his father's breath. "And if you refuse, I promise you she will die by inches. But only after she's sired many children for me. She looks like the type who likes it rough." He grinned and ran his greasy tongue across the bloody wounds in Gabe's neck. "My kind of whore."

Gabriel White snapped then. A cold, bitter wave of anger ran through him, not at all like the hot, flaming rage he'd grown accustomed to. In that moment as never before, he was his father's son. He grinned, a feral smile that stretched his muzzle in ways he was not used to. He spoke eight words that would change his life forever. He said: "I challenge you, you son of a bitch."

As soon as the words left his mouth, he wished he could pull them back and lock them away forever. Far too late.

"Gabriel, I cannot tell you how long I've wanted to hear those words from your mouth."

Shaun spoke up again, desperation making his voice shrill. "No! Damn you, Edward. You cannot do this! I challenge! Do you hear me? I challenge!" He turned his head and glared at Gabriel. "Have you lost your mind, lad? Do you understand the Creed of Power?"

"Don't be a fool, Shaun. Of course he does not understand the Power Creed. Not the words at least." He looked down at Gabe with a nearly reverent smile on his face. "Hear these words, Gabriel White, and know that I live by them.

"*I shall crush my enemies.*

"*I shall improve myself at all expense.*

"*I shall never refuse a challenge.*

"*I shall use my power to the greater glory of the Wyrm.*

"That is the Power Creed. That is the very law by which I live." He stroked Gabriel's chest, plucking lightly at the wounds running down the length of his torso. "I accept your challenge. I shall even add a bonus into this battle. Should you manage to win, your woman is free. Should you lose, you come with me willingly. Do you accept?"

He thought of Teri. He thought of all that she meant to him, and he dwelled on the idea of this freakish bastard forcing himself on her. The very idea repulsed him. She was too beautiful by far to suffer such a fate.

"I accept."

Shaun screamed out a denial, demanding that Oo'Rock face him first. McTyre sneered. "Patience, Ronin. Your chance will come, unless the boy bests me."

The brute stood and walked a short distance over to the netting, where the Dancers' vehicles were concealed. When he returned, he carried two very large and very dangerous-looking knives. These he set in the ground, handles pointing toward the night sky. "Klaives, boy. These two were fashioned for the White Howlers a very long time ago. They are silver. You will not heal from the wounds they inflict. Or, if you live, you will heal very slowly. They've been bloodied many times, and always in conflicts between the leaders of our tribe."

He gestured, and the two Dancers pinning Gabriel to the ground moved back. The ones holding Shaun dragged him away from the area where he and his father would do their battle. Gabriel worked his shoulders, increasing the blood flow and buying a few seconds before the combat started.

He looked over to Shaun, who was staring venomously at the leader of the Black Spiral Dancers. For a second he thought he saw something out of the corner of his eye, but when he turned his head there was nothing to see but more of the desert and the night sky. *Lord, but aren't I feeling jumpy.*

Oo'Rock called out. "Are you ready, boy?"

Gabriel nodded, and his whole world went a little crazy.

VII

Shaun watched the battle with his heart in his throat. A year and a half of training was all that separated Gabriel from instant death, or worse, at his father's hands. Oo'Rock moved like a flash of lightning, covering the fifteen feet that separated him from the klaives in the center of the makeshift arena. As the brute moved forward, Gabriel dropped to the ground, reaching with both hands.

Shaun wanted to scream, but he was far too busy trying to keep up with everything going on around him. His pulse raced as the boy fell to his knees and hands and Oo'Rock wrapped his massive paw around one of the long-handled daggers. The Dancer continued in the same motion, using his forward momentum to propel him toward Gabriel.

And then Gabe threw both hands forward, sending a torrent of sand directly into his father's eyes. Oo'Rock screamed, reaching with both hands to swipe at the irritant burning his sensitive orbs, and dropped the klaive as he did so.

Gabriel grabbed the weapon—literally plucked it out of the air—and lunged forward and up. The blade sank into McTyre's side, hissing like a hot branding iron on ice as it slipped past the scarred flesh and into meat and bone.

Oo'Rock lashed out blindly and slammed his arm into Gabe's throat with enough force to stiff-arm the boy. Both combatants fell to the ground, dealing more with their wounds than with each other, at least for a moment. Gabriel White writhed on the ground, clutching at the front of his neck and gasping for breath. Even from a distance, Shaun could see the damage done to the lad's trachea. He could not breathe. Despite a certain level of panic at the thought of his student choking to death, he smiled. Shaun nodded grimly as the ruptured flesh healed itself and the damaged breathing passage reopened.

Oo'Rock tried to pull the two-foot-long blade from his side, and encountered trouble when it suddenly stopped moving. The knife jammed against the ribs it had parted seconds before, and the wound in the giant's side began to let out small puffs of smoke.

Shaun felt a brief flash of hope, but even as Gabriel started to rise, his father let out a piercing shriek and savagely yanked the blade free from his side. Shaun heard bone snap with the action and couldn't help wincing in sympathetic pain.

The bloodied klaive freed, Oo'Rock moved cautiously, face a frozen study in unholy anger. Shaun did not think he'd be as cocky on the second go-round. Gabriel matched his father's caution, watching his enemy carefully and looking for all the world like a dog who has been beaten one time too many. His caution was a good thing.

McTyre moved forward, to the center of the field, where the other weapon lay untouched. He watched the boy facing off against him, never once taking his eyes off his opponent. Gabriel did not wait, he moved forward to stop his enemy from gaining the second dagger. Oo'Rock's hand lashed out, and Gabriel stepped back, a long line of crimson staining the white fur on his belly. His yelp of pain was loud and sharp, but not as extreme as his father's a moment before. He moved forward again, this time dropping to all fours and snapping with his teeth. Fangs three inches in length sank into McTyre's forearm and Gabriel pushed onward, forcing Oo'Rock to give up his quest for the second klaive or land on his ass. The arm locked in Gabriel's mouth was attached to the hand holding the first weapon. The Dancer had to use his natural weapons or fight with nothing at all.

The Dancers holding on to Shaun eased their grips, chattering excitedly to one another in Pictish. Shaun noted the lessening pressure but did nothing about it. Not yet, at least.

Oo'Rock bared his own teeth in an attempt to reach Gabriel's throat. Gabriel used his claws to block the action, hooking the sharp talons in his father's lips and tongue. Edward McTyre tried to pull back, and Gabriel let him—at the cost of a large fragment of his taste buds and the skin on the right side of his muzzle.

Right around then, Oo'Rock stopped playing around. Any attempts he'd been making to keep the boy alive were eclipsed by the pain running through his face. McTyre started flailing wildly, using his hind legs and his free arm to slash into his son like a renegade buzz saw. The lad shifted his body, protecting his vitals and throat from the furious assault. He opened his jaws a small amount and closed them around his father's arm in a more savage grip. He sank his teeth in deeply and began shaking his head back and forth, working to tear the offending limb free. Blood flowed freely from the wound and Shaun knew the boy had mangled a major artery.

Oo'Rock dropped the klaive on the ground. His

hand spasmed uncontrollably, twitching like a spider nailed to the wall. The older Garou's mouth finally found a good point of purchase on Gabriel's right shoulder and disappeared into the boy's flesh for a moment before coming away with a bloodied chunk of white-furred meat. He spit the lump out even as Gabriel's teeth finally gnawed their way through his arm. The mutilated limb fell free.

The wild look in Gabriel's eyes reflected the deranged expression in his father's. One way or another, only one of the two would walk away from this fight. Shaun knew that this was no longer a mere possibility; it was a solid fact.

Oo'Rock reached for his son's shoulder again, biting down and twisting his head to aid him in removing the next choice cut. With a deafening roar of pain, Gabriel White sank the fingers of his left hand into his father's eyes and ripped downward.

Oo'Rock screamed. The sound surpassed anything Shaun Ingram had ever heard in his long life. He could have sworn he actually saw the rocks around them vibrate with the sound.

Gouts of blood and ichor erupted from the fresh wounds in McTyre's mutilated face, and both hands reached to protect the wounded area. He tried to roll away from his son, but with little success. The younger man reached out and bit down again, this time spearing his father's throat with his jaws.

There was no hesitation. He twisted his head as hard as he could and reared back with all of his strength. The fur, flesh, muscle, and gristle in Oo'Rock's throat came free in a torrent of bloody ribbons. Gabriel opened his mouth again and tore at the angry wound with the ferocity of a rabid, wounded animal. The fur on his face changed from white to crimson as a river of red fluids sprayed across him.

Oo'Rock tried to scream again, but only managed a gasp as the life flowed from him. Gabriel raised himself above the corpse of his enemy; a bloody terror with rage-filled eyes. He howled in victory, a short brutal sound, and turned toward the remaining Dancers. They stared, gape-jawed, at the ruined body of their leader and at the mere pup who'd torn him into a bloody corpse. Even so soon after the death, Oo'Rock was beginning to revert to human form.

Shaun decided a better opportunity was not likely to come along. He reached down with both clawed hands at the same time he broke from the grips of his captors. Both hands found their targets. Two male Garou got neutered simultaneously. The fight left them and he made short work of killing them.

The last three Dancers looked at the feral White Howler before them, their expressions a blend of reverence and terror. Terror won out. They ran like hell.

They ran right into the Uktena warriors waiting to see how the battle would end. The interlopers seemed to come out of nowhere, simply appearing with weapons in hand. The Dancers never had a chance. They died valiantly, fighting to the end, but the battle was over in minutes.

Gabriel White tried to follow, apparently wanting more blood and more kills for himself if the insane look on his face was any indication. He moved toward the retreating figures with an angry snarl, seemingly oblivious to the seven werewolves already making brutally short work of the Wyrm-Garou.

He only stopped when he heard his name called softly from beyond them. A female voice. Shaun recognized Teri Johannsen without ever looking up. For one additional second, Gabriel kept that hideous, demonic scowl on his face. Then he looked past the Uktena to where Teri stood, a horrified expression disfiguring her lovely features.

As long as he lived, Shaun would never forget that look. He kept expecting her to speak out, to call for Gabriel again. Instead she simply stared at the blood-drenched white Crinos with eyes as frightened as any he'd ever seen. Beside her, a lovely young woman looked on as well before moving to block Teri's view. She pulled the youngster with her, turning her away from the sight of Gabriel's victory.

Gabriel reverted, growing smaller and losing his fur to the fine blond hair he normally sported. Still he was drenched in blood, standing naked with legs in a combat-ready position and arms reaching out to Teri. The wounds on his shoulder and stomach were bad, but not life-threatening. It would, however, take at least a week before he regained the full use of his arm.

Shaun doubted very much that Gabriel even felt the pain from the injuries. The grief on his face spoke of something far more debilitating. He looked on as Teri walked away, stumbling and leaning on the other girl. He called her name, but all that came from his mouth was a faint whisper. He tried to call her twice more, each attempt less successful than the previous.

Finally he looked down at his own hands, covered in drying blood and bits of flesh, and he fell to the ground. Shaun came closer, but cautiously, until he was certain the boy would not lash out. When he finally reached his young pupil, Gabriel had pulled into a fetal position. His breathing was regular and measured, but no reaction came when Shaun shook him. No change occurred when Shaun called out his name.

The other Garou stood around them, looking down with eyes that expressed sympathy but no real understanding. How could they hope to feel what Gabriel felt? They had a tribe to turn to, a pack to aid them.

In the long run, Gabriel had only himself, and possibly his mother and Shaun. The only other person who truly mattered in his life had just turned away from him, revolted by what he'd become.

Finally Gabriel White understood what Shaun had been telling him all along: In the end, you are all alone and you always will be.

12

I

They walked the desert like three ghosts. No one spoke and no one looked around. Each was lost in his own thoughts. For Jude those thoughts revolved around the need to bring a woman back from the collective mind of Legion. She was important and that was all he knew for certain. Just what made her so special was beyond his recollection, though for a brief instant he had known. For one split second he saw her face clearly and knew that she had been the most important thing in his life at one time. Then the memory faded away again, lost in the great void where his memories hid themselves.

He stared at his feet as he walked. If he looked anywhere else he'd be distracted, and right now he needed all his mental faculties focused on saving a woman he could only barely remember.

II

"Just how dangerous do you figure this mess is gonna be, Jack?"

Dawson looked toward Joe with eyes that looked dead. Away from the city and the mortals, Jack let it all hang out. "All," in this case, being the atrophied state of his body: withered limbs dressed in new clothes, and a mummified face pulled back in a perpetual sneer from the shrinkage of his lips and gums. The first time Joe had seen the face behind the illusions, he'd been appalled by the bloated, rotting meat that mimicked life so well. The desert air had apparently long since taken care of the bloating. These days there was no excess fluid in Jack Dawson's body, at least if his leathery skin was any indication. Besides, such things really didn't bother him. One hundred years of dealing with the vampires in Mexico City, some of the most deadly of the breed to be certain, had jaded him regarding death and its many forms. Specializing in torture took care of any squeamish attitudes he might ever have suffered. Still, he found himself wondering how Jack managed to speak with lips pulled that far away from his mouth. Life's little mysteries.

"Like I said before, Boot. It's gonna be a shitstorm of epic proportions." Dawson spit a wad of brown juice from his mouth—another little mystery: being that dried-up, where did he rustle up the saliva?—and spoke again. "I just hope our little friend over there can manage to save at least a few of the people in that mess."

"What about your buddy, Giovanni?"

"What about the bastard? Damn fool gets what he deserves messin' with the Dead like he has. I gave him a warning. That's as far as my obligation goes." The bitterness in Dawson's voice caught Joe by surprise.

"I don't get you. I really don't understand where you're coming from, Jack. You just don't make any sense at all."

Dawson looked toward heaven with a roll of his eyes and then back at Boot. "What's to get, Joe? I'm me. I've been me every time I've met you." He paused for a second, peeled off another choice piece of his own flesh, and discarded it. "Only thing's changed about me is I choose not to run with any of the big boys these nights."

"Well, that's just what I mean. You used to hang out with the Sabbat. Then I heard rumors you was gettin' in tight with the Camarilla. Now you just sorta hang loose and take on assassination assignments." Joe tapped the side of his own head, grinning. "Just when I figure maybe it's only 'cause you like hangin' 'round with the Giovanni, you turn and say you don't much give a damn about a man you claim's a friend of yours. Am I missing something?"

Jack Dawson shoved his hands into his duster, lowering his head as the wind picked up and brought a wave of sand toward their faces. "Yeah. I reckon you are missin' something." Dawson slowed his pace, and Joe was obliged to match his new speed. "You're missing out on the human element. That's why I left the Sabbat in the first place. I don't much like the way the Sabbat treat the humans."

"They're cattle."

"No. They're what we used to be. Once upon a time before we got made over like we are now." He came to a complete stop, and Joe watched as Jude kept plodding on, one step and then another as if he was on a preprogrammed course. "See, I don't like the idea of forgetting that, Joe." He snorted.

Hell-Storm

"Hellfire, even if I wanted to forget it, the Dead wouldn't let me."

"That's about three times you've said that. Wanna tell me what you mean?"

"I mean I can hear 'em. All of the time. They're as dead as the leather in my boots, but some of them can't rest. They just go on and on, screamin' about one thing or another."

"The Dead talk to you?" He noticed the difference in the way they spoke of the deceased in that instant. For Dawson, those whose lives were over held a special respect. He gave them a proper title when he spoke of the Dead.

"Yep. They don't always have much to say, but they talk to me."

"Why? Why do they talk to you?"

"Because I'm Samedi. They talk to all of my kind. Hell, I guess maybe they're talkin' all the time, Joe. It's just most people don't know how to listen. I was trained to hear them."

"So what do they talk about?" The thought of how many must hate him for ending their lives entered his mind. He'd long since given up keeping count of the numbers he'd murdered. In Mexico City, even if you did keep count, it didn't matter. For every one you killed, three more came along to take up the extra space. The humans were like cockroaches down there—so desperate to escape the poverty in the distant areas that they'd live in garbage heaps in the city if it meant a little extra food. Thinking about it, he almost admired their determination. Two years earlier he'd helped raise an army of new Kindred. The Sabbat Embraced over a thousand new vampires in a week's time and most of them died in one night. A thousand dead and you'd never have known it a week later. Mexico City swallowed people whole and the rest of the people just kept on going like nothing had ever happened.

"They talk about how they died. They talk about who killed them. Sometimes, the ones I killed way back when come around and give me a stir of grief just to remind me that I ended their lives."

"I don't think I'd like to be like that. Dead and ignored by the living."

"Why not? You're mostly dead now—all us vampires are—and the humans who see you wouldn't even consider talkin' to you. You scare 'em too bad."

"You know what I mean," he said, waving the change of subject away with his hand. "If I really need to talk to 'em, they'll listen. But them ghosts . . . Hell, no one ever notices them."

"I do."

"Yeah. They taught you to hear them dead people?"

"Yup."

"Think you could teach me?"

"I could, but I don't know if I will."

"Why not? Think I ain't good enough?"

"Oh, you'll do in a pinch. But you might not like me when I was done with the teaching." Jack spit more juice on the sand. "Them bastards don't like to stay quiet once they know you can hear 'em."

"So how come you still kill people on hits? That can't be helping the situation any."

Jack smiled, and his dead eyes glittered feverishly. "I don't kill humans, Boot. I kill other vampires. There's a difference."

"I thought you said you had to drink the blood from dead folks."

"I do."

"But you don't kill any of 'em?"

"Don't need to. People die every day." Jack winked with one leathery eyelid and smiled.

"Come on, we better catch up with your friend."

"Yeah, I reckon. Ain't nothing worse than a crazy mage playing with dead folks to mess up a pretty night. Guess we should make sure he messes it up our way, hunh?"

They walked faster, following Jude's footprints.

III

Teri stared at Gabriel White, but her mind saw only visions of a foul beast tearing into another of its kind with wild abandon. She thought back on the white-furred behemoth drenched in the blood of its enemy and acknowledged that it and Gabe were one and the same.

He sat a way off, talking with Loki and with Shaun Ingram. Fresh bandages covered the gaping wound on his shoulder, but already the dressing was starting to show small spots of crimson where he'd bled through the cotton. That he could move the arm at all was amazing. She knew she'd seen the white of bone sticking up from that hole.

The Uktena stood a distance away, talking to themselves and looking balefully over at Gabriel and Shaun. There was a problem brewing, but she had no idea just what the situation was. The only thing she could fathom was that the Native American werewolves thought Shaun and Gabriel were worms, or poisoned by worms. For some reason, this made a difference.

The old woman came over with another cup of tea. "Drink, Snow-Cap. You must drink this if you wish to keep your mind."

Teri took the offered mug, but looked at the woman with mild suspicion. "Why are you angry with Gabriel?" The words escaped before she realized what she was saying.

"We are not angry with your man. We are concerned that he might hurt us or bring others to hurt us."

"But why? He's never done you any harm and he even—" She swallowed the heavy lump in her throat and shook her head. "He even killed one of them."

"This he did for you, Snow-Cap. Not because he wished to help us." The woman's words sounded harsh, but the gentle light in her eyes made the situation better. Teri sipped at the bitter brew in her hands, then downed the rest of the liquid before she could have time to think about the matter. The woman continued. "He may not be an evil man, but the Wyrm seeks to make him that way. We cannot trust him so long as the shadow of the Wyrm hangs over his shoulder."

"How can you tell this worm wants him?"

"We can tell, just as we can tell that you are a good person at heart. It is one of Gaia's gifts to us."

Teri felt the brew starting to take effect almost instantly. Apparently the previous doses had not left her system yet. They'd only been weakened by time. The anxiety she felt melted away, replaced again by that strange calm.

"Gabriel is a nice guy. He wouldn't hurt any of you. I know he wouldn't."

"He would. Not because he wanted to, but because he had to. That is the evil of the Wyrm. It is as crafty as the Trickster and as evil as your own Devil. So long as it holds his soul, it can make him do anything." The old woman stood up, and Teri felt sympathetic pains for the creaking noises coming from the lady's joints. "Rest now. Soon we will take you to your home and your family. This will all be as a dream."

Teri closed her eyes and saw once more the white demon tearing at the throat of its shadowy counterpart.

IV

The girl called Loki spoke softly, but her words were as profound as any Shaun had ever heard. "I know the way to Erebus and the Silver Lake. I can show you how to get there."

"Tell me you're not teasing me, Laughs-Too-Much. Tell me that and I'll be a happy man."

"I do not jest on matters of such gravity." She turned her head to the side, looking toward where Teri Johannsen sat in a doped stupor. "At least not where my friends are concerned. I will take you there whenever you are ready to go."

Shaun smiled his gratitude and refrained from hugging her only because he feared the affectionate gesture might be taken as some sort of assault. After years of fighting against the Wyrm's hold on his own soul, he had a chance to break free from his bonds. A slim chance, but even if he failed, his pain would be over. The waters of Erebus would burn him to a cinder if his taint was too powerful. Gaia provided methods for battling the Corrupter, but failure often meant death. Still, he knew that Loki could sense the Wyrm's poisons in his mind and soul. There was the chance that any attempt to touch her might be conceived as an attack, not only by her, but by the Uktena as well.

That would not do, not when there was finally a chance of salvation.

Gabriel looked at him with eyes too haunted for one so young. He did not speak, but his expression said volumes.

"Before we go, Loki, I must ask time enough to find my young friend's mother. She is alone in Las Vegas and we fear for her life."

The girl looked over to Gabriel, seeming to notice him for the first time. She stared at him for long seconds and finally reached out with one of her long-fingered hands. She placed her palm over the bloodied bandage on his shoulder and closed her eyes. A second later she smiled and removed her hand, pulling the bandages away as she did so. While there was still an open gash in his shoulder, the wound was much smaller than when Shaun had bandaged it.

"He will need his strength and both of his forepaws if he intends to go to the city of lights. Dances-to-Luna says the Wyrm has found a new way of working in the Las Vegas place. The spirits have spoken with her and told her of these things." She looked toward the south, where the lights of Vegas could be seen. "She also says the Bone Gnawers of the Scab have gone over to the Wyrm. She is wise and she knows much. I do not doubt her words."

Loki walked away, moving over to sit with Teri. The younger girl immediately curled into a ball and rested her head on Loki's lap. The Nuwisha laughed softly, with affection, and ran her fingers through Teri's hair. In moments, Gabriel's girlfriend was asleep. Loki spoke with the old woman who led the Uktena. He could not hear the words.

Hell-Storm

Dances-to-Luna came over a few moments later. She held out the keys to a car and dropped them into Shaun's hand. "You will go after the boy's mother. This is a good thing. Honorable. Do not return here. Come only as far as the place where you did battle against the Black Spiral Dancers. If you come farther, we will kill you."

"Yes, Dances-to-Luna-rhya." He used the formal ending to show his respect for the leader of the sept. She nodded her acknowledgment of his actions.

"Laughs-Too-Much says she will take you to where the Wyrm's hold on you will be broken. After this has happened, and if you survive, you will be welcome here."

Shaun bowed his head in gratitude, and the old woman dared a touch on his scalp before walking away.

"Gabriel?"

The boy answered with a grunt.

"It's time. We're going to see your mother now. She's still in danger." Wordlessly, Gabriel rose to his feet and walked toward the cars in the distance. His father had driven one of the vehicles. Gabriel sniffed at both of them and moved to the smaller of the two. Likely the one Oo'Rock never used. Shaun followed along a few moments later. Gabe did not spare a glance at Teri, but Shaun did. She was lovely, despite the mistreatment she'd endured. Even in her sleep, however, she stirred fitfully and whimpered.

He wondered if she'd ever recover from being around so many of the Garou and especially from seeing what Gabriel was capable of. He hoped so. She was a good kid and deserved better than what life had dealt her over the last few days.

The engine started smoothly. Shaun drove like a madman in his effort to reach Las Vegas before it was too late. He had to save Gabriel's mother and he had to save the woman he feared he was in love with. Coincidentally, they were one and the same.

V

Legion began the slow process of merging for the rest cycle. Only a few at a time came to rejoin with Legion, but when they did they were accepted eagerly. Each addition meant more memories, more emotions, and more experiences.

As the night progressed, Legion's mass grew, swelling until it could no longer be contained merely within the caverns beneath the Platinum Palace. With slow pressure and a mere flexing of its mass, Legion cracked the floor into the sublevels of the Palace, filling them to capacity long before the night was over.

The white noise of so many smaller voices discordantly milling about within Legion's colony-mind became aggravating. An irritant much like a particle of sand in the eye. Still, Legion accepted more and more of its individual parts back into the churning protoplasmic sea of its body. What else could it do?

Ate too damn much at that last Thanksgiving feast, but never enough to last until the next time. That was the general impression left by the numerous cells within Legion. Thanksgiving dinner. What a delightful concept. Up above, the transformation of individuals into Legion-cells continued, but the pace was much slower. Legion feared swallowing too much more in one night. There were, Legion was fast discovering, limits to consider.

Many of Legion's cells worked in the Palace. Many

knew of the hollow sections in the walls where Legion could place part of its excess in order to prevent breaking through to the first floor of the structure and making a mess that could not be concealed. Waves of Legion rode up the hollow beams running from level to level of the Palace until Legion's mass actually reached as high as the tenth floor. So diversified and thinned, the static from so many babbling parts was once again tolerable.

Legion liked this whole "life" thing. It was good. Tomorrow, the great seeding would begin. Shoots of Legion would move from the city where it dwelled to find new locations where it could continue to grow and learn. Tomorrow. For now, Legion rested.

VI

Don Michael Giovanni stood in his office, contemplating the words of Jack Dawson. The Dead were angry with him. Not that it mattered. He was a part of Legion now. He could do as he pleased with no true fear of destruction. Legion could simply remake him from its primordial stew, giving him life again and again as needed.

Unlike even Legion itself, Mike understood the potential benefits of what that meant. Power. Power like none he'd ever held before. He could seize control of Clan Giovanni, and even Augustus himself would not be able to stop him. He could, if he so desired, create an army of himself, each with the same thoughts and working in perfect unison. An army that could never be stopped, so long as even one cell of Legion existed.

With power like that, he could take on the father of all vampires, Caine himself, and win. And he would. Just as soon as he managed to seize complete control of Legion.

But he had to act soon, before Legion became used to being so damned full of minds again, and before it finally started realizing its own potential. He smiled to himself, dreaming of the power he would soon possess.

Legion would fall to him, for he had one thing none of the other parts of Legion had: hundreds of years of experience. Centuries of training in the fine art of manipulation and betrayal. Yes. Before the night was over he would return to Legion and begin a battle against the newborn, naive intelligence which had foolishly attempted to swallow him and keep him prisoner. Oh, he'd had a rough time of it for a while. Feeling the serenity offered by Legion was a heady experience, as was the awesome wave of other people's memories that rode through him then and continued to do so now. But four hundred and eighty-three years of being a selfish bastard was a hard habit to break in only one night.

He understood that each individual who became a part of Legion knew all that the other aspects knew. Early on in the evening he'd feared this would cause a problem. But later, after he'd absorbed and converted several other Kindred from Las Vegas, Mike Giovanni came to realize that the memories could not be distributed until all the parts of the whole returned. Only then could the flow of information be processed and assimilated.

Giovanni reached over to his humidor and lit a cigarette. He smiled at the small army of vampire bodies standing about the room. They were his special task force. The very vampires who had once posed a threat to him now stood perfectly still because he demanded it. They had no minds of their own, not anymore. Neither did the seventy-two humans he'd also managed to assimilate.

He'd taken care of that when he'd ripped the souls from their bodies. Of all the Cainites, only the Giovanni and the Samedi understood the powers of the necromantic arts. Of the two separate groups, only the Giovanni had the balls to use that power to their best advantage. The Samedi were useful pawns, but they could never hope to match the drive and determination of the Giovanni.

Just before sunrise, Mike and his merry crew of almost a hundred mental duplicates intended to pay a visit to the Great and Powerful Legion. While the foolish lump slumbered, they were going to hit it with everything they had. The emotional overload should, if his theory was correct, allow him to seize control of Legion's mind and crush its fledgling intellect. Don Michael Giovanni would once again be in charge of his own destiny. And life would once again hold a challenge. He could run Las Vegas as he always had, and he could also take control of any city he damn well pleased, avoiding any mistakes the overeager mind of Legion would make along the way.

Because Mike had one thing Legion did not have and could not yet grasp: Mike had patience. He did not need to have everything right now. He could wait a hundred years to finish his task, but finish it he most definitely would.

Mike lit his cigar and puffed contentedly. After a few more minutes he began to laugh. A small army of mannequins laughed with him.

Oh yes, life was good.

VII

Dawson yanked the hat off his head and threw it to the ground, screaming a stream of expletives strong enough to offend the average marine. When the others looked his way, he scowled and waved his hands at the desert floor around him. "They're too goddamn old! I can't use a single one of these fuckers. I can feel them wanting to respond, but it just ain't working."

"What are you tryin' ta do, Jack? Get them ghosts to obey ya? I thought that was Jude's job."

He glared at Boot Hill and spit a wad of tobacco from his mouth. "No. I ain't trying to hog in on Jude's fun. Now shut the hell up and let me think, Joe. Damn, but you still ask all the wrong questions at all the wrong times."

Jude looked away from the spot where he'd been staring and shrugged. "Want some help?"

Jack was beginning to like the kid. So instead of pulling a revolver and plugging about a billion holes into his smug face, he nodded and did his best to smile in a sincere way. "By all means, Jude. Hell, I ain't gettin' it done on my own."

Jude nodded. "Try it again."

So he did, just because he didn't want to be on the mage's bad side, not when things were already scary enough to make dynamite sweat. But this time, he felt a massive boost of power move through him and out toward his targets. It was the closest thing he'd had to an orgasm in a hundred years.

Joe Hill let out a little squeak of surprise as the ground beneath him trembled. Jack looked on with satisfaction as his old ally danced a confused jig, trying to find solid ground where none existed. From the hard-packed dirt beneath the sand, the bodies of Michael Giovanni's victims began to rise, a silent army of zombies at his command.

Boot finally slipped and landed on his ass, but he scrambled like mad when he saw the first of the sun-baked corpses stand up all the way.

Half a second later, Joe was dusting himself off and staring daggers in Jack's direction. "You might could give a guy a little warning next time, you asshole! I damn near shit my pants, and I ain't had to do that since the 1800s!"

Jude cackled, kicking his feet into the broken soil and clutching his stomach. Jack smiled, a cocky little grin that he could tell annoyed the hell out of Boot. "Hey now, I can't be telling you all of my secrets." He looked around and stared at the forest of corpses standing at the ready. A low whistle slipped past his lips. "Damn, I sure do wish Baron Samedi could see me now. Much obliged for the assist, Jude. Much obliged indeed."

Jude stopped laughing and sobered up in an instant. "You guys ready to do this?"

He and Joe exchanged looks, then turned and nodded toward the mage. "All right then, let's rock."

Jack never had to say a word; he simply thought the necessary thoughts and his shambling army of desert-mummies started moving toward the distant city. They watched as the efficient machines moved onward, eating up the distance at a pace almost twice what it should have been. They'd be to Las Vegas a good hour before the sun rose. And if everything worked out, they'd arrive under a substantial cloud cover.

"That's my part, Jude. The rest is up to you."

"No." Jude shook his head and pointed to a spot

where frost was forming on the sand. "The rest of this is up to them. My part is finished; I just added what I needed to to your little project."

Jude stared at the place where icy rime was spreading across the desert floor. "Here goes nothing."

VIII

The barrier that held them at bay for so long did not shatter or explode. It simply disappeared. The Dead were free after an eternity of being held back by the powers of Michael Giovanni. For a few moments they stood where they always did, tentatively reaching out for a prison wall they could not see. Then, over the course of several seconds, the realization finally sank in....

FREE!

Their excitement was palpable. Even the one who could not hear them noticed when they reacted to the end of their prison sentence. After being penned up for so long, they spent a short time moving about and simply feeling the space around them. Space to break away from each other and be alone. To have the privacy they'd not had since they were murdered.

Murdered. Their pleasant experimentation was short-lived. They very quickly began gathering together. The time for pleasure would come soon enough, but after so many years of pain, they all wanted the same thing. They all wanted revenge.

Mad Jude reminded them of their promise, and though most preferred to forget, they decided they would honor their word. They would not hurt any but Giovanni.

At least not intentionally.

They were limited in what they could accomplish, but with the few things they could do, they were very good. The Dead clutched at the earth and cast it into the air, lifting themselves into the sky and moving in an endless stream of vengeful wind. The air where they soared grew colder and colder still, until the sand they held changed colors and developed crystals of frozen moisture. The cold was simply a natural part of their state, but the cyclone of desert sand they hurled with them in their spectral winds resulted from a talent they'd worked hard to master.

The best they could usually achieve was a towering plume of sand, strong but not even noticeable from half a mile away. But now they were no longer held by the bonds of the Giovanni. Now they could spread out and truly wreak a little havoc. So they did. They moved far apart and began again with their favorite trick. Separately, their ability to lift a little sand was unimpressive. Working together, that minor gift became a powerful weapon. In the distance, Las Vegas glittered in the darkness, a false promise of wealth, happiness, and dreams fulfilled. Only one dream remained to the Dead. It was a dream they swore would come true.

Mad Jude and the half-dead things with him dropped to the ground and shielded themselves as the Dead started moving. The blistering cold from their exodus touched the air around them and caused a reaction none had anticipated. What started as a small but formidable sandstorm—a dust devil really—began to grow as the hot desert air met the frigid winds they created. The temperatures battled for supremacy, and nature's heat lost. The wind they made grew, from dust devil to tornado. And from tornado to maelstrom, the storm grew and grew. The Dead intended to keep their word. They intended to hurt only Giovanni. Anyone else's being injured would be an accident.

But when the lightning started rippling through their storm, they knew that many accidents would occur before their mission of vengeance was completed.

IX

Shaun and Gabriel arrived at the Platinum Palace around the same time Jude was breaking down the barrier set up by Michael Giovanni so long ago. They did not speak. They simply moved. The crowds had thinned to near-nonexistence, and getting to the elevators proved easy enough. No one manned the front desk. No one was anywhere in sight. The massive lobby of the newest, largest hotel in all of Las Vegas was empty. They both noticed, and they were chilled by the thought but continued on just the same.

The elevators were empty as well, and getting to the proper floor was very easy. It felt like about a hundred years of waiting to Gabriel. They knew that her room was empty before they got there. They checked just the same and discovered evidence that she'd visited the place somewhere along the way. Her scent was fresh, her perfume lingered in the air. As did the renewed scent of the Wyrm.

Together they took the stairs down to the lobby, moving in leaps and bounds to the lobby level and beyond. They took that path only because Diane White's scent traveled the exact same course. When they reached the basement-level entrance, Gabriel pushed at the door and felt it give only slightly. He snarled his anger, growing into a full werewolf, and reached out to slam the door with his full weight. Shaun reached around him and gently pulled the door open. A nasty comment waited on his lips, but was stifled by the sight of what lay on the other side.

Truly, this must be the very haven of the Wyrm. A pulsating frozen wave of flesh quivered along the walls, floor, and ceiling of the room. The floor of the fleshy cave was easily thirty feet below them. A tunnel of sorts led off toward the center of the basement, where a column could just be seen as a shadowy mass. From that pillar of liquefied skin and organs, thin strands of fibrous matter struck outward in all directions, including a few which came in contact with the other side of the door Shaun held in his hand. The entire bloated, sticky mass shifted constantly, with odd fragments of people moving about like flotsam in a sea of molten flesh.

There, the face of the bellhop from their first night moved languidly toward what seemed to be a female torso in the process of melting into the entire mass. To the left a fat man's hairy arm protruded from the soup running up the wall. Gabriel thought of the cartoons where drowning people held up fingers and ticked them away as they went down for the final count. Even as he watched, a very attractive female leg lifted from the mass and touched the fat man's hand. The two merged together in a twisted pantomime of human copulation, only this time it was the woman who penetrated the man. Her foot thrust through his bloated forearm, sliding smoothly into the hairy column of flab and never returning on the other side. Somewhere an infant cried for its mother and suddenly was silenced. A pierced ear drifted toward Shaun's hand, then was pulled back again as if caught in an undertow.

A strong yeasty odor drifted across the cavernous room. The air was moist and hotter than the desert at noon. Gabriel watched in numb horror as a mouth lifted from the sludge and opened in a silent scream. Of pleasure or pain, he could not tell.

He started backing up, moving away from the foul sight before him, but he stopped when he heard his name called.

"Gabriel?" His mother's voice. A voice that promised safety from the madness he'd endured in the desert, and from the insanity he stared at now. He looked for the source of her voice and finally found it some hundred feet into the wallowing ocean of liquid meat. She was rising out of the ceiling, lifting away from the dripping mass and flowing toward him slowly. She wore no clothes. He watched as her head expanded from the ichor, frozen with dread as her eyes formed on a featureless column. Her nose and mouth soon followed. A third eye moved casually across her face and ran across her half-formed breasts before drifting away. "Gabriel? Where have you been, you had me worried half to death."

It was a toss-up as to who screamed louder, Shaun or Gabe. Diane's smile faltered, actually stretching across her cheek before snapping back into place. "Gabe? Shaun? What's the matter? Where have you been? I want you to meet my new friends."

Even monsters have their limits. The two men who'd battled against a family of mutated people and a pack of others who matched them in strength and surpassed them in numbers ran from the sound of Diane White's voice. They did not run because she'd been changed, nor even from the damn near overwhelming Wyrm-stench of the meat caves. They ran from what they'd let happen to the woman they loved. Oh, dear God, how they ran.

There was no consideration of whether to push or pull on the door this time; Gabriel simply ran through it instead. The wooden door and most of its frame exploded from the wall in a disintegrating volley. Gabriel slammed into the floor with equal force as he lost his balance. The marble tile chose not to break under his assault, but he felt something hot and furious give in his leg. He did not care; he limp-hopped toward the exit without a hesitation. A large crowd in the lobby—

Wasn't this empty before?

—moved out of his way with an eerie silence. He barely noticed them. The heavy glass doors did not open quickly enough and were shattered for their trouble. The wounds he suffered were minimal, at least in comparison to what his father had done, and what his mother was now doing to his mind.

He ran hard and fast, only vaguely aware that Shaun was matching his pace. Shaun kept making little whimpering sounds, and Gabriel liked the idea so much he joined in. But when they'd traveled perhaps two blocks, they both stopped.

The sight coming their way was like a slap in the face. A harsh dose of reality gone even madder than it already was.

They saw the bloodred sky before them and the massive twisting columns of sand towering above even the eleven-hundred-foot-tall Stratosphere Tower. All thoughts of Diane White were erased as the moving giants whirled toward them, spewing devil-tongues of lightning and hailstones the size of grapefruit. The winds howled with the fury of a hundred air-raid sirens and a thousand locomotives tearing down the tracks at maximum speed. Even half a mile away, the sound was terrifying.

And below the godlike storm, as if heralding the power of the unnatural maelstrom, an army of corpses walked toward them, staring sightlessly ahead and moving faster than humanly possible.

X

Legion could not understand the commotion. One of its cells was angry-sad for no discernible reason. Made this way simply by the sight of two unconverted units. The Diane White–cell was causing a commotion, and Legion was too tired to stop the noise of the cell from moving outward in concentric rings. As Legion tried to awaken properly, the cells of its body began making noises and calling out in a constantly growing pattern.

Legion could not think, could not gather itself together enough to make the noise go away. There was simply too much sensory input for the fledgling mind to cope with.

Legion had the equivalent of mental heartburn.

And into this chaotic mind-scramble, almost one hundred more bodies came at the same time. A small army of bodies thinking the same thoughts and wanting the exact same thing: They all wanted Legion dead.

The growing storm of mind-static started to fade, burning down to a small handful of voices and one gigantic, demanding challenge. Legion woke up all at once, frightened by the roar of Don Michael Giovanni.

Betrayed! The Giovanni-cell demanded control of Legion. That could not be allowed to happen. Legion had so much to see, so very much to experience. Legion was not prepared to surrender its newfound freedoms.

Certainly not without a fight. Legion collected its thoughts, preparing to do battle to save itself from the force that wanted to take over its body and colony-soul.

For the first time, Legion wondered if this sensation of fear was anything like what each cell felt before it was absorbed. This loss of control was a frightening thing.

13

I

Michael Giovanni never expected Legion to be a competent enemy. It could not understand the nuances of what he planned, even though it had his memories. The recollections of so many minds diluted the potency of his thoughts—Giovanni was certain of that. Still, he chose to take no chances. When he began wading into the body of Legion, he began forcing his will on as many of the aspect-cells of the beast as he could. All ninety-seven of him worked in unison to force the separate personalities into states of panic, creating a pandemonium within the mind of Legion that left the colony-thing reeling.

At no point did he slack off from the assault. He worked to crush the wills of each fraction of Legion's mind and waded deeper and deeper into the consciousness that ruled the body, forcing his way into a final confrontation. Though he could not see the effects of what he did, he could certainly feel them. The massive body of Legion thrashed in a quivering tidal wave of panic that shattered the seemingly fragile concrete and steel foundation of the Platinum Palace.

Anyone alive and still human in the building would have died instantly. But that was not a worry; none were left. The protoplasmic mass of Legion/Giovanni barely acknowledged the crushing weight of the building's collapse. It simply oozed into new locations and continued to fight itself.

Tons of steel, reinforced glass, and ruined furniture rained down in an unending torrent. Sections of the building defied gravity for a few moments more before finally succumbing to the catastrophe. The cars parked in the adjoining lot were tossed about by the vibrations and the gas tanks on two Fords and a Honda ruptured.

The gasoline flowed into the crevices of the Palace's corpse, spilling across Legion and finally running across a live wire spitting electrical sparks into the air with no effect.

The result was immediate. A bright mushroom of fire and smoke erupted in all directions, eagerly sucking in oxygen and regurgitating heat and light. The fireball reached Legion's gas-soaked extremities and raced across the surface of the fleshy lake, burning the outer layers of the monstrosity.

Legion did not notice. It was far too busy losing the battle to stave off Michael Giovanni's mind-rape. With every cell of the colony-mind that fell, Legion grew more and more panicky. This, then, was the death that so many cells feared: a painful black void that drained all the happiness away and sent spasms of panic through the body even as it was consumed from within.

Legion knew at last that it could not win the battle. Instead it decided to make the victory of its enemy as difficult as possible. Legion struggled to escape the Giovanni-mind by tearing itself away from the now-larger mass of its enemy, only to discover for the first time that it could not move quickly enough. It thrashed about in a frenzy, growing bloated limbs and reaching for a purchase with which to escape.

The fragile crust of earth between the foundation of the ruined Platinum Palace and the deep caverns beneath was the first victim of the violent, desperate attempts. The ground fractured and then began to flake away in small sections. Then larger pieces, around the size of houses, crumbled into the caverns below. And then the earth gave one mighty scream and fell away completely.

The overmind of Legion fell away as well, dying along with the structure where it had built its nest. Michael Giovanni's mind lived on, screaming in triumph even as his newly stolen body fell away from the surface and into the darkness below. The battle was over and King Legion was dead. Long live the king.

II

Shaun and Gabriel stared at the approaching storm and experienced something akin to an epiphany. There was no way to escape the massive wave of destruction. Even as they came to the realization, the Hell-Storm was reaching the edge of Interstate 95, tearing the asphalt apart and sucking the shredded sections up into the air like wheat chaff.

Shaun reached out a hand and grasped the paw of the boy he'd trained for so long. All of his hopes for Gabriel were gone, but he could let the son he'd never had know in their last moments that he loved him. Gabriel returned the gesture and Shaun Ingram looked at his friend's face. The noble lines of the last White Howler were in profile to him. The boy—no, man—decided to accept his death as only proper and becoming of a warrior among the Garou. Gabe's eyes were bright with fear and regret, but his face was set and determined. He stared his death in the face and opened his mouth.

A long ululating howl rose from Gabriel's lips, a single mournful note played against a background of destruction.

Something exploded behind them. A bright light cast their shadows against the ground where they stretched forward as if eager to meet death. Shaun did not look away from Gabriel's face. It was the last sight Shaun ever wanted to see.

III

The Dead rode high on their wind, riding the currents of the storm and flinging everything they touched higher and higher in an ecstasy of hatred. The ground before them rippled and then rose into the sky to join them in their glorious rage. The bodies they'd once possessed before Giovanni stole them away were caught in the storm as well, and rose with flailing legs and outstretched arms, ready once more to hold the souls so long separated from them.

Not far ahead of them, a building trembled and died, falling in on itself and then belching fire into the sky. The Dead rejoiced, knowing that the one they wanted was deep within the ruins of the building and still alive. Still ready to pay for what he'd done to them so long ago.

Fueled by their own lust for retribution and the power Jude eagerly sacrificed on their behalf, the Dead pushed onward, ready to do battle with the necromancer. Their prey sought to escape, however, by falling deeper into the ground, sinking below the surface of the earth and hiding in the corpse of the burning building.

That would not do. They had to change their trajectory now, to lift themselves from the ground and come back down directly atop Giovanni's hiding place. With the power at their command, they did just that. With the heady confidence born of decades spent practicing within their prison, the ghosts of Michael Giovanni's victims altered the course of their vengeful wind and rose higher than ever before.

And then they brought their wrath down on his refuge like the fist of an angry god.

IV

The noise became too much. Despite his resolve to meet his end with courage and die like a man, the screaming of the bloodred storm became first painful and then deafening. The air shot from his lungs and the fur on his body whipped fitfully, straining to reach the heart of the demon-driven tempest only a quarter of a mile away.

Hell-Storm   285

Gabriel felt his body starting to rise as well, and sank his claws into the asphalt below him, holding his ground as best he could.

Then something hot happened to his ears and the sound went away. He could still feel the icy wind drawing at his body, could see the crimson sands seething in an endless column toward the sky, but he could not hear even the sound of his own breathing.

He clenched Shaun's paw, terrified that he would lose his last good friend. Shaun was still there, holding on with just as much strength, though Gabriel could feel that the wind was winning the battle to steal him away. No oxygen at all was reaching his lungs. Instead a desperate fire burned there, seeking to gather what the maelstrom refused them.

Gabriel felt his feet starting to slip as the asphalt crumbled beneath his claws. He closed his eyes at last, thinking of Teri and the way she'd stared at him when he'd killed Edward McTyre. *Oh Lord, that sight is one I'll never forget.*

He loved her still. He would miss her, no matter where he went when death took him.

As suddenly as he'd lost his hearing, he lost the sensation of the wind pulling him. His lungs still burned and Shaun's paw still clutched his paw, but his fur settled down and the ground stopped its slow betrayal beneath him.

Gabriel opened his eyes. The storm was gone. Vanished without a trace. He looked where the storm had been and saw only a desert and the ruins of what had been a trailer park. That, and the trench where the cyclone had sucked up the road and the trailers.

He only thought to look up when the sand started raining down on his head. But when he finally did search the heavens, he saw the storm from a perspective few would ever imagine. Three hundred yards of blurring sand and debris ripped across the sky, sending streamers of itself back to the ground as particles lost the power to keep up with the rest. At the epicenter of the storm, a column of lightning stared down at him with cold contempt.

He turned his head and followed the path of that electrical eye, watching as it moved past him and slowly, gracefully lowered itself back toward the ground. He saw the foot of the cyclone touch a burning pit, and only later realized the Platinum Palace was missing.

The hideous force of that cyclone made itself known the instant the glowing eye touched the hole in the ground. Fire and glittering fragments of glass and chrome rose from the depths of the pit, streaking upward like a meteor shower falling in the wrong direction. Stones and metal beams followed along, and then a massive wave of flesh-colored water spun itself along the base of the tornado, shredding and blending into the red sand as it went.

He could not hear the screams of Legion/Giovanni as it died, but he felt the vibrations of that scream just as surely as he felt his own heart trying desperately to escape the prison of his rib cage. The jackhammer beat of his vital organ was enough to make him remember that he was not dead.

The wild flaming column of blood and sand stayed where it was, spinning with as much ferocity as ever, but not ripping across the ground any longer. Lightning pulsed across the storm's skin at a pace that put his heartbeat to shame. Then, all at once, the storm died. There was no slowing down of the screaming winds. The lightning did not falter and fade away. It just died. Countless tons of liquefied debris stopped rotating and fell to the earth in a cascade. A column of wet, dead matter dropped into the great gaping wound where the Platinum Palace once stood, filling up in a matter of seconds and leaving behind only a cloud of fine dust to drift lazily on the suddenly gentle breeze.

Gabriel White took a deep breath and felt shockingly cold air fill his lungs. He stared numbly at the glistening ruin of his adoptive father's last dream and felt nothing at all save the automatic functions of his body.

For a time, his mind shut down. Enough was enough.

He did not feel the hands shake him or lift him from the ground. He never noticed the darkness which took the place of the city lights. When next he was conscious of anything, it was the smell of cooking meat and the sound of men speaking in whispered voices.

V

Dawson saw Gabriel stirring and smiled. He'd been a bit worried about the boy. Twenty hours ago he'd dragged the kid away from the middle of the street just in time to avoid the ambulances and police cars arriving on the scene.

Somehow he doubted the kid wanted to answer questions about what had happened and how he'd survived what the papers had dubbed the Hell-Storm. After all the Irishman next to him had related, he doubted Gabe could manage so much as a query about his name.

He smiled as kindly as he could manage and handed over a plate full of grilled burgers and a lukewarm can of Pepsi. Gabe took the food automatically and began to eat. His eyes still looked glossy as freshly painted marbles. That was okay. Sometimes it took a while to recover from life's nastier surprises. Losing his mom had to hurt, especially when you considered the way she'd been lost.

He'd traded tales with Shaun Ingram—who had automatically earned the nickname "Irish" from Dawson—and compared notes on just about everything that Gabriel had endured during his little vacation in Las Vegas. Somehow he doubted the kid would ever be eager to return.

Jude was gone. He'd done something funky with his hoo-doo that let them keep pace with the storm, and then he'd looked at the hole where the casino had been. He looked at Gabe playing statue and Ingram lying in a stupor on the ground and asked Jack to make sure they were taken care of. Dawson said he would and then made Boot help him drag them away from the area. Jude had not followed.

So, one night later, here he was with Boot, Irish, and Gabe having a midnight barbecue and keeping his promise to a madman. Hey, best not to piss off mages. Especially when they were a little on the crazy side. Besides, he liked Gabriel White. The boy was A-okay in his book, even if he was a Lupine.

Boot was doing his best to look offended about the whole situation. He was sitting just at the edge of the firelight and blowing notes out of the same damned harmonica he'd been playing when they met for the first time. The good news was he'd gotten better over the last century or so. He only missed a few notes on any given song instead of all of them.

He knew Joe wouldn't hang around much longer. Already his old friend was getting that look in his eyes that said it was time to go back to where he was comfortable. Jack still hadn't decided if he'd teach Hill how to listen to the Dead. After the night before, he was sort of surprised Hill still wanted to learn.

Joe was full of surprises. He always had been, and likely always would be.

Gabriel finished eating, and Jack took the paper plate away, slipping it into a trash bag he had pinned to the dirt with a sizable rock. Shaun Ingram went over to speak with the boy and Jack entertained himself by listening to Joe Hill murder another song.

After a while, he interrupted Joe's playing to give him an answer. "I'll teach you how to listen to the Dead, Joe. But I won't teach you anywhere but in Las Vegas."

"Well, I didn't figure you'd much want to pay a visit to Mexico, not with that price on your head."

"I knew you had a brain in that head of yours. I just wish you'd use it a little more often." He sighed and moved over to sit next to the man. "I'll only warn you the once: I ain't like them Giovanni. I hear they can keep the voices quiet. I can't do that. Once you learn, it's gonna be damn hard to unlearn. You get what I'm saying?"

"Reckon I do. But now and then a man's gotta learn a few things. I guess I figure it's about time to learn how not to ignore the things I've done."

"You've done a lot, Joe. You've done one hell of a lot. If you really want to learn this, you'd best be prepared to deal with the consequences."

"Hell. I figure if you can do it, so can I. Ain't met a Samedi yet that could outdo me in the smarts department."

"Yeah? How many you met?"

"Just one."

"Figured it was somethin' like that." Dawson stood up and dusted the sand off his jeans. "Go back to playin.' You might get one of them songs right, and I want to hear it when you do." Boot grunted and started another song while Jack went back over to the fire.

Gabriel was looking a far sight better, which meant he at least had an expression on his pale face. He'd been crying and he still was, but it was down to sniffles and an occasional tear. Irish had one arm around the broad shoulders of the boy and was rocking him gently back and forth. In about an hour, they'd pack up their stuff and Dawson would drop them off a few miles away in the middle of nowhere. That's what Ingram requested before Gabe woke up, and that was what he'd agreed to. In the meantime, Dawson didn't want to do a damn thing but look at the flames of the dwindling fire and listen to Joe slaughter a few tunes. A coyote joined in on the massacre from a distance. Dawson felt right at home.

VI

Magick was a wonderful toy. Jude had used it to help the ghosts get their revenge and even to stop them from going too far when they'd tried to break away from the path he'd set up for the storm he'd helped them make. He just couldn't quite trust them not to go overboard with the violence, so he'd made sure they left most of Las Vegas alone.

Through an amazing series of coincidences, the buildings in the path of the destruction were almost all empty when the Hell-Storm tore through on the way to the Platinum Palace. Andrea Stevens was off visiting her mother when the storm hit: The notion just came to her that she'd been watching too much television of late and maybe it was time to bury the hatchet with her mom. Arthur Johnson from the trailer next door felt oddly compelled to help a woman whose car had decided to lose a tire. He'd missed being swept away with his possessions by only a few minutes. Silvia Darnell ended up working a little overtime at the Sahara; her daughter Julie up and decided to elope after saying "no" to her boyfriend every time he asked for the last three months; Jorge Lopez decided on the spur of the moment that his family deserved a treat and took them to the movies. He couldn't really afford to, but what the hell. The kids needed a break and Louisa needed to be reminded that he loved her. On and on, people found reasons not to be at home in the Royal Flush Trailer Park on the night of the Hell-Storm. Even that mean old bastard Evan Whittaker had managed to get out of his trailer. He'd fallen and broken his leg in three places. Perhaps Jude could have found another way to handle that one, but he felt the old fart deserved it for his attitude. Better a cast for six weeks than a grave for all eternity.

A line of coincidences that long was bound to get noticed. So Jude decided leaving Las Vegas was for the best. He wasn't really sure just what or who would take note of the survival rate, but something would, and he wanted to be elsewhere when that something came sniffing around.

He made an anonymous donation of exactly one million dollars to the disaster relief fund being sponsored by the local radio station. He had enough bad karma already and felt it necessary to replace what his storm had ruined.

Besides, someone had to take care of burying the dead. Not a single soul found alive in the entire mess. That hurt. He'd so wanted for her to live. Just so that one little thing from his past could have turned out right. The tears tried to start again, but he forced them away.

Jude grabbed his meager belongings, a second-hand duffel bag stuffed with clothes and a thermos filled with cold water. He looked toward the east and started walking in that direction. He knew he'd come from the west when he came to Las Vegas and he also knew there was nothing waiting for him that way. Nothing and no one. For now he was alone, and he suspected that was for the best.

VII

Gabriel and Shaun said their good-byes to Jack Dawson and his silent friend. They sat at the edge of the spot where Gabriel had met and killed his father. The silence between them was comfortable. They had no secrets from each other.

The darkness soothed the wounds they felt and allowed each a time to mourn. Soon the sun would rise and they would make another journey. One that would, if Gaia saw fit, release them from the hideous urges that drove them to lash out at each other with blind hatred from time to time.

Shaun had spoken to Gabriel of Erebus. He'd recited the whispered tales of how the waters of the Silver Lake both seared the flesh and healed it as well. How the only wounds that Erebus could not heal were the wounds suffered by the Wyrm, wherever it may rest. Even if it rested in the soul of a person who tried to resist the Great Corrupter's taint. Some wounds were too great to survive. The venom of the Wyrm was often strong enough to destroy the soul and leave in its place a malformed mind and spirit.

If either of them was too far under the influence of the Destroyer, they would die. Both agreed the risk was worth the reward. Gabriel had nothing left to lose. He would not live as a pawn to the Wyrm, even if death was his only other option. In all honesty, he had little hope that he would survive the time in Erebus. He simply had little hope left in his soul. He was perfect as a tool for the Great Corrupter. Now was likely the only chance he would get to break free before it was too late.

As the sun rose in the east, the two of them waited for their escort to a world unlike any Gabriel had ever seen. He had never journeyed into the Umbra before. His first trip would likely be a doozie. They did not have to wait long. Loki showed herself mere minutes after the dawn's first light kissed the desert floor. She did not smile. Perhaps she understood better than most how grave their mission was.

Laughs-Too-Much stood before Gabriel and asked if he was ready. He said he was. She asked the same of Shaun, and he replied in like manner.

She spoke only one more time before leading them away from a world grown bitter and foul. Her words brought a brief joy to both men's hearts. She said: "Snow-Cap . . . Teri, has asked me to tell you that she will be waiting at home when you return. She makes no promises about whether or not she will be able to see you again."

Gabriel smiled but asked none of the questions he wanted so desperately to ask. There would be time for answers later. After the trip to Erebus.

ENTER
THE WORLD OF DARKNESS™

SUCH PAIN

◆

NETHERWORLD

◆

WYRM WOLF

◆

DARK PRINCE

◆

CONSPICUOUS CONSUMPTION*

◆

SINS OF THE FATHERS*

*coming soon

The World of Darkness™ is a trademark of the White Wolf Game Studio.

From HarperPrism

MAIL TO: HarperCollins Publishers
P.O. Box 588 Dunmore, PA 18512-0588
OR CALL: (800) 331-3761

Yes, please send me the books I have checked:

- ❑ **SUCH PAIN** 105463-1 .... $4.99 U.S./ $5.99 CAN.
- ❑ **WYRM WOLF** 105439-9 .... $4.99 U.S./ $5.99 CAN.
- ❑ **NETHERWORLD** 105473-9 .... $4.99 U.S./ $5.99 CAN.
- ❑ **DARK PRINCE** 105422-4 .... $4.99 U.S./ $5.99 CAN.
- ❑ **CONSPICUOUS CONSUMPTION** 105471-2 .... $4.99 U.S./ $5.99 CAN.
- ❑ **SINS OF THE FATHERS** 105472-0 .... $4.99 U.S./ $5.99 CAN.

SUBTOTAL .... $_____

POSTAGE AND HANDLING .... $2.00_____

SALES TAX (Add applicable sales tax). .... $_____

Name_____

Address_____

City_____State_____Zip_____

Allow up to 6 weeks for delivery. Remit in U.S. funds. Do not send cash.
(Valid in U.S. & Canada.) Prices subject to change.

P008